Thru the Chairs

Carole Dee

Thru the Chairs

This is a work of fiction. Names, places, characters, and incidents are the product of the author's imagination and are used fictitiously. Any resemblance to actual persons, living or dead, events, or locales is strictly coincidental.

Published by Wheatmark®
610 East Delano Street, Suite 104
Tucson, Arizona 85705 U.S.A.
www.wheatmark.com

International Standard Book Number: 978-1-60494-147-0
Library of Congress Control Number: 2008930918

Contents

Book 1

The Rear Commodore

The Boat. 3

The Candidates. 5

May. 9

Blessing of the Fleets 14

The Visitation to Valley Crest 18

Yard Sales, Anyone?. 25

Relating the Story to George 31

Gearing Up for Labor Day 33

Mary Gets Involved. 35

Off to the Races 39

Is It October? 45

Election Time 50

Thanksgiving Preparation 53

Operation Reindeer. 57

Unwanted Children. 65

The Opening of Presents. 71

The Final Dance as Rear Commodore. 74

'Tis the Holiday Season. 77

A Final Toast 79

Book 2
The Vice Commodore

The Bar and Bartenders. 83

The Pink Panthers. 87

Darts and Pool 89

A Bad Experience 91

Rusty Scupper. 96

Blessing of the Fleets 99

Lazy Hazy Days. 103

Valley Crest Yacht Club. 104

Enter Pink Panthers. 106

Never Boring. 109

A Gift 112

The Confession. 114

The Storm. 120

The Repair 124

The Surprise Party. 126

The Invasion. 130

The Commodore's Wife's Casino Night 135

Jill 143

The Wrong Club. 147

Book 3
The Commodore

The Grand Umpa Makes His Claim to Fame 155

The Planning of the First Event Under the Commodore. 157

Palm Sunday. 160

Disappointment Sets In. 165

The Wedding 167

Early Morning. 169

The Fog in June 172

Lonely. 177

The Walk Out. 178

Jill's Departure. 185

The Fireworks and the Music 187

Dot's Fundraiser 189

Collecting the Stuff. 191

The Deadline 195

The Jumper Cable Caper. 200

The Results. 203

Summer Days 205

A Disturbing Lunch 209

Labor Day Came and Went. 214

The Fights. 217

Dot's Meeting 220

The Halloween Dance. 223

Time for Me to Make a Decision. 226

The Meeting and the Furniture All in One Day 227

The Cape Trip. 230

Tony's Final Days as Commodore 236

Book 4
The Past Commodore

The Cape House. 241

Tony's Tough Decision 243

They Came 245

Time Goes By 251

Pat. 253

The Wake 255

Paul Adler 256

Author's Note

"THRU THE CHAIRS" IS A TERM used to describe an officer's three-year journey in a yacht club. His first year as Rear Commodore consists of all the outside land activities of the club. His second year, if elected as Vice Commodore, consists of all the inside activities of the club. An officer's third year, if elected as Commodore, consists of overlooking all these activities and making sure they are fulfilled properly. Each year a new election takes place. If an officer completes all three years, he has gone successfully Thru the Chairs. Opposition can take place in the second and third year of these elections. This is called "breaking the chairs." If the officer who interjects wins, then the former officer is forced to leave his position. Breaking of the chairs is frowned upon in yachting. It usually occurs when the former officer has not been able to handle the position due to improper behavior or unforeseen circumstances.

This book is dedicated to all the Commodores who touched my life.

Book 1

The Rear Commodore

Chapter 1

The Boat

THE YEAR WAS 1988, THE YEAR of the boat. Tony, my husband, had purchased his dream boat. We had owned boats before, but this was the first new boat, the one with the great new-boat smell. People who have had a new boat know that if they could capture that smell and turn it into a man's cologne they would probably have a number-one fragrance.

Not only was 1988 the year of the boat, but it was the year of the yacht club elections. Tony was running for the position of Rear Commodore. Tony happened to belong to one of the best-located clubs in the New England area.

The club was known as the Briar Ridge Yacht Club. It was nestled in the womb of a bustling city. The club was a refuge that separated a person from all the sounds and feelings that the busy metropolis created. A cut out in the earth engulfed by the serenity of the ocean, a carpet of white sand to walk on, and the music of waves dancing in the background. One of the most captivating things about the club's location was its sunsets. People would stop and park their cars on the street, and members would sit in their boats just to see this event. These sunsets left people mesmerized. One could see different shades of red and orange splatter across the sky. It was like an artist took out a paintbrush and just kept changing his strokes until all the vibrant colors faded into the sea. This magnificent display ended with the sound of honking horns and clapping hands from the watching sun worshippers.

Many of the members of the club were in the trades. This, of course, was not a requirement. The advantage to being in the trades was that they had the opportunity to volunteer their services. For example, if one was a plumber and the club needed work, one would volunteer one's time. If members had no professional service to offer, they donated their time to help with many of the needed projects. By doing this, members kept the dues for membership at a reasonable level. Another huge advantage was that members got to meet a network of people they had something in common with other than boating, and it helped expand their careers in the trades. Tony was in construction. As a foreman he was extremely responsible and got the job done. When the club needed a new roof, he called suppliers he knew in the business. Once the products for the roof were delivered, Tony put together a crew of members and got it done in record time.

We had a great slip for the new boat. The new boat was a thirty-six-foot Wellcraft with twin engines. It was designed in red and white fiberglass. The colors were separated by a black pinstripe. The canvass that was used to protect passengers in inclement weather was also in the same shade of red that engulfed the bottom of the boat. This truly was a speedboat of distinction. We named her *37 Park Ave* so when contractors called to speak to Tony, I could say, "He is at *37 Park Ave*," and no one would know the better.

Chapter 2

The Candidates

ELECTIONS WERE WITHIN A WEEK. ALL the campaigning one sees on the national level was going on here, but of course on a much smaller scale. The usual mudslinging, fighting, and revisiting of events of the other participants' pasts were being used by all the candidates in an effort to gain the upper hand. Tony's opposition was a Jewish man named Sam. This was the first time a Jewish man had run for a major office. The prejudice toward his faith was started by a few members. Fortunately they were only a few. Sam owned a deli and had been called on many times to donate cold-cut platters or take part in members' upcoming weddings. Sam could not fix a thing—macho he wasn't. He had a gentle quality. When Sam walked through a room it was almost like he tiptoed. Sam walked like he was afraid he would wake someone up or disturb them. Sam's voice was barely above a whisper when he spoke, and he didn't have that rough-and-tough appearance most of the members had. He wasn't what one would call a boater, either. Sam was a cruiser, and when his boat broke down, crews fixed it. If Tony's boat broke down, no one dared to offer to fix it. This boat was Tony's baby; he took care of it. The boat made him a man in control of his thirty-six-foot domain; he was captain of his yacht. Everyone knows how some men need control, like never asking for directions. Men can drive for hours before they ask anyone for help. Everyone in the car knows they're lost. They know they're lost. But ask directions? How humiliating. How out of control and powerless. Compared to Sam, Tony's image looked great as a running candidate. The same few members that were hassling Sam referred to Tony as having Mafia ties. With all the beautiful arts, food, and music that the Italians have given to society, why does the mafia accusation always surface? But that is what happens in elections. Elections give some people the power to say what they want, and some feel it is their civic duty. Actually, it is only prejudice. The fact that Tony was in construction and had a lot of knowledge about building materials seemed to be one of the many feathers in his cap, but the real reason that Tony made a great candidate was his background. Tony's dad came from a small village in Italy. He was a fisherman. When he emigrated to this country, he was forced, as so many immigrants were in the early twentieth century, to live in row houses in the cities. Of course, the Great Depression did not help the situation either. Language barriers created even more problems.

When Tony and his four brothers were growing up, they helped their dad with small construction projects. They would do a back porch or fix a set of stairs, but the conversation always turned to Tony's father telling his sons how passionate he felt about boating and fishing. He wanted so badly to share these dreams with his sons. That day eventually came for Tony's dad, and the whole family celebrated. Uncles, aunts, and cousins gathered at the ocean to watch Tony's dad launch his first boat. They set up tables and chairs on the beach, and then the men went fishing. And fish they did. Tony was no more than twelve at the time. He was the youngest of the brothers. But when his dad put that fishing rod in his hands he knew he would catch that fish. The camaraderie that he shared with his family during those years was what this yacht club meant to him. It was an extension of boating, fishing, and male bonding that he inherited from his dad's dream. Unfortunately his dad could never be a part of it, as he had died a few years prior to Tony buying his dream boat. But he left a dream and Tony was part of it. Tony wanted this opportunity more than ever.

At the club there were more Italians than Jews, and our last name, Vendetti, was more than a shoo-in. The names of the past Commodores were mainly English or Irish. Italians had only come along in the past few years. However, the club members were not quite ready for a Jewish Commodore. As I said, this club was political, similar to the national system we have now. Going Thru the Chairs was a true test of leadership. If one completed the process, one also would be able to enter yacht clubs all over the country as a past officer in good standing. It is one of the highest honors in yachting. One would become a part of history in the yachting world, and one's picture would be placed forever with all the previous Commodores of one's club. This position could also be taken further. One could enter the same procedure in the Commodores Club of America. This was Tony's goal, but it was Sam's as well, and the campaign trail was going to be a long one.

Sam's background was different. His family also migrated to the United States. Sam's dad was a doctor. By the time Sam's dad came to this country he was very ill, and he died shortly after. Sam's mom made Sam go work for his uncle, who had a small deli. Sam had a lot of responsibility for his mom. She grieved his dad's death, but most of all she missed her homeland. She really never adjusted to the new world. Sam worked hard not only at the deli but at trying to make his mom happy. She died shortly after his dad. Some say she died of a broken heart. Sam was only sixteen at the time, and his uncle took him under his wing but expected Sam to work hard. Sam had no time for boating and fishing, but like Tony he still had a dream, and this election would bring him one step closer to that dream.

Campaigning was something I really did not want to get involved with. At this time in history, women were not considered members. However, I did feel my husband was the best candidate for this position. Out of respect I agreed to campaign with him. I had my banners, and I screamed out my opinions of why I thought Tony was the perfect leader. Even though I wasn't a member, who knew Tony better than I? I remembered the saying, "Behind every successful man there is a woman," so I made myself heard. I had posters made with all the work that Tony and his crew had done on the floats. Tony's previous position before running for Rear Commodore was on the Float Committee. This position involved a crew that Tony was in charge of. Their job was to make sure the docks were in pristine condition. It also involved preparation in securing slips for the members' boats. This was a tedious job, and the crew was at the mercy of the tides. A lot of this work was done in the off season. Sometimes the ocean would create such a hassle that the crew would have to wait for another time, and each postponement would only delay the necessary progress that had to be finished. I reiterated all this past experience on my posters. *Without the Floats There Are No Boats!*

Sam's wife really didn't seem interested in the election. I shouldn't say she did not care, but it was just that she was very rarely seen at the club with Sam. Some people who had seen her on rare occasions said she feared the water. She feared the movement of the boat when it swayed back and forth. Maybe she got seasick! Whatever Sam's wife's reason was, she made it obvious by her lack of appearance throughout the election that it was not her priority that Sam get elected.

When an election takes place people say it is not a popularity contest, but it is. The prettiest girl in grammar school and the handsomest boy always got elected. Tony had charisma. He learned it by being the youngest son. He had to fight hard for attention and had to face the hand-me-downs, the used toys, the last piece of dessert, and always waiting his turn for the one bathroom or the one fishing rod. He learned how to be charming, and most of all he learned how to get his way so he could survive. He learned how to get along because his older brothers had to be convinced to include him in their daily activities, otherwise he was left behind. Tony had no intention of being left behind.

Sam wanted to be Rear Commodore, but he was happy just being a part of the club. If he didn't make it, he would still have his boat, the smell of the ocean, and a break from the deli. And knowing Sam, he would try again.

Election Day finally arrived. The members gathered in the boardroom. Of course I was not a part of this. These elections were held in strict confidence. Each candidate spoke before the board on their final appeal for election. I was never privy to the details, but from what I heard through the grapevine, Sam was just a little weak in his final speech. The fact that it was not important to his wife that she be a part of the campaigning did not help his situation. It was a victory for Tony. There really was no doubt. One thing I realized in my campaigning was that member or no member, the club was still family oriented and wanted a wife involved. Remember, behind every successful Commodore, even a Rear Commodore, was a woman. My campaigning with Tony paid off.

Chapter 3

May

YACHTING OR BOATING IN THE NEW England area was a short season. All winter, boaters planned all the excursions they would take once the warmer months came. As the snow fell down and the icicles formed on rooftops, longing for the warm, sunny boating days and the ocean breezes were very common. When May came, many boaters, who were so weary from the very long winters, were extremely anxious to put their boats in the water.

There were two types of boaters: the sailors, who were the frugal group according to the club, and the loud noise makers, who owned motorboats. The motorboats ruled—they were the majority, and they became the most popular at the club. The motorboats could usually be seen flying across the ocean three inches above the water, if not more. I can only describe these boats in this fashion: These vessels glisten, they shine. Their names express tremendous pleasure, fantasy, and most of all escapism. *Zanzibar, Erotica, Virago* ... and then ours, *37 Park Ave* (the great elusive meaning). Sailboat names were usually something like *Sea Drifter, Wind Sail,* and *Flying Cloud*—the more relaxing, quieter side of boating. The men who owned the high-speed motorboats wanted a fast pace. They liked to open the engines full throttle and fly across the ocean. These men had to have all the toys that went along with motorboats. They treated their new toys with such emotion. Rubbing, shining, painting, and decorating their boats was a loving chore. It was expressed in the enjoyment on these men's faces. You could hear their laughter and excitement as they programmed lorans, fish finders, radar, and other gizmos that could be used to enhance their yachting adventures at sea.

If only a wife or girlfriend could get all this attention. For a wife, sometimes a boat was worse than a mistress! Don't get me wrong; I got a lot of pleasure from the boat. However, with all good things there was a downside. I got to run from side to side with a net when the big fish was caught. I got to be a Cyclops on the bow when the big fog rolled in. The best part was I got to be number-one swabbie, in charge of the cleaning and washing of the deck. Then there was the upside. After all, I was first mate. I got to inhale the salt air and feel the water catch my skin, which made me feel like a kid again. I also got to taste the great fresh fish we catch. And at night, I got to sleep like a child being rocked in a warm and comforting cradle. But the most beautiful sight of all was to look up through the skylight in the boat and see a sky full of stars. Yes, I loved boating.

It was our anniversary and Tony was anxiously trying to get our boat in the water. Of course, he had the responsibility of getting everyone else in also. He was hoping we could have a romantic evening, which meant no children. Our four children were teenagers, and my mother lived nearby and enjoyed them. She offered to babysit, and naturally we accepted her offer. This way Tony and I could celebrate our anniversary quietly and keep our sanity. Our teenagers had a way of making us *crazy*! We needed a break. I was also hoping to be alone with Tony for selfish reasons. I wanted a night of savage bliss, a chance to be carried away on a boat by my handsome pirate. We girls still had to create fantasies; I was on *37 Park Ave*, Atlantic Ocean, zip code xoxo.

Tony was on the dock with a crew, making sure that all the slips were marked. He was also checking on the security of the pilings. He had already done a final on the electricity. Tony's main man was Jim, who was also a good friend. Jim was a burly man. He had a crop of thick white hair. He prematurely turned gray at an early age. He was one of those guys with a dry sense of humor—told me he turned gray after his first year of marriage. He said his wife's demands were worse than the army. Sometimes I didn't know if he was serious or not, and I could only tell when I looked straight into his eyes. If they kind of curled up at the ends like a smile, then I knew he was kidding. It wasn't his wife that made his hair turn gray, it was his genes. Jim was also the best crane operator we had. Jim and two helpers would guide the boats into the water. This was a lengthy process, as it would take a couple of weeks to put all the boats in the water. They were all different sizes, and the larger yachts needed cranes to place them securely in their slips. The smaller yachts that were closer to the front were a little easier, as they could be guided by smaller prams and workmen who pulled them with ropes to their slip. Today they were concentrating on the larger yachts. There were four scheduled to go in the water. Sam was in the galley making pastrami sandwiches for the gang. We all felt that Sam had every intention of running for Rear Commodore again next year. I guess when Tony won, Sam realized that he truly did want the position and would make it happen. Sam would someday be Rear Commodore; there was no doubt in my mind.

I was up at the clubhouse watching the procedure when, what do you know, "Murphy's law." Our club received a phone call every parent dreads. I saw the Vice Commodore approaching Jim. Jim, who was operating the crane, stopped. He stepped down to greet the Vice Commodore and was told that his daughter had been in an accident. Her car had been rammed on the way to the club by a ten wheeler, and the impact sent her over a bridge and into the water. The car went down quick; a pedestrian jumped into the cold water but almost drowned himself. He was unsuccessful in trying to save her.

Immediately all work ceased. Tony took a shaken Jim to the accident scene. I hitched a ride with one of the crew. The police and firemen were there along with divers. They all knew Jim since he operated cranes for the city. Mary, Jim's wife, spotted me and rushed towards me with a tear-stained face. I took her in my arms. It took all my strength to hold her up, and she kept repeating, "My daughter, my daughter." My stomach had a pit in it, and I fought to keep a positive attitude in spite of the grim scene in front of me. The situation was bad. There was so much debris in the water near this section of the bridge that the divers felt the car was lodged, and they didn't seem to think anyone was in the car. There was a slight chance that maybe their daughter got out of the car because there were open windows.

By now Jim had arrived. He immediately ran over to Mary. The two of them entangled in each other as if they were one. My eyes began to water as I saw a blurred vision of a man and a woman united in a grotesque image. I heard a horrible moaning sound that permeated through the air. A sound as if everything in one's being was being drained out of them. There they remained, this piece of twisted flesh and bone on the bridge, my desperate friends, crying and praying between sobs that maybe there was hope that their daughter's body might surface unscathed.

Bob, the fire chief, approached Tony. He took him aside and informed him the chances were slim. The body was probably caught on some debris under the water. Bob had that weather-beaten face of a man who had spent a lot of time outside. He was a tall man who wore his uniform well. He had huge hands that if they could speak would tell how many people he had dragged to safety and how many he wished he could have saved. He estimated that in situations like this it usually took a few days before the body floated to the surface. The chief had been in the department for twenty years. His experience with rescue teams that involved drowning had been pretty extensive. He reiterated that it would take a few days before the body surfaced. Of course, if it was caught or trapped in heavy debris it might need the expertise of a diver to recover the body.

Tony had a lot of respect for Bob and knew this was a difficult announcement on Bob's part. Tony quietly advanced toward me. He embraced me and softly whispered in my ear the fire chief's assumption of what could be expected in the following days. I was speechless. I couldn't even fathom what I would do if one of my children were involved in such a horrific disaster. Of course Jim and Mary clung to hope and refused to leave the scene that stole their seventeen-year-old daughter's life. By eleven PM that night, a beaten and weary Mary and Jim left the scene, only to return the next morning. That same morning Tony showed up in support of Jim. Jim begged Tony to help, believing maybe his daughter grabbed onto a nearby boat. He hoped that maybe she passed out in one of these boats in the harbor. Tony knew Jim was hoping for a miracle, but he knew he would too if it was our daughter. Tony went back to the club. The Fleet Captain was handling the launching of the boats into the water, and a nearby yacht club, hearing of our dilemma, had sent over one of their crane operators.

By now at least eight boats were in the water, enough to put a small fleet together and form a search party. It was Tony's first month of official duty. He knew that the police department was out there doing everything possible to find Jim's daughter. He knew the fire chief had given him the reality of it all, but Jim was his friend, and if grabbing at straws was what Jim needed, then that would be what the club provided for him and Mary.

Tony stood on the dock and firmly issued his first command. A search party consisting of members from the club would assist in finding Jim and Mary's daughter. Tony knew chances were the body wouldn't surface for a few days—the police and fire departments were usually pretty accurate and experienced in their opinion of these matters. The members searched all day with every bit of hope, but to no avail. There was no body.

DAYS LATER, THE FIRE CHIEF CALLED. A fisherman had spotted the body close to where it had been predicted. The straw of reality broke, and the grief got worse. When I think of how excited Tony was to be elected, I realized that politics, whether on a small or large level, can put us in a position that might not be as pleasant as we wish.

We never know what the first role in office will be. Should one rule with the head? Should one rule with the heart? Tony did both. He handled the situation as he hoped someone would handle it if it were our daughter. I guarantee no one could have anticipated this, and it certainly put the seriousness of this position into perspective. It definitely took the hype away. The worst part was identifying the body. Jim asked Tony if he would help him. The police were very accommodating in showing identification, but the actual identity of the body was something that stayed with Tony for a long time. We never talked about it, but I knew a broken man when I saw one.

Chapter 4

Blessing of the Fleets

A MONTH HAD GONE BY SINCE the tragic death of Jim and Mary's daughter. In a few moments the Blessing of the Fleets would take place. The club was picture perfect. The sun was shinning and the blue water looked as though tiny white diamonds had been sprinkled like confetti all over the ocean. Each wave deposited these beautiful jewels and only enhanced their beauty as they rubbed up and down the yachts. The white sails on some boats looked like huge clean sheets that had just been washed and put out to dry. I looked over all the yachts that were lined up in the water awaiting the blessing. The blessing was a custom to guide boaters on a safe voyage. It took place every year. It was also a time of healing, reminding us of the many men and women lost at sea. It was a tribute to them. Many religious groups were represented to take place in the blessing. There were also representatives from the police, fire department, and a local politician, in this case the mayor. The mayor was seated in the front row along with the Commodore, the Vice Commodore, and Tony, the Rear Commodore. All representatives were in uniform. The healing started by the mayor issuing a moment of silence for Jim and Mary's daughter. He asked the community to reach out to them so they might find strength in their friends and family. This was followed by a prayer for all who had been lost at sea the past year. The Star-Spangled Banner was played and everyone stood. Our country's flag and the burgee of the club were blowing in the warm summer sky. The representatives from the religious groups proceeded to the floats. There they sprinkled holy water, said prayers, and reached out to the many boaters enjoying this traditional festivity.

After the blessing, the celebrating began. As I started to head for the floats, I saw Jim and Mary. It took a lot of courage to come to this function. Maybe they came because of what this ceremony stood for. It was a healing. During one's darkest moments, it was a salvation to know that people cared—thank goodness for friends. I knew in my heart it would be a very long time before the two of them started celebrating, but for the good of the club and out of respect they showed up for the start of a new beginning. After all, we were a family connected by yachting, and what other place to begin again but with the security of friends.

Down on the floats, cocktails were flowing. The appetizers were being gobbled up by children, and some people were dressed in costumes representing phases of nautical history. From Columbus to Captain Hook, one could experience sea-bearing heroes or villains. Patriotic music was being played, and the floats were full of members and guests doing little jigs and singing merrily. Every once in a while a salutation could be heard in memory of those who were lost at sea or past soldiers who died for our great country so we could have the freedom we so love. The more the liquor flowed, the more heroes were remembered. The regatta was definitely encompassing the ocean. Diamonds were now being replaced by lobsters. These huge crustaceans came from the many lobster traps surrounding the club. Nets of clams were being pulled and gotten ready for the steamer. Women were coming along with boiled corn and bowls of hot melted butter. The party continued into the night, with the stars becoming our glow balls.

It was late, and I was sitting on *37 Park Ave* when I was approached by a young girl no more than twenty-two years of age. This girl was fairly attractive in an almost fairy-like way. She introduced herself as "Jill." I looked into her face and saw sad doe eyes. Fearful eyes— eyes that expressed a frightened uncertainty. She said, "I am a friend of one of the members," and mentioned his name. The member I recall to myself was a real drifter. Then she asked a peculiar question. She asks if she might take a shower in my boat because she was on a sailboat and there was no hot water. I think this is quite unusual. She goes on to say, "I am very uncomfortable up at the public showers that the club provides. There is just too much excitement going on."

She promised me that she would be very quick. I was a little hesitant because I really did not know her and was not too fond of the member she knew from the club. I felt he was a drifter, and if she was with him she might be one too. I again notice a frightened look in her eyes as she spoke. I myself did not care to take showers up at the club either and was glad when Tony bought a boat with a shower and running hot water. I thought with all the partying and drinking going on, *What's one quick shower?*

I said, "Fine." She must have known I would give in for under her arm she carried a bag, from which she produced her own towel, shampoo, and soap.

"Give me ten minutes," she said. She kept her word and was in and out within ten minutes. She left the shower immaculate. I felt I did my good deed for the day. Before Jill left she looked up at me. I noticed how sad her eyes looked—almost like a frightened doe. I wanted to address her more, but she seemed unapproachable. I started to say something, but I could tell she wanted to be on her way. She thanked me repeatedly, almost like a child singing a song. "Thank you, thank you, and thank you." Then, as quickly as she had appeared, she disappeared.

As the party continued, the stars and moon radiated such a shower of light. It was these moments that made me glad to have a boat. Soon one of my dear friends, Pat, wandered over. Now, Pat was a Taurus. She was as stubborn as a bull. When Pat judged someone, she saw only black and white. Pat never saw gray. Pat was built solid and visited the gym twice a week. Pat had thick, curly blond hair and wore huge round-rim glasses. I felt they were too large, but Pat felt they made her look authoritarian. Pat also had no problem giving her opinion on any topic. Pat was also very loving. She was one of my true friends who would always be there for me. She would help me with any problems, even if she didn't agree with me. Of course, like most Tauruses she would try to convince me to do it her way. I loved Pat. Our personalities, even though different, complimented one another.

I asked her if she knew Jill. She mentioned that she was George's girlfriend. George was an electrician who did a lot of work on the docks at the club. He had a sailboat called the *Rusty Scupper*. The sailboat was actually his home. He vanished for periods of time—a real drifter like I thought. Pat said, "The rumor goes like this: Jill is a part-time waitress he picked up somewhere along his many questionable voyages. From what is assumed, Jill lives with him on his thirty-foot vessel. Jill probably has no roots, and at such a young age must be running from somewhere or someone. California was mentioned in a conversation I heard." Pat then dropped the conversation about Jill and we changed the subject. We started to pick apart some of the members as women do, got a little catty, and then had some wine and giggled profusely.

That night I retired, with a head full of wine and a rocky boat to boot. I couldn't sleep. I did not want to wake Tony, who had worked so hard all day making sure everyone's boat was taken care of. Therefore I went up on deck. I was holding my head and reminiscing of the laughter Pat and I shared when I thought I heard a ruckus on the *Rusty Scupper*. It looked like Jill and another man were having some words. I didn't think it was George because this man looked a little older. Being in a nosey mood, I took a double take and thought, *This can't be who I think it is.* He was a married man and very prudish when it came to his wife. He claimed to be the pillar of the community. Actually, this man was a bit of a bully in my opinion. The raised voice did sound like him, though. *Imagine,* I thought, *could this be Paul Adler with Jill, a girl young enough to be his daughter?* I really did have too much to drink. Both parties causing the ruckus went back into the *Rusty Scupper*. I decided to call it a night and put my wild and ridiculous thoughts to rest. Why would Paul Adler be on the boat with Jill?

Chapter 5

The Visitation to Valley Crest

MORE THAN A WEEK HAD PASSED since the blessing, and we were all getting ready for our first invasion of another yacht club. An invasion was when we were invited to visit a neighboring yacht club. Sometimes it was for a day, and sometimes it was for two days. The inviting club would entertain and feed us. It was always a lot of fun. The reason it was called an invasion was no one ever knew how many people would come. Sometimes they came from different clubs, and whether they were invited or not they invaded. However, boaters are usually very welcome. I knew this would be a great two days of festivities. We would be guests, and Tony had gotten twenty-three boats from Briar Ridge to take the voyage. The names of the vessels departing were posted on Tony's clipboard. He gave the Fleet Captain the list so he could line up the yachts for departure. The fleet was soon headed to Valley Crest Yacht Club. I noticed that the *Rusty Scupper* was among the vessels. Sailboats usually leave earlier than motor boats; they take longer because they are navigated by the wind. Sometimes some sail boats have a small motor that can expedite their arrival. The motor comes in handy when there is no wind. Of course, a true sailor likes to take their time and enjoy the hands-on navigation that is involved in this type of boating. On the other hand, speedboats were designed to do just that. These captains liked a faster pace. The majority of the fleet was excited that their speedboats would be there within two hours.

It was late June, and the weather was unusually hot. I was truly looking forward to a nice cruise to Valley Crest Club. The trip was as I expected—flawless. The ocean was like a blue carpet. There were no waves, just flat calm. We careened across its surface like a skier on new snow.

As we approached the dock entering Valley Crest, we saw a bright blue clubhouse with a wrap-around porch. Cascades of multi-colored flowers hung from huge wicker baskets all around the huge veranda. Officers were dressed in white uniforms, flags from all over the world blew in the breeze, and the Fleet Captain and his crew were ready to tie our boats safely to the docks. We were greeted with open arms. Of course the smell of hotdogs, hamburgers, and sausages permeated the air all around us. This was what yachting was all about—what camaraderie! Tony was immediately greeted by Valley Crest's Rear Commodore, who also presented me with a corsage. This I planned to wear later at the welcome dance held this evening. In the meantime, I was going to enjoy the fabulous food.

I was really looking forward to an evening of dancing and being a guest. There was a band. The night was devoted to all the music from the late seventies and early eighties. No sooner did I sit down when I heard someone yelling about a baseball question. Evidently a disagreement had broken out over who hit the most home runs on some team. I couldn't hear all of it, but I did hear someone say, "That damn George Dighton has had too much to drink," and the night was still young. The other culprit involved in this discrepancy was also feeling the effects of too much liquor.

"Let them hash it out!" someone yelled, and so we did. In the meantime, people were requesting songs. One was Dianna Ross's, "Stop in the Name of Love." The band had a young female singer who was doing a great impression of Dianna Ross, when, lo and behold, Jill appeared on stage and stood next to the singer in a see-through blouse. Jill's nipples were standing erect. Her hair had flowers woven through it. She truly looked like fairy material. The flowers were obviously stolen or borrowed from one of the centerpieces on the tables. She was belting out the same song as the singer. The only difference was Jill's movements were so superior that the crowd was truly egging Jill on. Of course, with all this attention Jill continued to make an even greater spectacle. However, the see-through blouse was starting to get the wrong attention. What started as a Dianna Ross song was turning into a striptease. All of a sudden the quiet, scared, doe-eyed girl was transformed into a stripper. The original singer was in awe and left the stage. The clapping and chanting continued, and the peekaboo blouse was becoming even more of an issue. I tried to find George, but where were men when they were needed? As far as Tony was concerned, he was in a pool game on the other side of the room and probably did not want to be disturbed. What a dilemma. Was there any way I could intervene?

I guess in a small way members of clubs were family. Even though I was not an official member, I was the Rear Commodore's wife. I had a responsibility. I shared a part of that office too, if only in my mind. So I did my best impression of Ginger Rogers, without Fred Astaire, and danced my way to the stage and placed a jacket over Jill. At that point I noticed her eyes. They were no longer doe eyes. They were Cleopatra eyes. Her pupils were heavily dilated—the size of saucers. She was drugged or she had just left the optometrist. I felt my first summation was correct, and I knew I had to get her out, and fast. I was surprised when the atmosphere calmed down. I guess I generated a touch of respect. The music stopped. Jill looked into my eyes, and just as if I had hypnotized her, Jill calmly left the dance floor, wrapping the jacket comfortably around her. I took Jill back to the *Rusty Scupper* and I checked to see if Paul Adler was part of our fleet. Fortunately he had not come. I was beginning to wonder if that was him the night of the ruckus; Paul's wife had said that these invasions were too rowdy. Of course his poor wife was always so sick. It was very difficult for her to enjoy any kind of fun. Then I felt bad—my conscience was getting the best of me. I had no right to assume Paul was on the *Rusty Scupper* that night.

THE SUMMER WAS GOING BY SLOWLY, and Tony's responsibilities seemed endless. From morning to night necessary plans were made. How many visiting clubs would arrive? Would there be enough slips to provide for everyone's boat? Would there be enough men to tie up all the in-coming yachts during the invasions of other clubs? What were the alternative plans if the weather did not accommodate us?

Tony's meetings with the Vice Commodore and Commodore regarding these decisions were constant.

It was July and the weather continued to stay hot. I had not seen Jill; rumor had it she was under the weather. Someone said they thought it was women's problems. I just loved that comment. It was such a large category. I could list women's problems from A to Z. Anyway, I needed to talk to her, so I decided to visit the *Rusty Scupper*. I had purchased some great lilies for my boat, and the smell was so intoxicating that I decided to donate a few to Jill. When I approached the boat I noticed all the little windows were covered in curtains. The curtains had miniature sailboats on them—how appropriate. They were drawn shut, and I took this for, "do not disturb." Just as I was about to leave, I noticed Jill pushing the curtains aside. I motioned to her to let me in.

I saw that she was extremely pale and that her doe eyes were back. Her Cleopatra eyes had vanished. She looked like a poster child for Save the Children. She knew by my expression that I felt awkward. First, because she thought I was going to lecture her on her past musical performance at Valley Crest, and second, because her only roots were on George's boat. George was responsible for her behavior, being the member. I could tell she feared that she was about to become homeless.

I said, "Hi, how are you feeling?" Her response was slow. I said, "Jill, I don't have to be a rocket scientist to know when someone is in pain."

"Would you like to come in?" she replied. "You know, I do not get too many women visitors."

I wonder why, I thought. As I entered the *Rusty Scupper*, I was totally aghast at what I saw. "Jill," I said, "this boat is in pristine condition. Who polishes all this teak wood? I can see my reflection, it's so shiny."

Jill smiled and then said, "I do. I love to clean. It makes me feel good when things are pretty. However, don't look to close because there is a film of dust. I just haven't had the strength lately to give the boat that extra glow. I usually lemon wax it, but the thought of smelling lemons right now makes me ill."

"Jill," I laughed, "don't tell me you made the quilts and pillows on that bed."

Jill put her head down sheepishly and barely uttered, "Yes, I made them last year. I haven't made anything recently."

I said, "Such talent. You could really make some nice money placing these in a consignment store."

"Do you think so?" she said as she raised her head up. Her eyes looked so helpless. This girl had no confidence in herself.

I again said, "Yes! Yes! These are beautiful." My eyes then wandered to some fresh flowers of the wild nature that grew along sidewalks or hung from fences. These were arranged nicely in a large, nameless pickle jar. This girl had definitely missed her calling. Merry Maids could learn a thing or two from this fantastic cleaner. I felt like a spy instead of a visitor. I wished I had brought her a cake instead of secondhand lilies.

When I handed Jill the lilies, she smiled and said, "Thanks, I just love their smell." She added them to her already perfect flower arrangement. "Let's have some tea," Jill said.

I said, "Only if I make it. You look very tired." She agreed.

"You know," Jill said, "I had a D&C." She put her head down again sheepishly. I did not respond. Sometimes it was better not to ask too many questions. I really did not know Jill that well, and this operation might be too personal to get involved with. Jill said, "I am so glad you stopped by; especially after my episode on the dance floor. I am so sorry about my actions, although I must admit I can't remember much. I had never tried cocaine, but George had some and I wanted to experiment. I knew I had to go for this operation, and I wanted to be happy that night instead of sad. I heard that taking cocaine can give you that effect. I didn't take much, and I felt so energetic and happy. I tell you this because I sincerely promise that I will never try it again. George regretted giving it to me. He screamed that he could be thrown out of the club. He said that drugs are really frowned upon everywhere, and especially in boating. He told me boats are another source of delivering drugs, and the club could be shut down if the police ever suspected drugs on the premises."

All I could think of was my husband. He was responsible for all outside activities concerning the club. Drugs would never go over well with Tony. Tony had already read our children the riot act. I would hate to see his reaction to this. I then decided to go into my mother routine. "Jill," I said, "forget embarrassing the club. What about yourself? Not to mention your selection of clothing that night. None of this was in any way appropriate." She nodded and again pleaded to me it would never happen again. I continued by reminding her that the episode was over. "However, Jill, I promise you that if I even have the slightest inkling of drugs here I will tell my husband, and I guarantee that the results will be devastating for you and George and anyone else involved. Now, I know you are not feeling well, so please let's learn from it and drop it." I then changed the subject. "Jill, you really look like you could use some TLC. Where is George?" I asked.

"He is on a job. Hopefully he will return in a couple of days." she said. I smiled, wondering if electricians usually stayed away that long—maybe if they were working on a huge project. Jill smiled and said, "I try not to question him too much. After all, I am so lucky to have a place to stay." I laughed.

"Jill," I said, "anyone who cleans and keeps a boat in this condition is lucky to be had. George is damn lucky to have you boat sitting." By now the tea was done, and I went to the refrigerator to get some milk. When I opened it I noticed one small orange and a heel of bread. These were not even included in the necessary staples to stay alive. I should have followed the rule of courtesy. When someone was ill, bring food. My mom would have been so disappointed in me. As we sipped the tea, our conversation was basically on how impressed I was with the interior of the boat. Jill mentioned that she likes to purchase a lot of things at the local thrift shop. Her hobby was to sew and sometimes redo things. I wanted to mention the peekaboo blouse but thought it best to let it go. There were two beautiful afghans present in the boat. Jill informed me that if she could get a good deal on yarn she would crochet. This was Jill's second passion. As she displayed one of her creations, I noticed her hands, or should I say wrists. They had scars running around them. It looked like the signs of a botched suicide attempt. I got a lump in my throat, and I thought it best to leave. I came up with some lame excuse. She must have sensed it, for she reached out and grabbed me in an awkward hug. I did my best to respond, but she really had caught me by surprise. I knew she was really trying to be genuine. When I left I could not help but notice how sad and pathetic this poor creature was—what a sad road she had taken. Maybe the sad road started the day she was born. Maybe a little kindness could go along way. Time would tell.

Chapter 6

Yard Sales, Anyone?

WHEN I RETURNED TO MY BOAT, my gal pals were waiting for me. Sometimes we would go to yard sales. We would usually come back with so much junk, but today we had a mission. The method to our madness was a function that the Rear Commodore's wife ran to raise money. We decided, my gal pals and I, to have an auction. We were allowed to have more than one function to raise money, and this money could be used to improve areas of the club. This money could also be used towards the charities that the club provided yearly. I had suggested earlier, "We would start a collection of items either donated or purchased at a low price. In order to come to this function you would have to go to your useless bin and retrieve an unwanted or unused gift to donate to the cause. We all have useless paraphernalia, and this gives us the ability to recycle unwanted or unneeded stuff."

Today was the start of collecting at yard sales. Pat was full of questions when I approached. She gave me her look of authoritarianism. Those damn glasses peering at me. As I said before, Pat saw only black and white. I just made a gray decisions. I was not bringing the episode of drugs up with anyone. I wanted to give Jill a second chance. Pat's main question was why was I coming from the *Rusty Scupper*, and I said, "Pat, Jill was having some women's problems and I thought I would just check on her. You know, Pat, very few people visit her."

Pat laughed and said, "Well, that should tell you something." I loved Pat, but sometimes I found her very opinionated. We have all had girlfriends like that. We loved them but sometimes they were so quick to judge someone.

I was always saying to Pat, "Don't judge a book by its cover." The funny part about Pat was that once she knew a situation, she tried to be understanding. Pat just had a habit of creating her own opinion of the situation without the facts.

"Pat," I said, "today is a very nice day. Let's not waste it with triviality." Pat looked at me with that head full of curls and that solid stance. I think she must have learned that stance at the gym. It was a stance where every muscle was flexed—a stance one might see on a *survival* show, when a bear was ready to attack someone. I just looked at Pat and smiled.

"I guess," Pat said, "you don't want to tell me what you and Jill were talking about.

"Pat," I said, "I want to go to yard sales. My conversation with Jill was limited to her health and getting better, that's all."

"Okay," Pat responded laughingly and broke her stance. "Thank goodness."

THE FIRST HOUSE WE VISITED HAD a fabulous garden. I thought of Jill's pickle jar. Imagine if she had these flowers to display. Pat was roaring with laughter as she held up a pair of mukluks. *For the person who has everything,* I thought.

"Hey," she laughed, "the price is great. Three dollars!" I agreed. If no one bought it at the auction it would still be worth the laugh. I then spotted a vase. It was fifty cents. It was crystal, but not the best quality. It sure was nicer than a pickle jar. I was such a softie. Just as I went to purchase it, I noticed a beautiful patch of black-eyed Susan. This perennial flower added so much to a garden. I then felt a tremendous pain in my inner upper leg. A bee had flown up my shorts and stung me. I let out a scream, dropped the vase, and grabbed my inner thigh. Pat ran over. Of course, being in such a precarious place did not help the situation. The woman who was running the yard sale came over as fast as she could with a small bottle of meat tenderizer. She immediately told me to apply it to the sting. Pat and I ran to her car.

"This is not going to be easy," Pat said.

"I really don't care," I yelled. "Pat, I am in pain! The pain is awful!" I hunched down in the back and removed my shorts. I then applied the meat tenderizer. Fortunately the stinger was not present, and thankfully I was not allergic to bees. But there was pain and I longed for ice. Well, it wasn't ice, but the woman managed to bring me some packaged frozen peas. Beggars can never be choosers. I accepted the peas. The best part was the woman felt so bad about my dilemma that she gave me the vase. I had dropped it during my mishap with the bee, but it remained unscathed.

By now the gals had an array of items. We decided after the mishap with the bee to do lunch at the Singing Fisherman. "Forget lunch, I am ready for a piña colada," I said as I limped to the watering hole. There we discussed the upcoming auction. We laughed over the crazy purchases, and true to common knowledge, I slowly forget the bee sting between my legs.

That night the saying, "one man's junk is another man's gold," was put into place. We had labeled the things we collected, but still our guests arrived with more donations. The rule was firm—no donation, no entry. Some gifts had been dropped of ahead of time because some people wanted to be incognito. I guess when one dropped off a book on Kama Sutra people might question one's athletic ability. Maybe Pat would purchase it—she had great athletic ability. After glancing at a few positions, I guessed one might have to be a contortion artist.

George came up to the donation table holding a huge wrought-iron chandelier. One thing about George—when sober he was a great electrician. In fact, George could be charming and tremendously helpful. He had a boyish grin that lit up his whole face when he was talking. He had watery eyes that seemed to make people feel he sympathized with them. I could see why Jill would be attracted to him. "What's up?" I asked. "Is this a donation?"

"No," he replied. "I need a favor. One of the yacht clubs in the area gave me this fixture to fix. Because of its size I need to find a place in the clubhouse. It is too awkward in the boat."

One of the members heard the conversation between George and I and intervened. "Not a problem," he reported. So George put the chandelier in one of the small offices where he felt it was safe and where no one would bother it.

I then decided to ask George about how Jill was feeling. George bent down to where I was seated, looked straight into my eyes as he placed one hand on my shoulder, and replied, "Jill is feeling much better, thank you for visiting her. In fact, you just might see her this evening. She needs a night off." He seemed very concerned. Actually, when he spoke so sincerely he caught me by surprise, but then again I knew the boyish grin and the charm he could turn on and off so convincingly. Then George gave me a wink and departed. I didn't care for the wink. Did it mean we had a shared secret? What scared me was that we did. The good news was Jill was feeling better and had gone back to work.

Tony was busy in the galley helping prepare a spaghetti dinner. The price was set for five dollars per person, and that included a meatball. Tony was on a stool overlooking a huge cauldron set on a gigantic stove. In his hand he had an oar from a paddleboat. I was told the oar was new and made a great giant utensil for stirring the sauce. This was one for the books. Tony was with a group of his mates in the galley cooking up a feast. Tony loved to cook for large amounts of people. A lot of the members liked to gather here—they called it the comfort room. The lowest mate peeled the garlic. The poor mate ended up being alone most of the evening after that venture. Then there was the pepper chopper, long, green Italian peppers only, thank you. Of course the best part was the official tasters. They decided if it was seasoned properly and that the meatballs were the right consistency. Nothing was worse than a sawdust meatball. That was a meatball that had too much bread, not enough meat, and not enough eggs. We knew when the consistency was right because the crew broke out in a chorus of moaning and groaning and licked their lips in pleasure. No one ever goes hungry at a yacht club; as I said, the galley was a place of comfort and camaraderie. As long as someone was cooking in the galley, the kitchen was open to all members and guests.

A huge bell was sounded and the auction started. The auctioneer was a very serious member. This was something he must have wanted to do in his prior life. He must have practiced for weeks on his oral presentation. He looked like he was from the Midwest, and he acted like he was about to auction cattle. He stood on a platform and had actually borrowed a gavel from the boardroom. I knew this gavel would definitely be used to keep the crowd from getting out of line and to keep the bidding in line.

The first items were three pairs of navy blue socks. They were stretchy high ups. They were probably donated because they stopped the circulation in most men's legs. Not a hot item, but charity always rings in the hearts of many clubs. Five big ones were collected—not bad. The next item was the unbreakable vase. I buy it for three dollars. I have a motive—it will be a replacement for Jill's pickle jar.

Next, the Kama Sutra book was on the auction block. After many laughs and a few positions demonstrated with attire on, the book goes to the quietest member of the club for fifty dollars. My mom always said to watch the quiet ones. As he clasped the book in his hands, he turned beet red. A couple of girls sitting at the bar called out his name. He turns to them and asks them if they would like to read the book with him. They started to get up and walk towards him, and he went maroon red in the face. They got close to him and put their arms around him. He grabbed them and started dancing, and then he did a split on the floor but couldn't get up. The gals help him and take him to the bar for a drink. Laughter was ringing through the room, and everyone was getting into a relaxed mode.

It was the mukluks that brought the next outburst after four dollars and a demonstration by the new owner. All of a sudden the place was screaming with hysteria over a huge wrought-iron chandelier that was being carted in by two members. I took one look and tried to get the auctioneer's attention. I had to explain that the item was not to be sold but fixed. But there was a group of people blocking my way, and they were bidding furiously. I needed a gavel now and looked for George to help me, but he was nowhere to be found. I started yelling for them to stop, but my voice was like a whisper in the crowd. This couldn't be happening. But it was. The gaudy chandelier went for forty dollars. Worse than that, however, was the arrangement that the buyer wanted to destroy the ugly fixture on sight. By now the crowd was egging the new owner on to destroy the fixture. With wild emotions in play, the glass beads on the chandelier started to fly around the room. Another member offered to pay ten dollars more to partake in the destruction of the gaudy light fixture. This continued until $125 had been collected and a naked chandelier was carried to its rest. The trash bin now held its remains. My heart was beating so fast. I felt so responsible, even though I had nothing to do with its demise. Everyone who partook reveled in their good deed. All I could think was that it would be impossible to explain and definitely not something I could cover up easily with so many people witnessing its destruction. No use ruining the evening now—there was nothing I could do. We have all put too much hard work into this event, and the horrible truth was that the chandelier was ugly. It almost gave me that eerie feeling of watching *The Phantom of the Opera*. I bet when the neighboring club found out what happened to their fixture a real phantom would appear.

The auction ended with a whopping eight-hundred-dollar profit. Tony and his crew departed from the galley and were greeted with a ton of applause. The food was great. I decided to stay silent about the hottest and most profitable item of the evening.

Chapter 7

Relating the Story to George

I HAD BEEN PUTTING OFF THE inevitable. It took a few days to finally get my courage up. I knew I had to pay George a visit and explain what happened to the chandelier. I would be very surprised if he hadn't heard the news by now. I also had the vase I purchased as a gift for Jill. Neither one showed up for the auction. I really was not looking forward to this. As I approached their boat I noticed an argument taking place. I almost walked away, but Jill's sobbing got my attention. I heard her say, "Don't make me do this any more, my body and nerves won't take it."

With that the front cabin door was flung open and George appeared. "How long have you been outside my boat?" he asked.

"I just got here," I reply. "Is everything okay?" He gives me a hopeless shrug, and I ask him why he didn't come up to the auction the other night. Before I could explain the purpose of my visit, he jumped off the boat and shook his head in disgust. I figured this wasn't the best time to add more salt to his wounds. However, I had the vase and thought it might cheer up Jill. I entered the *Rusty Scupper*. Jill was rolled up in the fetal position. She looked awful. Her eyes were sunken and had black circles around them. She appeared so frail. I was afraid that if she left the boat a gust of wind could push her overboard. I handed her my gift. She took it and smiled. She slowly went over to the pickle jar, removed the flowers from it, and placed them in the new vase. I must say it looked nice. The pickle jar was now like the chandelier—stripped of its purpose. I looked at her. "Jill, can we talk?" I could tell that she really did not want to respond. I knew I should put this off, but I had to get this off my chest. I decided to take the attention off her and put it on me. "Jill, I really need to tell you something. I know it is not a good time, but it is important that I tell you this. This has nothing to do with you; it is in regards to George. If you could just listen to what happened the other night. Jill, I really wished you had come up to the club; you would have experienced it firsthand. But maybe you can help me solve the problem anyway."

I thought with this approach she might feel needed, and I was taking the attention off her problems. It worked, and she started to respond positively. "Okay, let me hear what you came to say." I proceed to tell her the saga of the chandelier. When I was done, I noticed her expression. For the first time in a while I saw a smile. She then smirked. Then I saw a belly laugh so strong that I couldn't help but join in. She said, "This is so funny!" I realized that some of her attitude was revenge for her encounter with George, but all in all it really was funny. We were laughing so hard that tears were starting to form in our eyes. Then, with a choking giddiness she said, "Now let him see what it is like being up against it." I tell her I didn't really think it was funny, but it was kind of like an oxymoron. Now she was laughing harder.

"It takes a moron like George to know one!" she screams, and this type of craziness went on for quite a while. I thought in this case laughter was the best medicine for her. When I left, I felt good that I had taken the time to reach out beyond myself and not let myself be influenced by others. I made her laugh. She made me laugh. For a few minutes in time, we connected for the better. Maybe that was what it was all about, touching someone's life even if just for a little while and connecting for the better. However, George was another story. What would his reaction be?

Chapter 8

Gearing Up for Labor Day

As the fall season approached, a lot of members were deciding to pull their boats out of the water. Some of them got in their boats and sailed or cruised to warmer climates. And so without saying goodbye, the *Rusty Scupper* sailed off early one morning. Rumor had it George never paid his dues. I was sure it also had to do with the news Jill told him about the chandelier. The worst part was that as time went by talk on the floats implied that the club that owned the chandelier had accused George of actually stealing that gaudy fixture. The Vice Commodore intervened, feeling that the fixture was left in the premises of Briar Ridge and therefore the club was responsible and made restitution for the light fixture. One thing was for sure—the officers agreed that if George ever wanted to come back, he would have to make full restitution for the chandelier and for his dues. He probably would be required to do some extra chores to remain in good graces with the club.

Tony was gearing up for the Labor Day dance and the invasion of neighboring clubs. My job was to set the theme for this occasion. I was also to set up all the tables with the proper linen for the evening affair and make sure the centerpieces were of fresh flowers. I also was expected to raise a few coins for charity. I was thinking to myself how much time this would take away from my family. This was a busy time of year because I was getting all the children geared for school.

I sat down and discussed this with Tony. He told me there were a lot of members' wives and girlfriends who had asked to help the Rear

Commodore's wife. "Just get on the phone and ask, hon," Tony said. "You will be so surprised at the results." I decided to take him up on this suggestion. I would ask Pat if she would help me call a few girls. When Tony's reign as Rear Commodore was over, all the money I raised with the help of my team would go towards something for the improvement of the club. Or, as they say in cards, I could let it ride. It could also go Thru the Chairs. If Tony continued to go Thru the Chairs, the money would continue to grow as well, and at the end of his reign I would decide what improvement the club needed and dedicate the money to that particular need. Last year it was a new dance floor. I had plenty of time to think on this issue.

As Tony walked away from me, he bumped into Paul Adler. They both started talking about the upcoming events, and Paul seemed extremely moody. He felt George and the *Rusty Scupper* should return and face up to the chandelier incident. Soon enough someone would let the cat out of the bag and we would be facing an embarrassment. Tony laughed and reminded him that we had already paid for the damn light.

That night Tony noticed that I was preoccupied with how to get all the school shopping done and be involved with the Labor Day functions. He said, "Hon, I have an idea that would involve everyone. Members, wives, and girlfriends could all take part in this charity event to raise money." Tony's ingenious idea was to run a horse race as part of the Labor Day festivities. Tony, being in construction, said, "Hon, it would be easy to create and design six wooden horses. They would be similar to the ones children put between their legs and prance around with. Their heads would be rag mops trimmed to look like a mane. Your crew could paint the faces. We could collect various hats to portray the character and name of the horse and rider. What do you think, Hon?"

I grabbed him around the neck and said, "I love the idea. I will get on the phone tomorrow, Tony, and call the girls for help."

Chapter 9

Mary Gets Involved

I THINK THE BEST PART OF this idea was the phone call I made to Mary. I explained to her what we were going to do to raise money for the club on Labor Day. I told her about the horse races and what we needed. Mary said, "Jim and I would love to get involved in this project. Please count us in." My phone calling got a lot of other positive responses. At our next meeting, excitement filled the club. The best part was the appearance of Jim and Mary. They realized life went on, their daughter loved the club, and they needed to be surrounded by their friends, who knew and loved their daughter too. They were welcomed with open arms and tears. The best feeling went through my body. Imagine not having a place to go when you needed it most. This was when I loved camaraderie. Loneliness is the worst disease of all in my opinion. When you reach out and there is no one to hold you, talk to you, or feel your pain, what do you do? When a person feels they have entered the valley of despair and all hope is gone, is there someone to turn to? Is there someone out there that can relate to them and help them? May I, dear reader, or you, never experience this, but if we do, may we have the deep compassion that surrounded Jim and Mary at Briar Ridge Club that night. Human contact is so important, and it was displayed vigorously and emotionally that night.

It was known that many yacht clubs were havens on the water, places to escape from the heavy responsibilities that life could demand. It was very common to see family members on members' boats resting, celebrating, or just looking for a few moments of peace.

I had a different source of peace. I was lucky and had the galley.

There was an older past Commodore who would donate his time to just being a cook. My friend would stay late into the evening, preparing food for the following day. He loved Tony, but he loved cooking more. He looked very much like a cheff seen in many paintings. He was one of those jolly, fat, loving people who found a great deal of comfort in cooking. He even had a mustache that curled up at each corner. Sometimes I sat at night just talking to him while he prepared his next concoction. He would make my problems seem so insignificant. I had to laugh because each time he tasted the food he was cooking, part of it clung to his mustache like an ornament on a tree. He would say, "Why are you laughing?"

I would reply, "Your comfort in cooking creates such an aura that makes me feel relaxed and able to tell you my problems." I mentioned that I was having a hard time dividing my time between Tony, the club, and my family.

He smiled back at me and said, "Family is everything. Sometimes we get caught up in trying to make everyone around us happy. This is very difficult. You will eventually learn that people come and go. They touch your life for a reason. Sometimes these reasons are good, and other times they are bad. Sometimes all your hard-fought efforts will never be appreciated. However, your children and your husband will be with you for a very long time, God willing. If you feel you have time and energy after you have given your family their due, then let the rest of your time spill over to your friends."

I smiled and said, "Can I taste that?" He laughed as he handed over his latest concoction.

PAT WAS REALLY EXCITED AFTER MY phone call to her asking for her assistance in the Labor Day festivities. She asked if she could be in charge of all the trimmings that would identify the new wooden horses. Of course I agreed. Pat was dependable, and I knew the job would get done. The unveiling would take place at the club bar at cocktail time. We decided that around five o'clock would be respectable. I had to say that Pat's cheerful attitude over this event made me so happy that I really was looking forward to naming these cute little wooden creatures. The magical hour arrived, and so did Pat with her arms full of mysterious articles. As she entered the room, I couldn't help notice how her authoritarian attitude came into place. Pat actually marched over to the table and placed all the bags down in order. Each bag was labeled horse one, horse two, and so one. Six bags neatly decorated the large table. I thought to myself that if women were eventually allowed to become commodores, Pat would be a perfect candidate. She took the task extremely serious and wanted our stable to represent our hard work. Pat had such enthusiasm when she spoke. She held up the bag labeled horse one and explained its final décor. First she displayed a fireman's hat. Then Pat included a scarf with mini Dalmatians on it. The scarf was to be placed around the horse's neck or the neck of the jockey. This horse was named Fire Hose. Number two horse had a police hat and a shiny badge that would be pinned to the mane, which was of course a cut-up rag mop. This horse was called Car 54. We all snickered as we knew Pat had such a sweet spot for that particular TV series. Number three horse would have a cowboy hat. The chosen rider would have a cap gun and would be allowed to shoot it if need be. This stallion's name was Hop-Along Cassadici—the Italian influence was seeping in. Now the Irish girls wanted a horse, so the number four horse ended up with a hat left over from last year's St. Paddy's Day party. They also got a promise from Pat to find a shamrock pin. We girls name her Kelly's Pride. Horse number five had a hat with a huge purple plume. The mane would have purple beads threaded through it, and the horse would be called Mardi Gras. Pat finally pulled out her last few items, which included a pirate's hat and a patch for the chosen rider's eye. By now a few of the gals were getting a little inebriated and so very silly. Mary started laughing so hard. We were so happy to have her there with us. Mary was a tall, stately lady. She had a reddish crown of hair that she wore in a bun. Mary reminded me of Katharine Hepburn. She looked at us and between giggles said, "This horse must be the long short. Who ever heard of a one-eyed jockey running in a race?" She was laughing so hard that we all realized a part of her was back. "What eye should the patch be on?" Mary asked. She got up and did a demo of the jockey with the left eye patched. She pretended to smash into the rail, and we all started laughing. She then switched the patch to the right eye. She asked me to stand up and pretend I was riding the race against her. I was on her right side.

I started to laugh and said, "Mary, am I the jockey or the horse?" Now everyone was laughing.

Mary said, "Who do you prefer?"

I said, "The jockey."

Then Mary said, "How the heck would I know which one you are? I can't see out of that eye." We all laugh some more.

"Mary, we get your point," I said.

"Hey, Mary, I think it is a good idea if you name this horse," Pat yells. We all agree to let Mary name this horse. She got a little serious, looked over at Jim, who was playing pool at the other end of the bar, and then she put her head down. Before Mary said anything, however, she threw the patch into the rubbish. Then Mary blurted out, "The Lion's Paw!" We all looked at each other and tried to relate this name to the horse, but before we have a chance Mary continued, "It's like a lion's paw in your stomach when you lose a child, a gnawing that comes and goes. When this feeling occurs you feel you have to run, but sometimes you lose sight of what direction you're running in. The truth is, no matter how much you run or how lost you feel you always have the intuition to run home." When Mary finished talking it was amazing how we all sobered up.

It was more amazing how we all said in unison, "Number six horse, The Lion's Paw, and may she run home." Mary stood up and in her stately fashion replied, "It is good to be among friends. I try not to be so serious, but thank you for letting me express myself. I hope I did not destroy the fun we were all having."

Pat stood up, placed her arm around Mary, and said, "The Lion's Paw will be a credit to our stable."

Chapter 10

Off to the Races

LABOR DAY ARRIVED AND OFF TO the races it was. I had finally convinced my children to take part by telling them that I needed them. I decided to reverse roles. The boys could help set up the race track for me. The first question my older son asked was, "Mom, can we gamble too?" Considering it was for charity, I said I would think it over. My daughter would waitress.

My daughter wanted to know, "Mom, can we keep our tips?"

I said, "Half of your tips should go to charity. However, I will let you decide." With this statement, I prayed I was raising them properly and they would donate half their earnings to charity. I remembered a conversation I had with my friend the past Commodore in the galley. I had told him that I was so tired of repeating the same thing over and over to my children on the subject of proper behavior. His words came back to me.

He said, "Trust your children. As they get older the words that you have said to them become embedded in their brain. Ironically, they usually do the right thing. Have confidence in your teaching. Your job as a parent is to teach, and part of teaching is repeating the lesson." I was hoping that my friend was right; only time would tell.

The nice part was that I had my family with me. The plan was to divide a section of the club into six long rows with twelve huge squares in each row. This was all done in washable chalk. The horses would be lined up in front of each row, and their jockeys would be chosen by unusual circumstances. This was actually on of my son's ideas. He had thought of something he had experienced in camp. I asked what it was. He said, "Mom, every time we had to stand in alphabetical order, I was always the last person to be picked because my last name started with V."

I said, "Son, sometimes being last has its advantage."

He said, "What do you mean, Mom?" I told him a story from when I was a little girl.

I said, "Son, when I was little, polio was a very serious disease. There was no cure for it. My parents kept me in during the hot summer from one o'clock till four o'clock. At the time my parents and many doctors felt that the polio germ raged. How true that was, I do not know. I was but a little girl of six. What I do remember was a vaccine was invented. The children in my class were divided into groups. All the As through Ls were in one group. The rest of the alphabet was in the last group. You know my maiden name started with an R. The object of dividing the class into two parts was that we would all be vaccinated. Some of the group would get the real cure, and the other would get a water-based solution. "This is a vague memory on my part. However, my parents, along with many others, would try anything as long as it would not harm us. Polio was a treacherous disease that crippled the body. Son, I was in the last group. I got the real cure. My picture was in the paper along with the rest of the class from M to Z. It took a long time before the rest of the class could get the proper cure. As I said, I was little, but I was glad I was in the last group." My son smiled at me as if I was making this up. No one made up polio. My childhood memories were very real.

The jockeys were being directed on how to ride these wooden creatures. They would put them between their legs and would try to trot as best they could. The jockey's goal was of course the finish line.

In the first race, the first six people whose name ended with an M would be chosen as the jockeys. This was the letter my son and I arrived at. For the second race, the first six people with blue eyes would be the new riders. The third race was the race of lovers. All the new relationships that had blossomed in the past year would grace the floor. This was not my son's idea. I would like to believe he was too young, but according to his younger sister, he wasn't. The women would ride piggyback on their men, who were the jockeys. The fifth race involved all the handsome men in the club. What was cute about this race was how different women saw men. There were two older women who always sold raffles for the club. They were both widowers. Their husbands were past Commodores. Even though they were not members, they were welcomed at every event. They donated their time to selling raffles. It was a place to come that harbored great memories of their years as Commodores' wives. This was a very good position for them. These ladies knew most of the members, past and present, and their families. Mary thought it a good idea to let these two ladies pick our next jockeys. Some men really did need a full-length mirror. It was amazing how they saw themselves. Some of the men stood up to flex their muscles for the ladies. Other hopeful contestants ran fingers through their hair. The funny part was that some of these men were bald. The cutest scene was when one of the men grabbed the two ladies and started to dance with them. And guess what? Yes, he was picked. The two ladies were very kind. Most of the men picked were judged more on personality than looks. We had our jockeys.

The sixth race was all the Rear Commodores; this race would naturally include the visiting yacht clubs. We felt we saved the best for last. We picked these jockeys by taking the first five Rear Commodores who came though the door. The sixth was Tony. There were also six bookies. They would collect the bets. However, the payoffs would be arranged so that the house got most of the percent because it was going to charity. I decided to let my son, who had asked earlier if he could gamble, be one of the bookies. This way he could see how the house always won. He was very excited to be in this position. I told him, "Son, this is just for fun. This is a charity."

This particular function was going to the orphans' Christmas party. I and a few of my friends were helping the Vice Commodore serve drinks at the bar. All of the waitresses had agreed to put their tips toward the orphans' Christmas party as well. There was a small cage similar to a bingo cage or even a parrot cage. The cage had six large dice in it. Mary would shake the cage until each die landed evenly. Each row would advance whatever number Mary picked from the six shaken dice. We painted the dice in different colors to match the numbers on each jockey's back. For example if number one horse was yellow, then whatever the yellow die landed on was how far he advanced. The same rule applied to each horse, who had their own colors. The first to complete the twelve squares was the winner.

They're off! In the first race, Fire Hose advanced two squares on the first shake, Kelly's Pride one, Hop-Along Cassadici went backwards, so we rerouted him to the fourth position. Car 54 went to the second square in his row. Mardi Gras was on five in that row, but it was The Lion's Paw that went to six. The cheering for that particular wooden horse was so unbelievable. For one second I actually thought that the jockey was riding Sea Biscuit. In all the races, The Lion's Paw either won or came in second. I guess Mary gave the horse the right name. The little wooden horse and jockey wanted to run.

The third race was extremely funny. The girls had placed themselves on the men's shoulders. The men jockeys were expected to race in this position with the wooden horse between their legs. The things we do for love. One of the jockeys dropped his girlfriend off of Mardi Gras, and instead of helping her up he continued to the finish line to win. For some reason this upset her very much. She felt his priorities were off. He was trying to explain to his girlfriend that the object was to win the race. The girlfriend said he could sleep with Mardi Gras instead of her, and then the boyfriend said, "Fine, the horse looks better than you." She then took the beads that were around her neck and flung them at him. Fortunately, Pat grabbed the beads in midair. The best part was that when the girlfriend found out that her boyfriend had put a fifty-dollar bet on Mardi Gras, she agreed his priorities were in order and they made peace.

The best race was the last. The Rear Commodores decided to sing. They took their horses, mounted them, and belted out, "Home on the Range." They did change a few of the lyrics. *"Home, home at the club, where the boats and the officers play. Where never is heard a despairing word,"* and so on and so on. I must say that all these men in uniform really looked good. It was like having a barber shop quartet singing. They actually harmonized. I think it had to have been an officers' trait that they must automatically perform in the line of duty.

After each officer saluted each other, the crowd automatically saluted them. It was a fun night, especially since Kelly's Pride had a great singer. After the Rear Commodores sang, this guest sang "My

Wild Irish Rose." As usual, there was one in every crowd. The jockey on Hop-Along Cassadici fired the cap gun in protest. He preferred a different Irish song. He said it was a command, but nobody issued it. Finally he got his wish, and the great tenor that rode Kelly's Pride sang "Danny Boy." I laughed till there were tears in my eyes. It was hard to imagine that those six little wooden horses could create so much fun. Before the evening was over , our club Commodore stood up and thanked everyone for their hard work and dedication. He said he felt bad that he wasn't asked to sing. Naturally we egged him on to perform.

He laughed and said, "I will perform on the next occasion; I feel the competition with the Rear Commodores is hard to beat, but thanks for asking."

Tony and I sat on *37 Park Ave* after all the activities were over. The children got a ride home, and my mom was waiting there for them. You have to understand—my mom was all alone, and these children gave her a strong reason to feel alive again. Sometimes I was angry at her interference. I felt that it was to confusing having two moms, but now that they were getting older I realized that they were lucky to have both of us. My mom loved them unconditionally, and I loved them with many conditions. That was the difference between mother and grandmother.

Tony and I were realizing that the year was coming to a close. He put his arm around me. The boat was rocking back and forth. It was one of those soothing rocks that I welcomed when I was in someone's arms. It added to the feeling of being loved and comforted. That was probably why babies loved to be rocked—we probably carried the feeling from infancy. We started to laugh about our son's realization that the house always wins in gambling. Tony had tried to explain it to him mathematically. I said at the time, "Son, you watch too many TV shows. On TV sometimes you do not see the real reality in life. Gambling for fun is one thing; but as a habit it can become very dangerous."

Our daughter didn't disappoint us—she was more than happy to donate more than half of her tips to charity. Tony said, "Hon, thank you for being so supportive of me, but most of all thanks for our family. Our children are turning out okay, and I know it is you and your mom who put in most of the time." Tony then looked at me and said, "Sometimes I feel like I am neglecting you because of my desire to go Thru the Chairs."

I had to take a deep breath. I wanted to yell, *"Yes, I think sometimes you are!"* but instead I looked at him and said, "Tony, the children and I do not want to hold you back on your dreams. This has been a long-awaited dream. If you are happy then we are happy. I feel that as long as you give us your best the rest can spill over to going Thru the Chairs." Then to myself I thanked my friend in the galley. My friend was my past Commodore, chef, and mentor.

Tony and I stayed outside on the boat for a very long time. The sky was a velvety black. It reminded me of the piece of cloth that a jeweler puts on the counter before he displayed different stones. The jewels of the sky were much prettier, though. There was a diamond-encrusted Milky Way, there was a canary yellow diamond in the shape of the moon, and there were baby baguettes scattered all over the sky. That night was a jeweler's paradise. It was a grouping of rare gems.

The following morning after a restful evening of sleep, Tony and I discussed the upcoming events. For people like me who loved coffee, having coffee on a boat and watching the sun come up was one of the many wonders of the world. It was a true awakening of body and soul. First, the warm coffee warmed my inner body, and then the sun did the rest. It was such a pleasant way to greet the morning and the one I loved.

The Halloween party and the huge Christmas party were the next two functions on the agenda. I wasn't as concerned with them as I was with the Labor Day festivities. I had learned that I had plenty of help. I just had to ask for it. I also had to involve my children, and maybe in this case my mother.

Chapter 11

Is It October?

IT SEEMED ONCE LABOR DAY WAS over, people got more into their everyday routine and days went by faster. It was already October. This was always a fun month. Everyone usually loved Halloween. It was a chance for people to disguise themselves and get away with more mischief than normal. The club was planning a party, so I called different people and as usual the same people responded as had for the last function.

I think we can all relate to this. Some people say, "Call me if there is anything I can do," but it is just a term they use; they never show up to do anything. Our club was no exception. The good news was that it was only a small minority, and I had friends to help. And then there were those lovely ladies that I liked very much. They were the older ladies, whose husbands were past Commodores. They had played such a fun role in the last function picking out the studs that I felt I would give them a call. As I mentioned, these ladies loved the social aspect of the club because they always had a place to go. They always felt safe. Most of all, they did not have to depend on their families to entertain them. The club gave them a sense of independence because they had their own social circle. I found on some occasions that I was even asking them for advice. There were a lot of things I did not understand about the officers' duties, and through these ladies' past experiences I thought I might learn something. I felt that these women would be pleased to be involved, so I picked up the phone and called them.

"Hi," I said and proceeded with my spiel. What a nice response I got.

"Of course I would like to help," the first one I called said.

The second lady responded, "You know, dear, I feel my husband's presence when I am at the yacht club. Thank you for asking me to help." I decided to ask them to collect tickets for the different functions. The combination of the two women at the different functions was the best thing I could do. These ladies not only new every officer at the club, but they knew every visiting officer from most of the other clubs and their wives or girlfriends. These ladies were going to be the best guest greeters.

Within a few weeks, our meeting took place for the Halloween party. The colors were easy—black and orange. The centerpieces would be pumpkins. One of the decisions was designing the pumpkins with a candle inside to be lit at each table. The second choice was to just scoop the pumpkin clean and place fresh flowers in them.

"Let's perform surgery," Tony's requested. Then Tony announced, "If you place lit candles in pumpkins with dried leaves, it could be dangerous. People are having fun. You know that fire laws really do not encourage this type of centerpiece." I looked around at the committee that had come to help.

I addressed the issue and said, "What do you think we should do with these pumpkins?" Pat motioned to cut out the pumpkins.

Mary said, "I second the motion."

Tony laughed and said, "That is the decision." Jim, Tony, and a few other members would cut out the pumpkins. Pat, Mary, and I would purchase some glow-in-the-dark paints.

I asked Tony and Jim, "What are you using to cut out these pumpkins with?" Jim laughed and his eyes curled up at the corners. I hadn't seen that in a while and found it very comforting.

Jim said, "Drills."

I said, "I really would feel better with surgeons performing this task." Everyone laughed. I then looked up and saw Sam tiptoeing towards us.

He said, barely above a whisper, "I would like to help. I can make some sandwiches to serve while everyone is cutting up pumpkins."

Tony said, "Sam, don't ask—just do it. You do not need permission to do something good. Sam, please take control of the sandwiches." I guess Tony was trying to tell Sam that if he wanted to be an officer he had to learn to be more assertive. We all agreed Sam was really trying hard to be helpful, and we all realized that he wanted to be an officer of this club. I hoped he made it next year as Rear Commodore. Tony, for one, I felt would give him his support.

Time went by fast. Everyone showed up for the cutting-out party. Huge platters of salami, roast beef, and imported cheeses prepared by Sam were placed on a buffet table. Victor, a huge bulk of a man, was one of Tony's newer crew members. He almost looked like Barnacle Bill the Sailor. He had a huge black beard, and his eyes were piercing. In my opinion he looked very threatening. However, as I had told Pat in the past, "Do not judge a book by its cover."

Victor was flashing his knife back and forth like he was going to kill the pumpkin rather than perform a surgical task. In fact, he was making us girls a little nervous. I remarked, "Victor, maybe you would rather paint." He just gave me a sly grin, the kind that was almost a dare. I felt like Victor was daring me to take the knife away from him. I tried to let this feeling pass.

I noticed that the other carvers were creating some very good faces. Then Sam came over and said to Victor, "What kind of a pumpkin is that?"

Victor held up his creation and laughed in Sam's face. We were all shocked. Victor had made a Nazi pumpkin. He had created a mini Hitler with a swastika over its mini head. Victor laughed louder. He then stood up and said, "Hail Hitler." This statement sent Sam over the edge. The gentle Sam we knew had now become enraged with anger. Sam went to grab the pumpkin with every intention of demolishing it. Victor was so huge and so fierce that Sam did not have a chance of overpowering him. Victor took the knife he was working with and stabbed Sam in the wrist. This all happened within seconds. Victor was laughing, while Sam stood in shock. Then Victor ran out of the clubhouse yelling, "Hitler Rules!" A few members chased after him.

Tony was busy with Sam, wrapping his wrist up as best as he possibly could. Tony and his friends put Sam into Tony's car and took him to the emergency room at the local hospital. Sam was mumbling as he left, "I can't believe this happened in this day and age."

The rest of us were left at the club in shock. The pumpkin remains were on the floor. Part of the remains that had the swastika also had

Sam's blood. The scene resembled a part of the past. Something that we thought was over, but like the lion's paw it still kept churning in the society we lived in and in the stomachs of the people that it touched.

By now some of the men were at the hospital and some were chasing Victor. The girls that were helping me grabbed the remaining pumpkins and segregated them from Victor's. Then Mary literally destroyed all traces of Victor's sadistic creation. It looked like Mary was getting even with the lion's paw. We watched her take out a lot of hurt on that mangled pumpkin. Pat and I let her. We knew it would only help her for the time being.

Sam required seven stitches that night, and fortunately no nerves were severed. Tony told me later that night how Sam felt. He said, "Hon, mentally Sam is reminded of the prejudice that still exists. On the way back from the hospital Sam told me, 'My dreams of becoming Rear Commodore of this club are just dreams. It will never happen.'"

I said, "What do you think about Sam's chances?"

Tony became very serious. "I think Sam's chances are like anyone else's who has been held down in society because of prejudice. You can become an ostrich and stick your head in the sand, or you can fight for what you believe in. If Sam feels he would make a great Rear Commodore then it is up to him to convince the club. One thing about the club and any other club, no matter what kind it is—no one likes a quitter."

I then said to Tony, "What about Victor?"

Tony said, "The necessary channels will handle that. This has nothing to do with you, hon. Please don't worry about Victor. Your chances of seeing him again are rare."

"Tony," I yelled, "How did a knife-twirling lunatic get into this club?"

Tony put his arms around me and said, "Every day in every walk of life something falls through the cracks, and no matter how hard you try to avoid it mistakes are made."

SAM REFUSED TO PRESS CHARGES FOR the good of the club. He did not want to call attention to this episode. Tony told me how upset he was over Sam's decision—he disagreed with Sam regarding the police. Sam felt that enough charges would be handled by the club. Tony and Sam knew Victor would be expelled. Everyone who witnessed the horrific experience knew that the club would never tolerate that type of behavior. We all realized that the final decision would be made by the Commodore, and Tony informed Sam it was the Rear Commodore's responsibility to address the issue to the Commodore. Tony had said to me over and over again, "I know the club will handle this properly. The Commodore will never let Victor get away with what he did, but I still feel Sam should press charges with the police."

I commented, "Tony, the club is run like the police. He will lose all his privileges."

"One thing for sure," Tony said, "Victor's boat will be towed out of his slip and put on a mooring until he can make arrangements to have it hauled out." This, to a boatman, was a fate worse than death. The girls and I looked forward to watching this take place. No one had heard of or seen Victor since that terrible night.

The Halloween party finally took place with a cloud of uneasiness over it. Sam was there, and surprisingly his wife made an appearance as well. It was a great gesture. They danced, laughed, and showed us that fear was something they would not give in to. Sam and his wife were no ostriches. The evening got better when Mary and Jim took the best costume. Mary was a brick and Jim was a bricklayer. Leave it to construction workers to come up with that idea. The highlight of the dance were the guest greeters. They welcomed everyone with open arms. The hugging and laughter and trips down memory lane at the front entrance were wonderful. Those ladies were loved, and I hoped one day I would get that same respect.

Chapter 12

Election Time

I COULDN'T BELIEVE NOVEMBER WAS APPROACHING. It was that time of year again. Just as in the presidential elections, the club was making preparations for Briar Ridge's next vote. Tony' responsibilities would not end until the end of the year. I am sure Tony was not contemplating campaigning with all the work he still had ahead of him as Rear Commodore. However, I am sure this issue was in back of Tony's mind, as it was in mine. Tony's chances at Vice Commodore were good. Everyone felt he had done a great job so far, but the year was not over till December 31. I know that Tony wanted to start the New Year as Vice Commodore; he wanted to go Thru the Chairs. The club liked an officer who went Thru the Chairs. One thing for sure was that a Rear Commodore had a lot of responsibility. I had firsthand experience on some of the matters Tony was involved in. Another thing about the club was they were not too fond of someone who tried to break the chairs. The true test of leadership was the first chair, and in my opinion it was the hardest. However, at the upcoming meeting members would have the right to post their names for the various offices and positions opening up. We knew Sam would be running again for Rear Commodore, and Tony informed me that a lot of the members were backing Peter Flanagan and John Dunne. Both these men were part of the float committee, and both men had worked with extreme physical force to secure the arrivals and dispatches of boats for members and guests. This was quite an accomplishment considering the club had no boating accidents all year. Tony was pretty confident about being Vice Commodore, but once in a while someone tried to break the chairs. Usually they failed, and this year would be no exception.

Unfortunately, no matter how hard one tries, there would always be someone who had issues with one's performance as an officer. Garry, who was considered the club joker, took a bet from a few token men who felt Tony was not doing a good job. Garry was egged on to break Thru the Chairs and be Vice Commodore. Naturally, Tony was offended. He truly felt that he was beyond reproach. One night before we went to bed, he made this comment: "We all know that clubs have the helpers who work hard and the complainers who use criticism to prevent them from actually getting involved. These criticizers actually have no actions to contribute for the good of the club, just a lot of negative rhetoric. You know I feel I deserve to be Vice Commodore." I laughed it off.

"Tony," I chuckled, "sometimes you wish these characters would actually get elected. Then they would have a chance to see what leadership is all about." In the meantime Tony still had work to do, and I still had functions to plan. Therefore, I did not campaign. I felt if Tony was going to get elected he would succeed on his own merits. My husband had done and was doing a good job in my opinion.

The first week in November arrived. Tony went to the club for the elections. It was a landslide win for Tony! He stayed for a small celebration but could not wait to come home and really celebrate it with me and the children. Even my mom came over and had a glass of wine with us. I said, "It is very hard to break the chairs. I had faith in the club and faith in you, Tony."

Tony said, "One bit of sad news. Sam didn't make it as Rear Commodore." I would never know the reason since the final elections were held behind closed doors in the members' boardroom. Tony was not about to go into detail about why Sam didn't make Rear Commodore. Peter Flanagan had a landslide win. Peter would be the new Rear Commodore. I guess the physical aspect of hard work seemed to prevail more than the culinary skills that Sam had to offer in the galley. Even though the year for us still was not over, the excitement of 1987 and Tony making Vice Commodore was something I and the children were proud of. The best part was that Tony felt he could involve the boys in this position. They were teenagers, old enough to work in the clubhouse. Tony said that for a few hours during the week they could help him set up tables and chairs for the different functions. Our daughter, on certain occasions now that she was getting older, could waitress. My mother did not look so happy over this decision because she liked to stay close to home and was not a social person. She loved her family. The thought of not having her grandchildren constantly around her bothered her. However, my husband wanted her to get used to it. He knew as I did that once they were in their late teens and early twenties we would probably see very little of them. Once they were driving, which one of our sons was, they would always want to take off with their friends.

Chapter 13

Thanksgiving Preparation

As I mentioned before, our club was big on charity, and Thanksgiving Day was no exception. Pat, Mary, and I purchased turkeys that were stuffed and precooked. We distributed them to several nursing homes the day before Thanksgiving. The weather had been nasty, dropping several feet of snow in our wintry New England area, so this mission of delivering turkeys on nasty, snowy roads would require some manpower. Tony received a call from Peter Flanagan, our future Rear Commodore. He offered to drive some of the turkey committee to the various nursing homes. Peter was a young, happy-go-lucky sort of guy. Things didn't seem to bother him much. He was always laughing about something. In fact, I never really saw him in a bad mood. He had sandy hair and wore it in a Dutch boy hairdo. It was as if he had taken a Tupperware bowl, put it over his head, and trimmed around it with scissors. One of the great things about Peter was that he had a plow on the front of his truck. He felt he could accommodate us quite nicely on these icy roads. Pat and I decided to ride with Peter. Tony and Jim took the rest of the girls and turkeys. With a happy thanksgiving feeling we sent out towards our destinations. Ironically, the nursing home that Pat and I went to was Belford Housing for the Elderly. As we entered this lonely facility we heard a meek little voice welcome us in. As I turned to see who had spoken, lo and behold it was one of the past Commodores, Joe Pissano.

His term was over twenty years ago. Our club portrayed pictures of all our Commodores, and even though he had aged there were still recognizable traits. The rumor around the club was that he had bouts with senility. Evidently his family felt these bouts were severe enough for Joe to be placed here. I decided to spend some time with Joe because to me loneliness was a horrible disease. I tried to go down memory lane with Joe, but all I could remember were passed on stories. I was a young girl then with no real connections to the club. It was funny how memory loss impacted what he had for breakfast, but the past for Joe was zeroed in. After all, his future certainly looked glum since he was in a nursing home. So I relived Joe's famous memories about the early stages of the club. Joe couldn't wait to go back in time to when youth was so taken for granted.

During Joe's reign the men had a special area for their lockers. This area was confined to officers only. One night when Joe was departing from the club, he heard some heavy laughter. This particular locker area was undergoing some renovation, so access to the property was easier than expected. It was not common to witness a few break-ins. Most of them involved teenagers looking for a place to drink or smoke. Being an officer, Joe decided he should approach the situation. He proceeded quietly. Perhaps to quiet, because he saw his Rear Commodore with a woman, enjoying the pleasures of life. Joe was so startled that he let out an, "Oh my God!" The officer in question was so stunned that he hightailed it through the window, leaving the lady in a terrible position. She screamed and ran. However, the Rear Commodore had one problem—he was naked. Joe ambushed the both of them on the other side of the building. The lady in distress was holding the majority of her clothing, and when she looked up Joe realized that it was his sister. The Rear Commodore was still standing in his birthday suit, but he immediately covered himself up with a two-by-four from the construction site. Joe gave the Rear Commodore a severe flogging, interrupted only by pitiful sobs from his sister. She left the scene half clad, screaming that she refused to marry her fiancée, that she felt it was an arranged marriage, and that she was madly in love with the Rear Commodore.

Now, I had heard many versions of this story, but Joe looked at me and said, "My sister was right. My dad was forcing her to marry a man she didn't love and who was twice her age. My dad was so afraid that she would get pregnant and embarrass the family. He arranged the marriage when she turned nineteen."

"How very sad," I replied.

Joe then said, "The funny part is I agreed with my sister. I liked the Rear Commodore. He was a young boy who I think liked my sister. I went to my father and told him that he was making my sister's life miserable. My father said to me, 'Joe, you handle your sister.'"

I said, "What did you do, Joe?"

"Three months later the Rear and my sister were married," he said as he smiled.

So, I thought, *what started out as an embarrassing situation ended in a happy occasion*. Of course people always wondered whether the Rear's career was at stake in the club. Joe was a powerful Commodore in his day.

No one would mock his sister, and if word leaked out that she was having sex in the locker room with the Rear Commodore, Joe could say, "She was overcome with love." The marriage, according to Joe, lasted long enough to produce a niece. The couple moved to Florida, got divorced, and his sister was still there with her daughter. Joe's eyes watered. I didn't know if it was because he missed them or if they had lost contact over the years. Joe himself never married. I guess after devoting so many years to his political ambitions, he lost his desire for family life. In the end this was the only place for him to be taken care of. Again, I had heard the story many times from different sources, and each time it got bigger and better. I guess Joe told the story because it was better coming from him—that way no one could question it. I wanted to believe Joe's version, especially the part about speaking up against his father's decision. No one should be forced to marry someone they didn't love. As I looked outside, I noticed the snow was piling up. I gave Joe a hug and a sad farewell. I had a lot more turkeys to drop off.

When I got home, I was exhausted. Tony fixed me a drink, a Hot Toddy. I then proceeded to tell him my encounter with Joe and retold him the story. Tony mentioned that years ago people at the club felt that if the Rear Commodore in question had not married Joe's sister he could have been tarred and feathered. This led Tony and I into hysterics. We laughed because each time the story was heard, it got funnier and funnier.

TONY STILL HAD TO GET THE rest of the boats secured for winter. Most of them were out of the water, and some had left for warmer places. The *Rusty Scupper* was long gone, and I hoped Jill would have a decent winter. I had no idea where she and George were headed, but Florida was usually where a lot of the boaters from our area went. Tony was on the floats with a crew that was shrink-wrapping the boats as they came out of the water. There were men hauling other boats into the boatyard where they would be stored for the winter. Victor's boat had finally been picked up by his brother.

When asked where Victor was, his brother replied, "I don't know and I don't care." As I was watching all this action take place, I saw Pat passing by. Pat came over and reminded me that she and Mary wanted to know about the Christmas bazaar, the orphanage Christmas party, and the members' children's Santa party. I got so tired just thinking of the planning that still had to be done.

I looked at Pat and said, "For the first time this year, Pat, I want it to be over. I never realized the responsibility Tony has as Rear Commodore. I hope Vice Commodore is not as demanding."

Pat laughed and said, "This part is fun. I know you—you love children. This is the best time of year, and you are in a position to make it extra special. Mary and I are here for you." I reached out and gave Pat a big hug.

I said, "Pat, you and Mary are my closest friends Thanks for putting my priorities in order. This is the best time of year."

Chapter 14

Operation Reindeer

THE NEXT DAY I GOT ON the phone. I called some members and their wives asking for donations. I especially needed baked goods and crafts. One of the members had a pattern on a reindeer that had a wooden basket for a body. I asked him if he could drop it off at the member's lounge at the club. Tony could make anything out of wood, and he would be happy to look at the plans. Tony had a cute shop over our garage where he and our children had created some very special projects over the years. This would be a great idea, and I could involve the children. Everyone I called was so responsive—I guess Christmas brought that out in people, and the club was usually very supportive when it came to charity events. The pattern of the reindeer was dropped off within a few days, and to my surprise Tony fell in love with the reindeer project. Tony agreed he would get his crew together and they would start construction as soon as possible. He asked the boys to help. Reluctantly they agreed. They really were becoming teenagers.

I would need my own crew to be creative in painting faces on these wooden does. The finishing touches would include varnish to give them a shiny personality. Pat was dying to paint the red noses. Mary got so excited that she wanted to go into the woods to collect pinecones. Mary felt that after the reindeers were varnished we could place the pinecones into the basket bodies of the reindeer. Tony felt he could construct one dozen, so Operation Reindeer took place. A few days later, Jim gave Tony a call and said Mary had vanished into the woods singing, "Rudolph the Red-nosed Reindeer." She came back carrying a large basketful of pine cones. Jim told Tony he had a small band saw that would be great for the reindeer's antlers, and as Jim laughed, he said, "Tony, involve me in this project. This is what the holidays are all about."

The bazaar was scheduled for December 19th, and it was November 30th. Within the next two days the first four reindeers arrived and were placed on my dining room table. I had covered the table with a small tarp, and the paints and brushes were on the table waiting for creative hands to make reindeer faces. The varnish was in a ventilated area in the garage. What fun we were about to have giving all the Rudolph's their own individual personalities.

Pat arrived and said, "I have the red paint and I am in charge of the noses."

I laughed at her and said, "I am in charge of the eyes, the temple of the soul."

Mary joined in and asked, "I know my responsibility is filling the basket bodies with pinecones, but I want to do the mouths." We put on our smocks, set up our palettes, and began creating.

When we were finished no two were alike. Some had long eyelashes, and some had redder noses. Mary gave some of the reindeer's fuller lips than others. Jim took the antler cutting to a different level when he announced, "Hey, I am the best suited to paint these. I did design them." Jim then started painting.

Mary replied, "How come some of the antlers are brown and some are black?"

Jim looked right at her and with a straight face said, "How come some eyes are blue and others brown?"

Mary answered back, "How come some hair is white and other hair is red?"

Then Jim said, "Mary, are you referring to my white hair? I told the girls it happened the first year we got married."

Mary said, "Jim, are you telling me I caused your hair to turn white?"

We all screamed out, "Jim, it's genes!"

Jim looked up and started to laugh. "These reindeers have some pretty cute genes."

One thing the reindeers had in common was they all had huge red bows. They also had plenty of pinecones tucked in their middles.

They truly were precious. As we continued with each batch, we started to get attached to them. Tony said that at a later time the crew could make more for family and friends, but these reindeers had a purpose—they were destined to be sold. The main reason for these creations was to raise money; however, they were still our little babies, and we fell in love with them!

A few days later I received a package in the mail. It was a box similar to a shirt box, and it was from Marathon, Florida. I didn't know anyone who lived in Marathon. It took me no time to open this package. It was a baby's sweater, and in the box was also a hat and mittens crocheted in lemon yellow. It looked like it was for a newborn baby. There was a small note attached to this package. The note read: *This is for the bazaar. I hope you like it; miss you, Love, Jill.* I was overtaken with surprise. First of all, who did she miss? I took time to be kind, but was it because of my husband's position? What was my true feeling for Jill? I thought about my friends who were less than hospitable towards her. This girl needed a friend. She was, in her own way, trying to reach out. She really had no family. Of course, this conclusion was from bits and pieces of information that I had heard and pieced together. Jill was making an effort. I decided to start with that. I thought that the little bit of attention I had given her might be the best attention she had received in a long while. How sad. I decided I would ask my friends to try to have some kindness towards Jill, and I hoped that Jill would return the following boating season. I wanted my feelings to be sincere. I would also ask my friends to give Jill a chance. This was a priority—I would put it on the top of my to-do list! Then I noticed there was only Marathon, Florida on the return address, no street. Of course they were living on the boat and George would never get a post box for such a short time. They were probably on a mooring. They might be at a yacht club, or they could be at the end of a pier at someone's home. My chances of getting in touch with Jill to thank her would have to depend on the *Rusty Scupper* returning to the club.

My thoughts were soon interrupted by a phone call from Pat. "I thought you would like to know," Pat said, "that the orphanage is sending a group of seven-year-old children to the party."

I responded, "Pat, that age is tough. Very few people want to adopt children that age. Most families prefer babies. Parents want to mold the child's personality at an early age, preferably infancy." Pat said, "These kids believe in Santa, and they need us." Pat then went on to give me the rest of the information. Seven girls and fifteen boys would partake in our Christmas party. At one of our meetings we had decided that the girls would receive Barbie dolls and the boys would get race car sets. Our Santa would be a member, Wally. Wally was a happy, jolly, lovable sort of guy. Actually, Wally resembled Santa, and it would take very little preparation to turn him into St. Nicholas. Wally had seven kids of his own. Wally also had a great deal of patience—patience could be Wally's middle name.

The party would take place in one of the smaller areas of the club. The meal would be prepared by a few of the officers. Tony would make his famous lasagna along with a healthy salad. Dessert would consist of make-your-own ice cream sundaes. I wanted to be in charge of this and planned to get the basic strawberry, vanilla, and chocolate ice creams. Then I would add mini dishes of jelly beans, jimmies, marshmallows, and M&Ms. The best part would be all the different sauces (hot and cold). I also thought we should use some fresh fruit. I thought about what children liked. How about adding bananas, strawberries, and blueberries? Sounded good to me! Of course, the squirt of whipped cream would be the finale. It was always so much fun to watch children make up their own little dishes of dessert. Their little personalities took over. Some were so very neat, and others got so excited that they clumped everything together. One thing is for sure—children love ice cream.

This event was scheduled for December 21st, two days before the members' children's party. That was a much easier event because the members' children had parents, and their parents would become Secret Santa and secretly provide gifts for their children. These presents would be capped at five dollars. The same meal would be duplicated. I had to stop thinking. I wanted everything to go smoothly, but this was all too much to digest at once.

Tony's feelings at this point were also being tested. He had just completed winterizing the outside of the club, and the boats were off the floats and stored away for next season. Victor's boat was finally out of the water, but the whole episode between Victor and Sam still did not sit well with Tony. He really felt Sam should have pressed charges against Victor. Also, physically Tony's muscles were aching. Working on the floats was very strenuous work. Tony still remembered the horrible incident of the loss of Jim's daughter. Worse was the fact that Tony had to identify the body. All these events were starting to take a toll on him. Recently the Commodore had held many meetings involving financial matters. Tony did not go into detail with me regarding these matters, but when he came home he appeared very stressed. When I did bring up how stressed he looked, he just replied, "I took on a responsibility, and part of responsibility is stress. I'll handle it." So I decided to handle these upcoming events as best as I could without putting too much pressure on Tony.

I realized that there was very little credit, if any, given to women at the club. I also realized that a time would come when women would have an opportunity to go Thru the Chairs. This, however, was not the time. I did see teenage girls at the club who were very close to their dads. Some of these girls had strong feelings for the club, and I knew it was just a matter of time before these young ladies would assert their opposition to an only men's club. These particular young girls were active at the club. They knew boating and fishing, and they loved the camaraderie they received by just being with their dads and their friends. My children never adopted the love for boating that Tony had as a young boy. Tony tried very hard to involve them, but they just had other interests. Our children came with us to the club many times when they were younger, but boating was work and as they got older our children chose to put their efforts into other hobbies. As parents we knew that no matter how hard we tried to entice our children with school, friends, and sports, they were their own individuals. Tony and I never forced this issue as they got older, but I always knew that in Tony's heart he was a little disappointed. He wanted that camaraderie with his children, be it our daughter or our sons.

Our daughter took after my mother. My mother was the epitome of femininity. Everything my mom wore matched. Her shoes, dress, jewelry, and makeup all blended to perfection. My mom looked like a movie star when she entered a room. I sometimes wondered if she was disappointed in life because she didn't follow that career. I remember finding my mom looking into the mirror on her dresser and crying. I was a teenager at the time. I questioned her sad mood, and she just smiled. Then I knew it was time to go shopping. A new dress and shoes would make her smile. What a shopping adventure it was. The whole ensemble consisted of a dress, shoes, makeup, and hair pieces that matched to perfection. They would all be purchased with such enthusiasm. Then we would have the best part for me. Lunch! I was not like my mom. I loved gardening. I loved getting into the dirt with my hands and feeling the soil run through my fingers. I loved boating as well, and I didn't mind putting the bait on the fishing rods. I was feminine when I felt I had to be, but there was a tomboy in me. Every once in a while I decided that I had to let that part of my personality come out. I don't think my mom liked it, but she never said a word. She just would point to a piece of dirt on my clothing or a wrinkle in my dress. I then knew how my mom felt. She was disappointed. When my daughter took after her, it really was a blessing— the pressure was off me. My mom now had a little protégé.

The boys, now that they were older, wanted to be with their friends. The boys enjoy boating provided that their friends could come along. The only drawback was that Tony only allowed the boys to invite one friend. Tony felt that six people plus himself was enough on our boat. Tony was very particular in what friends could come on the boat. First rule was whoever came on the boat should know how to swim. The second rule was they had to wear a life jacket. This sometimes created a problem. The waters in the New England area could change in an instant. A drop-dead calm sea could turn into a thick blanket of fog in seconds. Anyone who knows the ocean knows that it is the most unpredictable body of water that has ever challenged man. Tony did not compromise his feelings on these rules— when it came to boating, he was strict.

The day of the bazaar was freezing. I hoped the weather would not interfere with the day. I had high expectations in mind regarding this upcoming event, and we had all worked hard to put this day together. The club had set up ten tables; one of the tables would sell raffle tickets. On this table we placed a huge handmade Raggedy Ann doll three feet tall, a champagne basket, and a hand-crocheted afghan for a queen-size bed. Tickets were ten for five dollars. There were craft tables with handmade silk flowers, aprons, and small stuffed animals. Some of the tables were confined to specific items, like the baby table. This table brought such pleasure to everyone. It looked like a rainbow of pastels. Each item was handmade with love. And Jill's lemon baby set was plunked right in the middle of this awesome display. Jill would have been proud if she could have seen how beautiful it looked. A few men who created the reindeers were standing around that table. I could see how proud they were. Tony had a twinkle in his eye, and his expression reminded me of old Santa himself. There was also a large selection of baked goods, sandwiches, and cold drinks. All the tables were full of exciting things. The most excitement, I had to say, was the atmosphere itself. We were all having fun!

I was taking pride at how nice everything looked when I saw Mary and Jim enter the bazaar. They went right over to the reindeer table. Mary looked up and said, "I have to have one of these reindeers!" I couldn't help but overhear her request. I walked on over to the reindeer table and arrived just in time to see Mary lifting one of the reindeers up as if it were a new baby and placing it in her arms. Pat wandered over and repeated the exact same thing as Mary. Tony glanced over at me, but I nod no. If one of the reindeers was left over at the end of the day, then Tony could buy it for me. I felt that these reindeers were truly in demand. I also knew that Tony could always make me one. However, it was these first editions that would be hard to repeat. Later ones would never have the spark that the first twelve had. There was something about the effort that went into creating those faces, making those ribbons, and the enjoyment we all shared. Some moments were hard to repeat in life. Like I suspected, halfway through the day all twelve reindeer had been sold. We really could have taken orders—that was how much people liked them. I knew if we had made twenty reindeers they would have sold. But I had other things that needed tending to. I knew that our goal would be met; all the other tables were looking scarce. Our hard work was paying off. Jill's baby set went for twelve dollars. Jill would be happy to know how much it was appreciated. I hoped I would have the opportunity to tell her.

The day was winding down, and I was hungry. The pizza looked great, so I sat myself down and indulged. I looked around and laughed. It looked like locusts had attacked the tables. They were bare. Mary won the afghan and donated it back because she felt she had the reindeer and that someone else deserved to win. I knew Mary had twin beds. We winked at each other. It worked out well, and a young couple getting married won the afghan. Everyone was happy as the profit hit the one-thousand-dollar mark. I was beat, and it was time to go home. As I departed towards my car, there in the window of an adjacent car was a reindeer, looking straight at me. If I hadn't known better, I would have sworn he winked at me and said, "Good job," but I knew wooden reindeers couldn't wink.

Chapter 15

Unwanted Children

TIME WAS PASSING SWIFTLY. IT SEEMED every day the demands and priorities got harder. Tony promised the children he would go with them to get a Christmas tree, but that night the Commodore called an emergency meeting. Tony scheduled the tree search for the next night, and that night I had a meeting with the girls because the party for the children of the orphanage was coming up. One way or another we were managing to get everything accomplished, but the stress was getting worse. Sometimes Tony and I snapped at each other, and I would find his patience running very short. I prayed that this pressure would soon be over, and the following week the pressure stopped. For the first time in a long time, Tony and I experienced one of the most memorable events of our lifetimes.

The day had arrived. The orphanage had delivered the children, and they were meticulous. Some looked up at us as they entered, but most held their heads bowed low. I guessed it was hard to have confidence when they were born without the security of parents. When Santa approached, the atmosphere seemed to improve. Santa belonged to everyone; we were now on familiar ground. The girls were all around him, but the boys still kept their distance, as some boys did at that age. Children could be resilient, and no one knew better than Santa. He did his best to bring their little personalities out. Once the children spotted the lasagna, they become hungry. They all sat down and were enjoying the feast prepared for them in the galley. The dessert department was one of the best experiences, as always. I really could have eliminated the ice cream because the toppings were going like hot cakes. It was so much fun that we decided at have the children all participate in making dessert for the adults. The dessert that was created for me consisted of one large scoop of strawberry ice cream, three baby spoons of jimmies, marshmallows, chocolate sauce, and jellybeans. I looked at the cute, freckled, redheaded little boy named Mathew, who made this masterpiece of calories, and dove right into the dessert. I then looked down at Mathew again and said, "This is soooo gooood!"

He looked up and said in a meek voice, "Thank you, ma'am." Our clothes along with our hearts were covered with love and food. Two stains were on my skirt, and I hoped they would never come off. I wanted to remember this day. Santa played his role, and all the toys were a big hit. Some of the requests, on the other hand, that Santa received were hard.

One little boy said, "Can you make a mommy and daddy come and pick me?"

One little girl refused to get off Santa's lap. She said, "Please, Santa, let me come with you to the North Pole. I can help the elves make toys." Santa told both children that he would try and do his best, but today he could not make that decision. Trust me, they expected more from Santa. These two children were on the verge of tears. They did everything to be brave and hold back those tears. If they cried they looked like they would cry an ocean. They were like two balloons. Someone just let all the air out of them. But they couldn't cry because at seven years old in an orphanage they were all cried up. The problem was I wasn't all cried up. I was so selfish in wanting to rush these events when these innocent children were so excited and hopeful for some kind of recognition. Eventually these children fell into the regime of accepting disappointment and going on with their everyday activities, hoping that maybe something good might happen to change their lives. When Santa was done giving out all the gifts, he wandered over to me. His eyes also were watery. Wally was a good-natured man, and he tried to lighten both our somber moods.

Wally said, "Someday these children will be teenagers. We all know teenagers. They can look at you and say, 'I hate you. You don't understand me. I wish you weren't my parents.'"

I said, "Wally, I don't think these children are cut from the same cloth."

Wally laughed. "Maybe you're right, but teenagers are tough. Even the best have their moments." I sighed and looked around. The good thing I noticed was that these orphans had formed a bond with each other. They were the closest they could be to being sisters and brothers.

The children departed the same way they entered. I did notice that some held their heads a little higher. It was their day with Santa. Sometimes functions like these were harder for adults. I knew if I just avoided it, it made it even harder for these children. These children needed attention. How much could they be forgotten? What better time than Christmas to reach out and make a child happy, even if it was only for a short time? This time gave a child a moment to know someone did care. I had something else to add to my to-do list. Everyone loved the Easter bunny, and maybe we would have an Easter egg hunt; I would bring that up with the new Rear Commodore's wife next year. Then a strange thought came into play. What about Jill, was she an orphan? Maybe when or if she came back I would downright ask her. Was that why she held her head down? Was that why she had those sad doe eyes? Had Jill's eyes run out of water too? I learned something that day. When I saw those faces on TV for Save the Children, they were very real. The eyes they were the windows of the soul. Those faces stayed and haunted me, and I found myself giving so much to children's funds. Of course, it is easy to give money and hard to give time. I tried to do as much as I could, but that first event that I was so involved with was stamped into my heart.

THE DECEMBER DAY WE CHOSE FOR the children's party and adult dance was going to be no exception to New England's wild winter weather. A nor'easter was on its way. It was suppose to occur in the middle of the members' children's party. That same night was the adult's dinner dance. I guess I really did cram a lot together. After my experience with the orphan party, I wished I had spaced these events a little better. December was a hectic month. It was a month of holidays and parties. I had my own personal parties to go to, and I pushed the club's activities as close together as I could. Today, I feared, I might be paying for that decision. All I could envision was swirling snow and blankets of whiteouts. My mental vision of a Grandma

Moses picture-perfect winter scene, I was informed, was not about to happen.

I guessed there was a lot to be said about prayers, because the children won out. The newest of weather reports now stated that the snow would blow in later that evening. That, I laughed, would be during the adult dinner dance. I arrived at the club a few hours early, as I knew many parents would be dropping off their child's present. Of course, the children assumed that jolly Santa was the bearer of their gifts. We tried to instill the cap of five dollars, but no matter how hard we tried there was always someone who had to make an impression by spending more money. This sometimes made matters difficult and created havoc. This, I was sure, occurred in every club. Ours was no exception.

Garry, Tony's only opposition in the race for Vice Commodore dropped off his son's gift. As I mentioned before, Garry was the club joker. He always had a comment to make. He made it sound like a joke, but in reality he was mocking either some member's actions or deeds. I found people who did this did it to take the attention off of them. Usually these characters had very little to offer other than their big mouths. As Garry placed his package under the tree, he looked up at me. Garry was a very lean man—pencil thin. His Adam's apple was very large. When he laughed with his sneering tone, his Adam's apple went up and down like a yo-yo. When this happened I always had to laugh. Garry thought my laughing was at what he said, but ironically it was at what he looked like. Garry looked like an idiot.

"What do you think is in this package?" he asked.

I looked right into his eyes and said, "I don't know, Garry, but I hope that it is in the five-dollar-maximum range." Now he came even closer to me and looked right at me with his beady eyes.

"What if it isn't, Mrs. Rear Commodore? What are you going to do about it?" At that moment I knew that the package had all the makings of trouble. I had to compose myself because I was about to lose my temper and give Garry a strong piece of my mind. I hated men who tried to bully women. They did it in a sneaky fashion, coming up real close as if they were giving a nice compliment. Then they looked into the woman's eyes and almost threatened her. That was how Garry was making me feel.

I turned my back on Garry, and as I walked away I spoke softly, but enough that he could hear me. "Garry, you joke about members who work hard at this club. You are a horrible role model, and I feel bad for your son."

I know I infuriated him because he spun me around. "Listen to me," he said. "You are a guest, not a member, so be careful who you address in that fashion."

I smiled through gritted teeth. "Garry, you be careful, and get you hands off of me. I hate to tell you, Garry, but you have more enemies than friends." And with that I walked away. The episode with Garry was not going to interfere with my day. Garry was a bully, and with bullies it was just a matter of time before someone got the better of them. I hoped I had achieved getting the best of Garry mentally.

Santa was in the members' lounge getting dressed. Santa was to be played by another member, as Wally wanted to partake in the party with his own children. We had asked a retired fireman to fill Santa's position. He loved it when he had the opportunity to be involved in any children's activities. Two of my younger children actually got involved as two elves. They did not do this willingly. My daughter and her younger brother were going to receive confirmation in the coming year, and part of the lessons they were learning to prepare for this sacrament involved community service. This was their first assignment. They had to put in fifty hours. They had eight months to prepare. Tony and I felt this was a great start. They stood, on either side of Santa, helping to hand out the presents. My daughter had her hair in two ponytails. My mom had woven streamers of red and green ribbon through these pony tails, and she looked very cute. She was even smiling. Her brother was having a little more difficulty. It might have been the elf hat that Tony had stuck on his head. He was trying to be a good trooper, but it was obvious that if he could be somewhere else he would. Tony decided to bring along a camera that developed pictures on the spot. He wanted each child to have a memory of their visit with Santa. It was funny. Tony said to our son, "Smile!"

Our son yelled, "Dad, please, my image will be destroyed!" Everyone laughed.

Tony said, "Someday you will enjoy this picture, son."

"Ya sure, Dad," was his response.

When Santa took his seat, all the children gathered around him. Santa's first challenge was with the little babies. They usually tried to pull off his beard. Sometimes these little babies were very afraid of Santa. We were glad when my young elves tried to divert the crying babies' attention and make them laugh. Hopefully Tony got some good pictures.

Chapter 16

The Opening of Presents

THE CHILDREN WERE HAVING FUN AS they opened their presents. Some children had puzzles. I pictured many missing puzzle pieces. In the end, the dumpster would end up inheriting the missing puzzle pieces. A lot of Barbie dolls appeared (the four-dollar doll with the hundred-dollar accessories). There were race cars, trucks, toy telephones, jack in the boxes—all kinds of fun toys. But then it happened! Garry's child opened up his present. Lo and behold, a BB gun. Every mom said the same thing: "That boy will shoot his eye out, or better still someone else's eye!" All of a sudden the attention Santa was receiving got diverted. The older boys were engaged in the splendor of Garry's son's new gun, but soon enough all the glory of the new gun would come to an abrupt end.

Garry's wife interrupted the moment by immediately taking the gun out of her son's hand. At that point she repeated the familiar saying, "What do you want to do? Shoot your eye out?" Then she looked at her husband angrily and said, "We will discuss this matter later." Garry gave us one of his shit-faced grins again. One of the members reacted to Garry's facial expression, and a few unnecessary words were exchanged by both parties. Garry, his wife, his son, and the famous BB gun departed. The only lesson here to be learned was that for once it was better not to get a BB gun. Garry's son's face did not have the expression of happiness. The little boy was embarrassed, and we all knew it was not going to be a good experience in that house later. The children felt bad for Garry's son. We all felt bad for Garry's son.

We needed a mood change. The party was getting a little somber after the BB gun experience. What did all children love, I wondered? They loved ice cream. I decided to announce to everyone present, "It's ice cream sundae time!" And with that we all share in the makings of ice cream and candy. We tried to recapture the makings from our last ice cream buffet, but this was different because of the younger babies. This was fun as we watched the babies cover themselves in ice cream and whipped cream. Fortunately I eliminated the jelly beans and other candy that babies could choke on, but the M&Ms still remained a great treat and mess. I made a note—next year, bibs for all. When all the children left with their parents sadness set in my heart. I thought how different each group of children's parties were. The first party was quieter. The children didn't know what to expect at first. It took the children awhile to adapt and trust the people having the party. They all related to Santa. Even if Santa couldn't fill their wishes, they felt he wanted to. The orphan children were so appreciative for what they received as gifts. They would not let a morsel drop to the floor, never mind a gift. They took nothing for granted, and worst of all they knew this might be their only party for a very long time. I compared the members' children's party in my mind. Most of the older children knew they were getting gifts, and the children knew that they would have more parties. The children *expected!* I thought of all the people who adopted children. I wished more people did. I have often said that loneliness was a terrible disease, but I had never before realized children got it too. I asked Santa for a Christmas present. *Please make more people who have no children adopt one instead of buying a pet. Or better still, do both!*

IT WAS NOW FOUR IN THE afternoon, and the children's party had weathered the upcoming storm. Our dance began at six with the officers' cocktail party. By now I had heard two conflicting weather reports. One channel on TV reported that the storm would definitely blow out to sea. The other report said possible sleet and freezing ice along the coastline. What to do in a situation like this? Call on Jake. Every yacht club had that old, salty-dog fisherman. These sea captains knew the weather like a witch doctor knew his medicine. Their method was simple. They went by the feeling in their bones and the compass they kept with them at all times, and they even wet their fingers and then pointed them toward the wind. I wondered if someone did this for the Farmer's Almanac. So I decided to give Jake a phone call. I knew he would give me his prediction. Jake answered the phone with, "Yup, it's Jake."

I said, "Hi, Jake, this is Mrs. Vendetti over at the club. I was wondering what you think about the weather?"

Jake calmly responded, "Nor'easter starting around 10 or 11 PM." His final words were, "Have the party, we are a tough crew," and so I did. I started to laugh as I hung up the phone. I could see Jake, wearing his old sea captain's hat, going over to the window and opening it up. I could visualize him wetting one of his crooked, aged fingers and sticking it out the window. He would wait until the wind came up. I knew as he talked to me on the phone that he was probably still looking at that crooked, old finger. I had never seen Jake without his old, torn sea captain's hat. I wondered if he slept with it on his head. I laughed to myself and thought the only thing that might be holding it together was the salt from the ocean. If he ever took it off or washed it, it may never be the same again.

Chapter 17

The Final Dance as Rear Commodore

ALL THE WIVES AND GIRLFRIENDS OF the officers had prepared their favorite appetizer. I did something simple because I had been so busy with the children's Christmas party. This recipe was so easy. I will share it with you.

Get an eight-ounce jar of sweet corn relish and mix it with eight ounces of whipped cream cheese. Place the mixture in a cute dip dish and serve it with Ritz crackers. Amazingly, this was always a hit.

Tony made sure that all the officers' wives had corsages. They were holly berries with baby pinecones. The corsages arrived with some beautiful poinsettia plants. The poinsettias were the center-pieces for each table. The red tablecloths, white dishes, and green napkins looked quite festive. I forgot that the centerpiece has to be given away, so Pat quickly made snowflakes. They had eight points; it is hard to get that six-point theory, and no matter how many times I folded the paper over the flake it still has eight points. Pat couldn't conquer the six-point snowflake either. I ran around placing them under one chair per table, and then everything was in its place. I then decided to join the cocktail party in the officers' room.

I entered the party feeling really refreshed, despite the fact that I had engaged in Preparation H. I had placed this medicine under my eyes to relieve the puffiness. After a few sleepless nights going over and over all the preparations that Tony and I had to do, I noticed I had very baggy eyes. I had heard somewhere that models used the medicine, and I wanted desperately to look good! My dress was red, how appropriate—I was ready for an adult party. The men all looked so good in their dark, formal uniforms. As I mentioned before, there was something about looking at a man in uniform. My thoughts wandered. *I hope it snows early,* I thought, *Tony and I can use a night alone.* My mom had taken the kids, though it took a little bit of extra coaxing. My mom had trouble looking up at the boys now that they had outgrown her. This, she said, was difficult if she felt she had to discipline them. My mom felt she was shrinking. One thing I knew for sure—our boys would never disrespect my mom. Why? Because my mom still used the wooden spoon.

Enter Frisky Lisky. He was a past officer, and the ladies gave him his nickname. His real name was Thomas Lisky. Why did the ladies give him this name? Frisky loved to help the ladies pin on their corsages. His hands moved quickly over bosoms as he helped the ladies with their corsages, and his hands moved in all the wrong directions. By the time a woman realized Frisky's motives, Frisky had gotten his pleasures.

Tony and I had conversations over Mr. Lisky's unacceptable behavior. In our last conversation I said "Tony, let me remind you about the time he stuck Mrs. Simpkins in the left breast with the pin from the corsage. Then, instead of backing off of poor Mrs. Simpkins, Frisky proceeded to rub the infected area. Do you remember this, Tony?"

Tony started to laugh. "Hon, do you remember Mrs. Simpkins' reaction?" Then Tony laughed even harder. "Hon," he continued, "Mrs. Simpkins wasn't protesting until she saw Mr. Simpkins approaching."

I said, "That is not the point."

Tony said, "What is the point?"

I said, "You know damn well that this man is a pervert and needs a talking to."

"All right, I will speak to him. However, all you gals know about him, so avoid him." I had certainly hoped Tony had remembered our past conversation. So far Mr. Lisky was handling himself in a respectable manner. Tony must have noticed how nervous I was. He approached me and said, "Don't worry, I spoke to him." Then Tony started to smile. "Have a cocktail, honey, and relax." So I did, and I started to unwind. After a short time a giant bell rang. That was the signal that it was time to join all the members in the formal party area for dinner. There were no scenes of bad behavior from Mr. Thomas Lisky. Tony kept his word.

Chapter 18

'T is the Holiday Season

ON ALL THE CHAIRS WE HAD placed song books. We would later use them to show off our musical talents. This was fun, I was unwinding. I was going to be waited on. The usual format was always family style, which meant I could have seconds, thirds, etc. No one ever left these affairs hungry. First course was minestrone soup, made fresh in the galley. Delectable carrots, celery, potatoes, and little pieces of meat were flavorfully simmered in a huge caldron all day. The taste was warm and inviting. If you sprinkled some grated cheese on top, it enhanced the soup incredibly. This was followed by a caesar salad. The croutons were also made in the galley—day-old Italian bread cut into small pieces and simmered in garlic and virgin olive oil. The main course was roast beef. Two huge platters encompassed the table; one was rare for the lions in the group. The other was a combination of medium and well-done portions. Naturally the baked potato accompanied the meat, and here you had a choice of sour cream or butter and bacon chips. Fortunately we had a break before dessert. This gave the band a chance to play their music and also help us digest this wonderful food. The music started and people approached the dance floor. Tony would never be the first one on the dance floor. It must have been a man thing. Many people were starting to dance, so Tony reached for my arm and led me to the dance floor. We danced to a much-loved holiday song, appropriately "White Christmas."

And speaking of a white Christmas, Jake's gravelly voice soon broke over the microphone. "Folks, it's going to snow later, so enjoy

the time we have here. I am sticking to my original forecast." As Jake
stood in the spotlight, I noticed that he had on blue corduroy pants
and a cranberry sports jacket. He also had a white shirt and a cranberry tie. And yes, the sea captains hat. I thought, *Jake might be short
on conversation but he has a lot of longevity on knowledge.*

Tony looked at me on the dance floor and said, "Jake is a character, isn't' he?"

I laughed. "Tony," I said, "Jake is a true salty-dog sea captain. If
someone was to make a movie about old sea captains, Jake would be
the first person cast."

THE MEAL WAS GREAT, AND JUST the fact that I didn't have to partake
in the preparations made it taste even better. The band informed us
that it was sing-along time, so we reached for our books and started
with a peppy version of "Frosty the Snowman." But the best was
yet to come. All the singing officers of the club did "Rudolph the
Red-nosed Reindeer." They placed antlers on their heads, but it got
even better when Mary appeared with a bright red nose and a set of
bells. She joined in to give the song a more ringing sound. All I could
wonder was if it was a tribute to our twelve reindeer babies. We all
got louder and the song got better. The night passed by with such a
holiday feeling that we had all forgotten about the storm.

Jake's gravelly voice broke over the microphone for the second
time. "Folks, it's snowing." I think Jake liked the notoriety. Tony took
the mike from Jake and announced that under someone's chair at
each table one snowflake had fallen. Whoever had a snowflake under
their chair won the centerpiece. A lot of commotion took place as
chairs were tipped over and anxious guests looked to see if they were
the lucky winners. Some people who won actually gave it to someone
else at the table who might have wanted it more. The holiday season
was being spread all around.

Jake appeared one more time. "Folks, I am leaving. The roads are
getting icy, safety is an issue, and to all a good night." And with that
Jake departed. Tony seconded the motion and called it a night. It was
almost eleven and we had had a full day. I was ready to retire and
spend some time with the almost-past Rear Commodore.

Chapter 19

A Final Toast

TONY AND I ARRIVED HOME SAFELY. Jake was right—he knew when it was time to leave. We were warm in the confines of our home, and we decided to have a nice nightcap of cognac. We toasted to leadership and all that we had learned. We toasted to the theory that there truly was strength in numbers. We toasted to friendship and how lucky we were to have so many good people working with us. We toasted to unity—even though sometimes we didn't all agree, when the chips were down we acted as a club. We thought of John and Mary and the loss of their daughter. The club had been side by side, member with member. That was probably the most unified and saddest experience. With a tear in our eye, we toasted to each other. We had done our best, and we hoped we were better people for it.

Tony looked into my eyes deeply and said, "Hon, we just experienced one chair. Do you think that I am ready to go through the next chair? Do you think that I have what it takes to be a Vice Commodore? I think I handled myself well, but what about next year? Have I taken too much time away from my family? And what about you? Do you want to continue this journey with me?"

I laughed, "Tony, these were questions you should have asked me before you ran for elections. What can I say now? You are already Vice Commodore. Are you having second thoughts?" Tony took on a surprisingly different expression. Usually a man with such confidence in himself, Tony now looked perplexed. He looked like he was actually questioning himself. I raised my glass of cognac to my husband and said, "You are a great husband, a great father, and were a great Rear Commodore. I enjoyed my journey with you in this past year. It gave me an opportunity to be involved with a lot of wonderful people. It also gave me an opportunity to observe officers in the line of duty. I watched my husband perform difficult tasks and decisions; I see how proud the children are of you. Do I think you made the right decision? Yes, because it is something that you have always wanted. It is your dream. If you do not do this you will always feel less of yourself. You will feel that you fell off the chairs." Tony laughed at this comparison.

He grabbed me in a bear hug and said, "Thanks for the confidence. Every once in a while even the strongest personality needs someone to make them feel good about themselves and make them feel that the people closest to them are on their side."

With that I said, "No regrets," and we made one more final toast to that.

ON NEW YEAR'S EVE, WE SAID a farewell to Tony as our Rear Commodore. We welcomed the new challenges ahead as Vice Commodore and prayed for a great year with strong leadership.

Book 2

....

The Vice Commodore

Chapter 1

The Bar and Bartenders

IT WAS OPENING NIGHT AT THE club. One of the Vice Commodore's first assignments this evening was to make sure both the upstairs and downstairs bar was fully stocked. Of course, being in charge of the bar made him also in charge of the bartenders. So far Tony felt that everything was under control. He had met with the bartenders the previous week to insure that all would go well this evening. The room was all decorated, and I must say I was again glad that this was not my responsibility.

Briar Ridge looked so exquisite this evening. What a fabulous view of Boston. I could see the tall buildings of Boston against the warm sunset of the early spring evening. The sky had a purple and light pink color. It wasn't a vibrant color but more like a whitewash on a new piece of canvas. The skyscrapers in the background cast a grayish look, almost like an artist had charcoaled them in. I was glad that winter had passed. It had been long and cold, and this event was going to be welcomed. It was a chance to see people we hadn't seen in months. It was an opportunity for some laughing and socializing. I called it "the catch-up party," but Tony referred to it as, "the latest gossip gathering."

Tony and I entered the officers' cocktail party. The Rear Commodore's wife had added a new attraction. There stood her good friend Dolly, who was a very voluptuous gal. Dolly was also a past officer's wife. Dolly had volunteered the role of pinning the corsages on us ladies. As I watched her do this, I wondered if she was one of the victims of Frisky

Lisky. This might have been why she took her job so cautiously. When she got to pinning on my corsage, she smiled and said, "Don't you think it's better to have someone assigned to do this?"

I grinned and replied, "Most of us can put it on ourselves, but it is nice to have someone so concerned to help." I then decided she definitely was a victim of Frisky. Tony had to excuse himself, as one of the waitresses had beckoned him into the kitchen—there was a phone call he needed to handle. The call was from one of the bartenders. The bartender said he was ill and could not work this evening. Bartending was not a course that one could learn quickly, and though most of the members drank beer, the ladies had a tendency to get into those cute fancy drinks like a Stinger, Boxcar, Sex on the Beach, etc. Well, Tony put in an emergency call to a neighboring club to see if we could engage one of their employees for the evening. Fortunately, they were very responsive to Tony's plea. First problem of the evening was solved. Tony came back to the cocktail party and related his phone conversation to me. He also explained that a new bartender was on the way.

The appetizers looked great; I had to say the new Rear Commodore's wife really put out a fabulous display. She had notified all the ladies she wanted in her crew, and they made some super delights. I added my usual cream cheese and sweet corn relish dip, but Betty Flanagan, the Rear Commodore's wife, won the prize. Her crabmeat dip with roasted almonds encrusted in phyllo dough was mouthwatering to say the least.

This is another recipe I will share. One can of crab meat (eight ounces), an eight-ounce container of cream cheese, two tablespoons of fresh chives, a teaspoon of milk, and a dash of horseradish. Mix everything in a bowl, and then roll the mix in almonds until it is a ball. Wrap the ball in phyllo and bake at 375 degrees for fifteen minutes. This was yummy. Betty was in like Flynn, or should I say, Flanagan.

Tony added a nice taste to the cocktail party. He sent waitresses around with fluted glasses of champagne. However, I think he wanted us to quench our thirst on champagne rather than ask for the funny ladies drinks, which would have put more pressure on the bartenders. Tony felt that the newly recruited bartender was doing just fine.

The evening passed graciously, with mellow music in the background. I could see the laughter and tears as people reacquainted themselves with all the events of the past winter. Who died, who got married, and who got divorced—Tony's gossip gathering. In the background at one point I heard the name *Rusty Scupper*. I started to lean in that direction. I then got up from my chair. I walked in the direction of the Fleet Captain's table and overheard the Fleet Captain telling one of the members at his table that the *Rusty Scupper* was headed back to our club. He also said loudly, "Jill and George called me to see if there was any kind of employment that the club might offer." The Fleet Captain reported replying that the club was not too responsive to them, and he then continued saying that Paul Adler had said, "That bum called asking for employment; tell him he can wash dishes and mop up floors." Then both men at the table laughed.

I felt guilty for eavesdropping. I went back to my table. I would be glad to see Jill, and I hoped she was somehow getting her life together. I also really wanted to thank her for the ensemble she donated for the Christmas bazaar. But most of all I wanted to have the courage to come right out and ask her if she was an orphan. I had made myself a promise after the children's orphan party to be more sensitive. I thought, *What better way to start than with Jill?* As far as George was concerned, he had a lot of apologizing and working to do to get back in the good graces of this club.

The DJ was announcing the last dance, so I grabbed Tony and swayed to "After the Lovin'" by Engelbert Humperdinck. It was a great opening night, and on Tony's part the bar took in a tremendous profit. Tony enjoyed his new position. It was less laborious and much more social. He smiled down at me as we danced and said, "I like this part of the chairs."

Tony had made a commitment when elections were taking place, and it was now time for Tony to keep his word. The upstairs members' lounge would be turning into a sports bar. This was, however, news to me. One night he sat me down and explained what he planned to do. He had suggested to the board of officers that it would be beneficial and profitable to bring in a few TVs. He had also suggested more than one pool table. He then thought that a few dart boards could be added. He went further to suggest that we have dart and pool leagues, which could give the club competitive games with neighboring yacht clubs. These were suggestions he made to his fellow officers while running for Vice Commodore. He said there was no reason to discuss it with me until he had a chance to make it happen. He now had the chance. At the last meeting, the officers gave him the green light to go ahead with this project. Then he said to me, "Guess what, I would like to take this a step further. While we are having our pool tournaments, why don't you and a few ladies get involved in some dart tournaments?"

I said, "Tony, this encouragement to involve us gals in this project is great."

Tony then said in a strict officer's voice, "Remember, this is a man's club. As long as the men have no dart games scheduled then you can use the dart boards. I suggest you have them on the same night we have the pool tournaments and invite some ladies from the same club that the pool tournament is involved with."

I said, "I understand, Tony, but will this be a problem for you?"

He said, "I don't think so. I think it would be nice for couples to get together socially and have some fun." I became excited. We would have our own dart league. I decided to take inventory on what girls to call.

Chapter 2

The Pink Panthers

AFTER SEVERAL WEEKS AND A LOT of planning, the Pink Panthers were born. We had seven women who were very interested. I was glad that two of my closest friends, Pat and Mary, were on the team with me. Tony had worked hard. The sports bar attracted a lot of interest. Many members were present to do anything they could. This was exciting—it was a new frontier. Not only could people be on their yacht, but they could go upstairs and watch any sport they wanted or play pool and darts.

Once we all decided on the name, which wasn't easy, Mary took over. Seven was an odd number and we had to vote on the name. We had a final choice between the Pink Panthers and the Roadrunners. The color pink seemed to sway us. The vote five to two made it possible. It took Mary one week to create our uniforms. Mary made all seven participants pink jerseys with sequined panther faces. Each shirt's panther had one paw held high. Was it a reminder or symbolic sign of her daughter's death? Was it a memory of a churning, pawing sensation that one feels in the stomach when tragedy strikes? Was it the feeling of running? Or maybe Mary just felt this was part of overcoming an obstacle. Every one of us had the same guesswork going on in our mind about what Mary's reasoning was with the paw but no one questioned her. Mary was getting involved with life. This to us was far more important. We had Mary back with us. The night after she gave us the shirts, Pat called me and said, "What do you think about the paw?"

I said, "I feel it's a reminder of her daughter's death. We all love Mary, and we should do anything we can to get her through this terrible ordeal. Pat, if this helps her release her emotions, then let it be."

Pat said, "I agree. The paw stays. I do think it is a bit depressing, though."

Chapter 3

Darts and Pool

OUR FIRST MATCH WAS WITH A neighboring club. We were all gathered in our pink shirts. Mary looked at us and asked if Jim could take a picture of the team. Of course we all agreed. Mary then said, "These shirts are a symbol of strength and love, but they are also a symbol of loss."

I said, "Mary, what do you mean?"

"I mean that we are a strong team brought together by love and might have to accept the fact that we could lose a match here and there, but through our strength and love we will always be united." It was a lot for the team to digest. Mary was very deep in her explanation, but then again none of us on that team had experienced what Jim and Mary had.

We were *hot*. We started with a bang. Two darts in the wall, and one flying over the pool table. This shot almost interfered with an eight-ball shot. That would have been awful. One of our members was about to win a game of pool. Just imagine if on our first appearance as the Pink Panthers we ruined a pool shot in a men-only club. Fortunately no one commented on the flying dart. Pat was up, our Bull's-Eye Princess. She was deadly with her aim and brought us to our first victory. The men were not as fortunate during their pool tournament and lost. We hoped it wasn't because of the flying dart. We all agreed that this was a great format. The men playing pool and the girls playing darts was a great combination. The thing that really was enjoyable was that each couple brought a casserole, and at the end of the evening we had a huge buffet of all types of concoctions that delighted the palate. This hopefully would be repeated once a month. In case someone was not able to show up for darts or pool, we had our fill-in people just waiting for that phone call to join in the fun. And this was fun, though just how much fun I could never have imagined.

Now that Tony was so involved in the inner sanctum of the club, I found myself spending less time on the boat and more time at the clubhouse. Tony had to have a second pair of eyes to see all the things that were going on in the new sports bar that he and his associates had created. Not only did we have more TVs, but we had enhanced the atmosphere by adding more pools tables and dart boards. This created more people and more drinking. Tony also had to increase the bartenders from two to three. The most difficult part of being Vice Commodore was making sure that everyone that was drinking was responsible enough to drive. If this was not the case, members would usually stay on their boats. However, there were usually a lot of guests and Tony, along with the bartenders, had to stay alert. If they failed, the club would lose its liquor license. The name on the license was the Vice Commodore's, and needless to say if anything went wrong Tony would be held responsible. This was his duty as an officer.

Chapter 4

A Bad Experience

THIS EVENING WAS TO BE SPENT with friends in the members lounge. Unfortunately I was about to witness firsthand the effects of too much alcohol. It probably would never have happened if Pat hadn't asked me about my daughter. I happened to be sitting with Pat and some other gals when Pat said, "Tell me, and how was your daughter's prom?"

I said, "Pat, it went well, and I just happen to have some pictures." Naturally I passed them to her. I was very proud of how well my daughter and her friend looked. My mom had taken her shopping, and my daughter and her grandmother found the most beautiful lavender dress. It was in tulle, almost like a ballerina skirt. It had little sequin stars that were gathered along the bodice. The hem was in different-size points. It reminded me of something Tinkerbelle would wear. Actually, my daughter looked like a fairy princess. The finishing touch was a tiara that my mom had worn when she was a young girl. This truly complimented my daughter's long black hair. She had Tony's eyes—they were like large, black olives—and that beautiful Italian skin the color of polished almonds. Her date was dressed in a black tuxedo with a lavender cummerbund to compliment my daughter's attire. He was very handsome. He was much taller than my daughter, and he had light skin with a dusty blond crop of hair. His eyes were as blue as the sky. What I liked about this young man was his warm and friendly smile. He was the boy next door. Both children grew up together, so it seemed appropriate that they would spend this special occasion together. They truly made a handsome couple. It was just hard for me to imagine how two children who used to play in a sandbox had grown up so fast. Like all mothers, I was so happy to show off these pictures of the prom.

All good moments end, however. A grubby, overexcited, babbling idiot came up to Pat. He had obviously reached his alcohol limit. He brazenly said, "Hey, can I see the pictures?" Before Pat could reply, he quickly grabbed them from her hand. Pat tried desperately to retrieve them, trying hard not to damage the photos in the process. I looked at this stranger quizzically, but before I could say a word he started slurring obscenities. "Hey," he said, "does this girl put out?" Then he dropped the pictures and proceeded to make another vile comment. "Hey, she has bedroom eyes." He then continued on, but I couldn't make out what he was saying.

I asked Pat, "What is this man mumbling?" We were both having difficulty understanding the purpose of this conversation. Both Pat and I agreed he was definitely out of line. I was in semi shock—I couldn't believe what my ears were hearing. Pat immediately got up from her chair, picked up the fallen pictures, and walked over to Tony. I watched her whisper something in Tony's ear, and then I noticed an awful expression on Tony's face. I don't think I had ever seen my husband react the way he did that night.

He walked over to the intoxicated, scrubby culprit as the stranger was arguing with the bartender because he had been refused more liquor. Tony, with a strength I never knew he had, lifted the man up and bodily dragged him to the backdoor exit of the club. Then Tony pushed him out the door and slammed the exit door with all the anger and might in his body. He then said, "That is where all rubbish goes." In the meantime, the culprit managed to get up and was banging on the door while yelling more profanities. Fortunately, one of the members had called this unwelcome intruder a cab, and hopefully it was on its way. Eventually the banging stopped and the cab driver told one of the members that we could relax—he was driving this menace home.

The evening calmed down, and my beautiful pictures were back in my handbag, safe and sound. I went over to my husband and asked Tony why the man had been saying these awful things and if I had understood the words correctly. Tony said, "Hon, forget about it." He paused and then said, "I want to know whose guest this degenerate was. Whoever invited this man to the club will have to answer to me personally and then the club." Members were responsible for the actions of their guests. Tony then looked up at me with those olive eyes that somehow told me it was the end of this conversation. Of course we all know clubs and the gossip that spreads around. It would not take long before the unpleasant events of the night filtered through the club. Eventually I would find the pieces to the puzzle.

THE PUZZLE WAS SOLVED A FEW days later. Jim called Tony and said, "Tony, it seems that the culprit's name is Andy Bower. Guess what, Tony? He wants to be a member of the club. Boy, did he blow his chances!" Then Tony heard Jim laugh as he went on to say, "Andy was hoping to be sponsored by the member who brought him over the other night. Can you imagine this, Tony?"

Tony said, "You know, Jim, we could have accepted the fact that he had too much alcohol, but when Andy looked at the picture of my daughter, he made severe sexual comments regarding what he would like to do to her. It wasn't easy for Pat to whisper to me some of what this man said to her. The only good thing was that my wife only heard bits and pieces of his conversation, but even that made her angry. Imagine if she knew how bad his intentions were."

Jim said, "This guy will never be a member. Oh, by the way, Tony, the member that sponsored him is fairly new and is biting his nails over this situation. He is afraid he might get a suspension over this incident." Tony thanked Jim for the info and hung up the phone. He then approached me to relate his conversation with Jim.

"Listen," he said to me, "this type of character, this Andy Bower—that is his name—and this type of behavior would put me or any other father into a spinning rage. This is my sixteen-year-old daughter. When Pat told me what he said I was furious. I knew at that moment that I had to get him out of my sight and so I did." He continued, "Hon, I was glad at the time that you didn't fully understand what Andy was mumbling because you would probably have split his head in two." He paused. "I promise you this," Tony said, "he will never be a member of our club."

I said, "He wants to be a member?"

Tony said, "Don't worry about it. After the other night's display, he does not have a leg to stand on."

I laughed. "Tony, the way you tossed him out, he is lucky he is standing." Tony smiled, and then we decided to stop our conversation about Andy Bower.

ABOUT A MONTH LATER, ANDY BOWER applied to the club for membership. The member sponsoring him felt he should be given a second chance. Andy had sent a letter to the club asking for forgiveness for his rowdy behavior. This was immediately brought to Tony's attention. That night Tony came home and told me what was happening. I looked at him and said, "Tony, how did it get this far? You promised me that this degenerate would never be a member of the club."

He said, "Listen, when the committee meets to discuss the future of a new member and someone on the committee feels strongly about refusing the applicant, a blackball is thrown on the table. It takes three blackballs to eliminate the person's application. That is the procedure at the club. I feel that when Andy applies he will be blackballed."

I said, "Tony, what if he isn't?"

He hugged me and said, "Have faith in what the club will decide." Boy did I wish I could be a fly on the wall at the next meeting.

The night of the meeting approached. Needless to say I was a nervous wreck. Pat and Mary came over to keep me company. Tony had promised that as soon as the meeting was over he would call with the results. After several hours and no phone call, I was getting worried. I then heard Tony's car in the driveway. I looked at Pat and said, "This must be bad. He came all the way home to break the news to us." When Tony entered he had a huge smile on his face.

"I had to come and relate to you what happened." Tony then proceeded to tell the story as we waited with baited breath. "Well," he said, "Andy Bower presented his application. All the officers and the board acknowledged it. Andy then took a moment to apologize again for his unruly conduct, saying that maybe he had a little too much to drink. There were no emotions showing in any of the members faces. There was not an ounce of sympathy towards him. As far as the way he portrayed himself that night, this man could be a pedophile going after young girls. The best part was Andy's sponsor could not make the meeting due to sickness in the family. Did I forget to tell you who the sponsor for Andy was? Let me tell you. It was Garry, the breaker of the chairs. He was my one and only opponent in my race for Vice Commodore."

Pat said, "You're kidding."

"No, he just won't stop. Though, I think now he knows he went too far. He is going to have a hard time facing the club."

Mary said, "Tony, you are being challenged by him. Garry is trying to break the chairs again."

"I certainly am, Mary," said Tony. "Now girls, let me tell you the best part; justice prevailed. Andy went out in the lounge while the members voted. Andy felt he was a shoo-in. Wrong! Not three but six blackballs were thrown on the table. Three people brought their own balls to show respect for our situation."

Pat laughed. "Who did these balls belong to?"

Tony smiled at us and said, "I'll never tell." Andy Bower became history. We reveled when we heard the decision. Tony was right to have faith in the club and its officers. We decided to have a victory drink to celebrate.

Chapter 5

Rusty Scupper

OUR BOAT WAS FINALLY IN THE water. All the slips were starting to fill up. The *Rusty Scupper* was back, Jill was doing some local house-keeping, and George, after pleading with the club, managed to be in good graces again. He was a great electrician. That night we decided to have a float party, which was when everyone came down to the dock. We all sat outside our boats and talked about the events that would occur during the summer. Jill came over and sat next to me, and I thanked her for yellow baby gift set. I said it was a well-appreciated donation. We were just starting an informative conversation when Paul Adler appeared. I was surprised to see him. Paul did not have a boat, and during the winter months Paul was sort of a recluse. Tonight I noticed he was dressed rather nicely, however, in that collegiate style. Khaki pants, boat shoes, navy sweater, and a pin-striped shirt. He was somewhat handsome for a man in his forties, though I was surprised to see his hair was starting to thin. Paul gave Jill a smirk. He then asked, "Hi, Jill, how are you?" She instantly nodded an okay and proceeded to depart towards her boat, leaving me alone with Mr. Adler. Paul ignored me and quickly started to follow Jill. Then he hesitated as if realizing my presence. He also saw the expression of surprise on my face.

I finally blurted out, "What's up, Paul?"

He stuttered at first and then said, "You know, the winter was so long and lonely that I decided to come to the club and see what was going on. I was getting cabin fever locked up in the house, and it was such a nice late spring evening. I just decided not to waste it."

I decided to bring up a new subject. "Paul," I said, "how is your wife?"

He just shrugged, looked at me, and replied, "She has her good days and her bad days. Unfortunately, the bad days are taking over. She rarely leaves the house."

I said, "I did not realize that she had an acute illness."

Paul said, "My wife likes to keep to herself. As you know, even when we first came here she very rarely came to the club."

"Paul, you know maybe some of us girls could go visit her."

Paul gave me a second shrug and said, "When you feel as ill as my wife does, it is hard to put on a happy face and greet people I think that is why she prefers being alone."

I said, "Well, if she has a change of heart let me know."

"Will do," he said. My radar was going off. I knew damn well he was there to talk to Jill. He continued to make small talk, and all the while his hands were twisting and his eyes kept turning towards the *Rusty Scupper*. Then he excused himself and left. I put the whole experience on file in my mind. I knew eventually this would play out.

A half hour passed, and then Jill appeared again by my side. I just blurted out, "Jill, are you friendly with Paul?"

Jill mentioned, "Yes, Paul has a network of friends who have slips in different parts of the country. Paul occasionally helps me and George when we need a place to dock George's boat."

I said, "Jill, is that your only connection with Paul Adler?"

"What do you mean?"

I said, "Listen to me, Jill. It was very obvious that Paul Adler came down to the floats to see you." I paused and then said, "I know that Paul was Fleet Captain a few years back, but for the past few years along with him being semi retired he has been semi seen. Now, Jill, he is here. I know he came to see you." Jill looked at me with those big, sad doe eyes and immediately changed the subject. I changed it again and asked her, "Jill, what part of California are you from?"

She answered, "All over," and before I could have any further conversation George appeared and the two of them headed toward the food table that was being set up. I realized that Jill had a lot of secrets and that she was living a very unhappy existence. I then realized I needed a glass of wine. This was supposed to be a happy occasion. I involved myself with a few happy campers, and we chatted and laughed. I did not talk to Jill the rest of the night. She stayed very close to George.

The night was so beautiful, especially the sunset with the Boston skyscrapers in the background. Tony and I decided to sleep on the boat. We had the children with us—tomorrow was Saturday. The boys decided they might like to fish off the pier. Our daughter wanted to tan herself, and what better way than in the bow of the boat. I just hoped she hadn't brought that itty-bitty bikini she had recently bought. Tony would have a heart attack. I had told her it was inappropriate. She wanted to wear it in the yard where it was private, and that was okay. The bathing suit was definitely short on material and would cause a lot of heads to turn on the floats. I prayed she had made the right decision.

Even though our boat was a good size, it was still close quarters with all of us aboard. Around four in the morning, I decided to go up on the deck of our boat for a breather. I heard yelling, and it was definitely coming from the *Rusty Scupper*. Jill sounded like she was begging George for something, but before I could make anything out; Jill emerged from the sailboat and ran toward the parking lot. I noticed George did not follow. Tony poked his head out of the cabin and asked, "What's happening?" I start in by mentioning Jill, but before I finish the sentence he says, "Please come to bed. Haven't you heard a lovers' quarrel before?" I agreed. *Mind your own business,* I said to myself, and I joined the kids and Tony in the cabin. Night-night!

Chapter 6

Blessing of the Fleets

THE BLESSING OF THE FLEETS WAS approaching. We were deciding on how we would decorate our boat. Now that Tony had more time, we could really get into the activities on the floats. Our children wanted to get involved as well, and they asked if we would help them. Our daughter thought that Betsy Ross making the first flag would be a nice theme. Tony and I were so glad that the children all wanted to be a part of this occasion. My mom and daughter worked hard making Betsy Ross's costume. My mom had an old white wig that my daughter wore. It was difficult because of her long black hair. We worked hard hiding her hair with a huge selection of bobby pins. My mom also donated a large apron that had stars and stripes on it.

One of my sons dressed up as Uncle Sam. He took an old top hat and decorated it with red, white, and blue stars and stripes. Our other sons blew up balloons and made cardboard stars. The stars were stapled to the strings on the balloons. I had an old Singer sewing machine—my grandfather, my mom's father who had passed away a long time ago, had been a tailor. I had I kept his old machine for sentimental reasons. Tony carried the old sewing machine to the club and placed it in front of Betsy Ross. I had to say that our boat was decorated with such love and enthusiasm. My mom came down for the day, and she actually cried for joy. I guess her apron, wig, and father's sewing machine just brought out that sentimental feeling. It was nice to see her happy. She had her camera, which was almost as old as the sewing machine. She took picture after picture of her grandchildren holding balloons and stars and mimicking Uncle Sam and Betsy Ross. I looked at Tony and said, "Are Betsy Ross and Uncle Sam in the same era of history?"

Tony laughed and said, "Hon, I don't know, but they sure make a great couple."

That day was spectacular; the weather was in our favor. All the boats in the harbor were decorated. Pat's boat was done up with mermaids, and her husband was Barnacle Bill the Sailor. He stood on the stern with cheese and crackers, greeting the clergy as they passed through the floats blessing the boats. Pat's husband was shy, and he just nodded his head and never got into conversation.

Our kids did a great job. Red, white, and blue streamers blew in the breeze while Betsy Ross worked tediously on the new flag. Uncle Sam greeted the guests. We placed next to our boat a small table decorated with stars and stripes and set with homemade lemonade for those in need of a drink. Our young boys were astonished that some of the people were giving them tips.

The boat that was a real stitch, however, was Jill's, or should I say George's. It looked like a mini Noah's ark. She had stuffed animals everywhere. She had a huge bowl of Tootsie Pops for all the children parading by. When they approached, Jill glowed with excitement. The babies really turned her on. As the day progressed I noticed fewer and fewer animals on George's boat. I also noticed a lot of children hugging stuffed animals as they played among the floats. I was sure by nightfall George's boat would no longer resemble Noah's ark, and I didn't think I had ever seen Jill so happy. Every time Jill looked at a child hugging one of her stuffed animals, she wrapped her arms around her own body as if she was hugging one of those children. Her eyes were not doe like that day but bright and cheerful. The lines in the corners of her eyes formed an upswing. Her face formed a smile.

Mary and Jim came down to our boat after the official ceremony for a bite to eat. They had their niece and her new little baby. They had named the child Kathleen after Mary's daughter. This was a great gesture for Jim and Mary. It was like a part of their daughter lived on, right down to the small crown of red hair the baby was developing. Mary's daughter had also had red hair. Today was a good day. It was a "10." It was a day we would all remember as special. I would remember Mary holding Kathleen like she was her daughter. Mary's face was so expressive, like someone who was so intoxicated on love. I thought to myself, *This is good because love is like a drug. It is intoxicating. One just can't get enough of it.*

We were planning to invade the Valley Crest Yacht Club in a few weeks. Also, the Pink Panthers would be competing in their second dart game. Jill had previously asked if she could be a substitute player, I asked the girls and they agreed. I had stuck to my to-do list and asked the girls to give Jill a chance. I felt we should get to know someone before we were quick to listen to gossip. Mary smiled at the fact that she now had another opportunity to be useful. She could make another Panther shirt. We all agreed Jill would look great in the shirt. Our main concern was, could Jill throw a dart?

Luck came Jill's way when one of our teammates had to attend a graduation and informed us that she would not be able to play darts at the upcoming tournament at Valley Crest. We all decided that we needed to practice before this tournament. I arranged a night that we would all meet at the club and practice our dart game. I informed Jill that there was an opening for the upcoming event at Valley Crest. Jill promised to attend the practice meeting. That night we all started concentrating on the bull's-eye. Jill watched intently.

Jill was quiet until Mary asked, "Jill, how long have you been crocheting?"

Jill mentioned, "I have been crocheting since I was a little girl."

Mary asked, "Who taught you to crochet?"

Jill said, "My grandmother." Then Jill changed the subject. I wondered if she really had a grandmother, but I decided to let that thought pass. Then Jill asked "What is the exact format of the game?" Mary explained the rules and the point system to Jill. Jill then got up and threw her three darts. One hit the board the others went askew. Jill then hit the seventeen. We explained to Jill the numbers that were involved in winning the game. One of the numbers was seventeen. Each number had to be hit three times. If the other team hadn't hit one of those numbers three times, then our team could make points by repeatedly hitting that number over and over again until our opponent hit it three times. This included the bull's-eye. The rules applied for both teams. The first team to get all numbers and bull's-eyes completed won the game. Jill seemed enthused, and we continued to practice.

I asked Jill, "How did your winter go?"

She gives me short, quick shrug. However, she began to say, "I am very excited over this new afghan pattern that I learned this winter, and I am about to make a new blanket with it." Jill smiled and continued, "I was able to purchase some quality yarn in lavender and sage green. These colors are so beautiful together." Jill then promised to show us what she was working on when we were on the floats. She actually asked for our feedback on the placement of these two colors. This was the first conversation all of us girls were involved in with Jill, and it was nice. It was going well. Mary knew what questions to ask Jill. Mary had a sensitivity and kindness about her, and it spilled out that night during dart practice. Mary had a gift for making people feel welcome.

Chapter 7

Lazy Hazy Days

THE DAYS WENT BY WITH THE usual summer fun. Tony really enjoyed running the bars and function rooms. Every weekend involved some type of celebration, and the majority of guests and members using the club's facilities seemed to be happy. Tony had been working hard, and word on the floats was the new Vice Commodore was doing a great job. This gave the Commodore peace of mind and more opportunity to engage in all the political and important matters on improving yachting.

Chapter 8

Valley Crest Yacht Club

VALLEY CREST WAS ABOUT FORTY-FIVE MINUTES away by boat. For the journey, Tony had our boat equipped with a well-stocked bar. This was our welcome gift. The Rear Commodore, working diligently with the Fleet Captain, had arranged the departure of our small fleet. There were about twenty boats in this procession. All the boats were flying their burgee, which had the club's insignia on it. Tony and the Rear Commodore had an added flag that distinguished them as officers. Our Commodore would meet us at Valley Crest since he had been invited to three different yacht club extravaganzas. He would definitely attend the officers' cocktail party at Valley Crest. The Commodore knew he must make appearances at the different functions out of respect for his fellow officers. This involved all the yacht clubs in our area. As I mentioned, before politics were politics. The Commodore's position was the highest honor in yachting, and officers, members, and guests looked forward to the Commodore's arrival and the words of wisdom he related to his fellow comrades and guests.

The ride to Valley Crest was on a calm sea with soft breezes. We could not have had a better cruise. We had to apply a lot of suntan lotion. Even though the breeze kept us cool, the rays of the sun were like an electric blanket turned on high. Occasionally a spray of water came up on the bow, and we welcomed the cool feeling. When we arrive we received a warm welcome. The air was enhanced with the smell of sausages, hamburgers, and hotdogs simmering on the huge grill. Valley Crest had a view overlooking the beautiful Atlantic Ocean. Between the smell of the saltwater and the food grilling, we all felt this was what yachting was all about. Tony unloaded the boat and helped set up our club's gift, the well-stocked bar. Then Tony became a guest. "Boy this is fun," Tony said. "It is nice being waited on." We all indulged in a great barbecue. There was anticipation and excitement because the ladies' dart and men's pool tournament would start shortly.

Chapter 9

Enter Pink Panthers

AFTER STUFFING OURSELVES WITH DELICIOUS FOOD, we started to relax on the beautiful floats of Valley Crest. After about a half hour, there was an announcement. "Let the games begin!" announced the Rear Commodore of Valley Crest. One of the ladies from Valley Crest escorted our dart team to the ladies' room. There we were able to change into our appropriate attire for darts. I was getting my Pink Panther shirt on while Jill stood next to me with her new panther shirt on. I had to make a comical statement.

I smiled and said, "Jill, much better attire this year than last." Jill puts her head down, and then we both let out a laugh. "However," I continued, "I am afraid some of your audience from last year will be disappointed."

She then said seriously, "Can we forget that night, *please?*"

"Okay," I said. The team we were playing was the Rattlesnakes. They had a little more experience than we did and had been playing darts in competition for much longer. However, I smiled, we had fortitude. I felt we were going to win. The Rattlesnakes were in black shirts with a red cobra dominating the front of the shirt.

Jill looked at me and said, "They are very intimidating."

I looked at her and replied, "Did you ever see what a panther does with a snake?"

"No."

"Jill, they pulverize it."

Pat started to laugh, but Mary mumbled, "Pulverize it." We started the game, and as a matter-of-fact we were doing okay. Jill was doing well. She seemed to hit the same number—seventeen—and in this game we needed it hit three times. Pat got up, and I announced, "Well, what can I say Bull's-Eye Princess." I kept saying "Bull's-Eye Princess" and Pat kept hitting the bull's-eye. I liked the power of suggestion. I don't recall how it happened, but it certainly brought tears to my eyes. Jill was trying for a seventeen, a much needed number. In the mean time, one of the gals from the other team, who I might say had a huge posterior, got up to pick up her napkin. In the process she must have leaned on the table for balance, because unfortunately the table tumbled. Then the commotion began. Jill only added to all the confusion when she lost her train of thought and the dart she was throwing went askew. The problem was that it landed right in the posterior of the gal trying to retrieve her napkin. The screams caused a total cease in all games, including pool. Jill panicked and did the worst thing she could possibly do. Jill ran over and pulled the dart from the woman's behind. The screaming woman was then identified as Maggie. Someone emerged with ice, but between all of us no one dared to apply the ice to the poor women's behind. The worst part of it was Maggie was actually accusing Jill of doing it on purpose. Now the men were getting involved. One of the members from the opposing team was a male nurse, and he convinced Maggie to go in the officers' room with some of her friends and he would determine the extent of damage. He soon emerged from the officers' room and informed us that Maggie should be fine. The dart did no go in that deep, though she should still get a tetanus shot. Jill immediately offered to take Maggie to the nearest hospital, but Maggie would have no part of Jill's offer and left with the male nurse. The men continued their pool game, so we continued our dart game. In the meantime, we were trying not to break out in spastic laughter. We all felt it was an unfortunate episode, but Maggie caused this herself. It wasn't Jill who caused her to loose her balance and knock the table over. The scene of her bent over with the dart stuck in her buttocks would be the talk of our dart league for some time.

The dart game became more serious. Our team of girls tried hard to stay focused. Jill was very quiet. This was her second visit to Valley Crest, and neither visit had gone well for her. Our team was supportive and stayed close to her. We encouraged her when it was her turn at darts. I think she felt secure knowing we knew it was an accident. Jill helped us win the tournament that night, and we left on a quiet note. When we got into our boats, however, and we knew no one could hear us we all roared with laughter. Jill lightened up, and she started to laugh with the rest of us. We didn't think much of our chances of being invited back. Fortunately, the next night the cocktail party and dance went well. It was nice to say goodbye to Valley Crest and head home. All in all we had a good time. Maggie would recover and hopefully forgive Jill. It really was an accident.

Chapter 10

Never Boring

ANYONE WHO HAS EVER OWNED A boat, kept it on a slip, and belonged to or was associated with a club knows the different array of characters clubs attract. In this case, the character's name was Rocco. He was single, divorced, fat, and middle-aged. He was the type of man that no matter what clothes were put on him he always looked messy. He was like a crooked coat hanger—clothes never hung right on him. He owned an old wooden boat which served as a part-time home and source of pleasure. Rocco was a fisherman. The boat was about thirty-two feet long and had its own peculiar stench. I was glad our boat was not near it. A young couple with a couple of children had the slip abutting him. They were extremely tolerant in my opinion. The children loved watching Rocco clean his lobster traps. If they were lucky, they would end up with some crabs to play with. Crabs had an uncanny way of creeping into lobster traps, and they were very unwelcome guests. However, children liked to play with them. Rocco usually departed at about 5 or 5:30 AM for his fishing expeditions. Sometimes he would not return till three or four in the afternoon. So, needless to say, on this particular day around eleven o'clock in the morning the last thing I expected was Rocco's boat approaching his slip with a bunch of beautiful girls who were clothed sparingly. The ladies were dancing to loud, overbearing music. This certainly got everyone's attention. Rocco was in the middle of this soirée while a younger version of Rocco manned the boat. As the boat approached the slip, it was amazing how many men came over to help tie and secure the boat. In fact, there were more men than rope. I had to say the girls were all beautiful, but their skimpy attire left no room whatsoever for imagination. The audience of men was happy to escort these young girls off Rocco's boat. Now on the floats, the girls, along with Rocco and mini Rocco, continued to party. The music was blaring. By now a lot of the female population at the club was getting annoyed. They were telling the girls that their clothing was inappropriate, and they also did not like some of the dance steps the girls were performing. I found it rather funny; however, I was afraid it might get out of hand. I was right. The trouble started when the men on the floats decided to dance with the girls. Tony approached the floats to see what the clatter was all about. As Tony went passed Rocco and his revelers, even he did a little ditty with the girls. But then it happened. The music changed and the girls started doing a little strip tease to a rare version of "Happy Birthday." I was getting concerned seeing that they were already half clad—what more did they have to work with? It seemed the girls were part of a strip club in the area, and the younger version of Rocco was Rocco's son. Why wasn't I surprised! His son managed the strip club and thought this would be a different present for his dad. I certainly agreed with his son.

Unfortunately, the two young children who had the slip next to Rocco appeared. Their faces were stunned! One of the children cried, "No crabs! Just girls!" To make matters worse, one of the girls was topless. She did, however, immediately dress. The rest of the girls stayed clad, and everyone started singing "Happy Birthday" to Rocco. The dance steps improved, but I knew this episode would not go unnoticed by many of the members. This was a family club, and this was certainly not considered appropriate behavior, especially around eleven o'clock in the morning. Finally the girls, Rocco, and mini Rocco embarked on a departure cruise. Things settled down. However, Tony knew that this whole scene would be brought up at the next meeting. The final result would be determined by the officers and the Commodore. Tony felt that Rocco was a decent member. Hopefully a warning would be all Rocco had to face.

ROCCO RETURNED VERY LATE THAT NIGHT. His boat crept into its slip. Something strange happened during that late evening after Rocco returned. Rocco's boat, which was named *Fish Teaser*, was renamed by an anonymous painter. This painter and prankster had very little time to do this, but in the wee hours of the morning, when Rocco finally fell asleep, the boat was renamed. I could not believe it was named *Strip Teaser*! Tony smiled at me when I asked him how it was painted so quickly. I said, "Tony I noticed it this morning when I was departing from our boat. I saw a group of people around the stern of Rocco's boat laughing. Who did this, Tony?"

Again Tony smiled and said, "I'll never tell." Guess what—Tony never did.

Rocco got a warning, and we all got a lesson—be careful what you wish for. The fish gave an awful smell, but the perfume came with a high price to pay, or maybe to watch! The Commodore felt no one got hurt. The Vice Commodore felt it was a first offense. The Rear Commodore didn't appreciate a sex education for the young children. It was noted that as soon as the stripper saw the child she immediately dressed. This was just pieces of guesswork that filtered down to the floats. The truth would come in a letter to Rocco. I did know through Tony that a warning was issued. The details of that warning were privy only to the club's officers and Rocco.

Chapter 11

A Gift

MARY AND JIM VISITED THE CLUB a few days later. The hype of the wild dancing on the floats had died down, but the heat and humidity had not. We welcomed our friends' company. Jim and Mary asked permission to board our boat. There was a slight breeze, and we found it enjoyable being rocked softly. It was like being in a cradle of comfort. Mary was holding a large package and presented it to Tony and me. Of course, like everyone else I loved presents, so I anxiously opened it. I was taken by surprise! Mary had made a huge eight-foot banner—it was the club's burgee. Mary asked if it could be hung across the top of our yacht club. Mary felt this was a giant symbol of what we stood for. Mary wanted Tony to hang it the night before the next invasion took place at our club. Jim felt it would be a nice ceremony. He wanted Tony, as our Vice Commodore, to have that honor. Jim asked Tony if he would place the burgee on display upstairs in the members lounge until the invasion took place. This way everyone would have a chance to see the fantastic job Mary did. Tony said, "Jim, let me run it by the Commodore, though I feel that there should not be any problem. Also, I am extremely moved not only by how hard you worked, Mary, making this burgee, but by the fact that you both would like me to hang it up in celebration." Tony then said, "In the meantime I will place it safely in the officers' lounge upstairs until a decision is made by the Commodore."

JILL STOPPED BY OUR BOAT THE next day. She had in her hands the new afghan she was working on. I had to say her choice of pattern and colors was perfect. I was genuinely impressed. I said, "Jill, you have a knack for creating some beautiful handmade work."

"You think so?" she replied.

"I know so." I said.

"Well," Jill said, "I want Mary's opinion too. I just saw her burgee up at the club, and she would be a good person to ask because she did such a nice job. I find her very sweet, don't you?"

"Mary," I said, "is one of my best friends." I agreed with her on Mary's burgee and told her Mary would love to see her afghan.

Then Jill asked, "Can I participate in the next invasion?" I told her to check with Betty, the Rear Commodore's wife. There was going to be a raffle table, and I knew that anything Jill made was always appreciated. I asked Jill if she would like a cup of tea. When Jill said she would, I knew that she had something else on her mind. Call it woman's intuition.

Chapter 12

The Confession

WHEN THE TEA WAS BREWED, WE sat down at a table inside the cabin of my boat. I then looked at Jill and said, "How are things going with you and George?" Before Jill could answer, she burst into tears.

She cried, "I hate my life. George and I are just existing—we rarely speak to each other."

I told her, "Jill, you are not married to George and you could exit anytime."

She put her head down and said, "It is not as easy as you think. I have done a lot of things I am not proud of, and sometimes when you do these things people have a hold on you."

I said, "Jill, what do you mean by sometimes someone has a hold on you? Please define that."

She put her head down on the table. Her hair was wet from wiping her eyes and pushing her hair out of her face. Her nose was running, and at one point she looked like water was going to explode out of every orifice in her face. I immediately got some Kleenex. At this point I regretted asking her the question. I might have pushed to far.

I said, "Jill lets take a break and just sip on some tea." I then gave her a warm, wet face cloth and told her to just relax a bit. I felt I had started an interrogation.

After a few moments, Jill regained her composure. She then looked over at me and said matter-of-fact, "It's Paul Adler who is making my life miserable."

"Paul Adler?" I asked. "I knew he was up to no good. Jill, what kind of a hold does he have on you?"

Jill still kept her head down as she said in a broken whisper, "I do things for him and his friends so George and I can get slips and work when we travel. Sometimes we don't have enough money to pay for these things. I want to stay at safe areas when we travel."

"Jill," I said, "how safe can it be if Paul is making you unhappy? What does he make you do?"

Jill looked up with those doe eyes and again the tears started to flow. Jill had soft freckles that were splattered on her face. I thought with all these tears they might just wash away. She was slight, but not frail. She reminded me of one of those hopeless characters in books who were always taken advantage of. But then it came—all the pain and all the shame. It came like a roar when Jill let it all out. "*I give blowjobs to men!* Now what do you think of me? I prostitute myself for favors. I look into the mirror and I hate what I see. I am a piece of trash. I feel so bad because I have taken advantage of you and your nice friends; you have made me feel welcome. I have abused your trust. I want to be needed and loved, but it's too late—I just got lost along the way." I must say Jill definitely took me by surprise. It wasn't that I was that naïve, but I guess it was the actual words that made me lose my concerned expression and have one of horror. Of course, as soon as Jill realized my reaction, it was exit stage right.

I tried to regain my composure, and I grabbed her arm. "Jill, don't leave," I said. "Let's talk. Maybe there is another answer." All I could see was a reminder of why I thought there were cuts on her wrist. I didn't know for sure, but I was beginning to think that my assumption of her attempting to commit suicide might have been true. I did not want her to leave this boat with such a low opinion of herself. I said, "Jill, Tony might be on his way here, and I really feel we should talk a little more. Why don't you and I take a nice walk? I think we could breathe in some nice salt air." She agreed.

The two of us started walking past the floats and past the yacht club, heading to nowhere in particular; I was just trying to get Jill to talk. Maybe if she talked and let all this unpleasantness out, she could start changing her life. I didn't even know why I was doing this. I guess I felt bad, or maybe I felt that she needed someone to vent to. Whatever the reason, I was there and so was she.

After a few moments of extreme silence, Jill said, "I lied to you regarding my background. I was raised in an orphanage, and from eight years on I went from foster home to foster home. I am not from California. In fact, I lived in many trailer parks. Most of those parks were in Texas."

I said, "Jill, if this is too painful for you to talk about, you don't have to tell me."

"Please," Jill said, "I need to tell someone about my sorry-ass life. I don't want to have a pity party, but I need to know that maybe someone like you can understand and maybe just maybe point me in a different direction. You're a nice lady and maybe you have a little compassion."

I said, "Jill, I don't know the answers, but I do know that you have a worth. We all have a worth—it is the one thing that separates us from everyone else."

Jill said, "How can I have a worth? I was abused around eleven years old, and I learned that if I shut my mouth and acted like a *good little girl*, sexual favors had their rewards. I would be treated to special treats. This meant ice cream, movies, and even a pony was given to me to take care of for a short season." I was beginning to understand the lion's paw. My stomach was churning. I wanted to vomit. To think that in life someone had the power to steal a child's innocence made me sick.

"Why didn't you tell someone, Jill?"

"I did," said Jill. "That sent me back to the orphanage, only to be sent to another foster home. The only time I got lucky was when I was in a home where they made me take care of the old lady. She was very old and could not get out of bed very often. I used to bring her bedpan and bathe her. She liked me and taught me to crochet. I stayed with that family for two years. They made me do all the household chores, but I didn't mind. They worked both the woman and the man. The old lady's name was Alice. I really liked her. She died after two years, and then they sent me back to the orphanage. I was almost sixteen then. Those were two very happy years for me."

"So," I said, "that was where you learned to crochet."

"Yes," said Jill, "from Alice."

"Then what happened?"

"I ran away. I lived with a group of runaways, and we stole food and clothes and survived until I met George."

"How old are you, Jill?"

"I am twenty-two and all used up. There will be no wedding dress for me. I am just a used piece of rubbish."

"Jill, please listen—you have a worth. First let us count our blessings. You are healthy and attractive. You have a talent with your hands. You have the ability to work and pull your life together. It won't be easy, but it can be done." I then asked, "Jill, when did you meet George?"

"I met George after I had been through a nasty relationship. I was barely eighteen at the time, and I decided that George was my meal ticket out of Texas. I had never experienced living on an ocean. It sounded so clean, and the thought of living on a boat and moving from one place to another really appealed to me. I had no real roots, so who would ever miss me, never mind realize I was gone?"

When Jill made this last statement, I thought to myself how awful it must be to never be missed. What a lonely existence just live in other families' shadows. Jill then continued her saga with George. Jill said, "In the beginning me and George's relationship was exciting, as all new affairs are, but eventually reality set in. He began drinking more frequently, and then he would bring up my past experiences. He would remind me that I had already done sexual favors when I was younger and ask what the big deal was for me to do them now. He then started begging me to help him out, either for money or work, by doing what he felt I did best—performing sexual favors. Try to understand that I thought George was different. I thought maybe, just maybe, I could have a new beginning. So now that I was traveling unfamiliar surroundings, I became afraid and submitted to George's requests. This did not happen a lot, and when it did he would be so grateful to me and really treat me special for long periods of time. But these past years, his expectations of me are wearing thin. My nerves are knotting up to the point that I want to twist myself into a pretzel and stop all the blood from flowing into my body. I want to escape, but the second part of me has tried that once before without success." This was getting very hard for me to digest. I was not equipped to handle this type of erratic behavior. The thoughts of how Jill's wrist had cuts on them were coming back. With Jill's last sentence, I was almost positive she had tried to kill herself. One part of me just wanted to reach out and hug her. The other part of me was, I was sad to say, afraid.

I said, "Jill, have you thought of speaking to a councilor?"

"Yes," she said, "except who would pay for it?"

I said, "They must have programs where you could get some help."

Jill laughed. "Where do you start?"

Then I said what came right to my mind. "A church."

Jill laughed harder. "Do you want the walls of the church to come down?"

"Jill," I said, "Do you know who Mary Magdalene was?"

"No," said Jill, "and I really don't care."

Okay, I thought, *let's try another approach.* I continued to ask Jill questions. I said, "How does Paul Adler fit into the scenario?"

Jill replied, "I was introduced to Paul Adler, who made my situation worse. Paul was putting demands on me. He wanted to be with me even when my sexual services were not required. Paul haunted me in every way, and I knew if George found out that I was not accommodating Paul's advances that Paul had the influence to have George's boat removed from the floats. Paul also had the power to interfere with any plans that we might need in the winter. George relied on Paul to help him find a place in the warmer climates to work and have a slip for his boat. After all, Paul Adler had a lot of connections from here all the way down to Florida. George is very jealous of Paul's hold on us. George promises me that as soon as he gets settled in one place with regular work and pay that Paul Adler will be history. I guess this is his way of showing me that he does love me." At this point the vomit is going up and down my esophagus. I felt I was getting a preview of the latest soap opera. Jill also mentioned that this winter Paul had a friend down the Florida Keys who had a small marina. Paul's friend could use George, even though this was in a little fishing village. George could help Paul's friend take care of some of the boats. Paul also felt there were a few motels that could use chambermaids and Jill might be needed. "So," Jill said. "This is my life. I have no parents or family to run to."

What could I say? How could I judge? Fortunately I had never been in Jill's shoes. All I could come up with was, "Jill, let me think about your situation. This conversation will go no further." Then I took her face in my hands and said, "Jill, everyone has worth. Please concentrate on all the beautiful things you create with your hands." I gave her twenty dollars and told her to go buy some yarn. I then told her that when she felt troubled she should pick up her crochet work and just repeat to herself, "I have self worth." At the time it seemed like a good idea. That was one positive area in her life.

Jill said, "Since I have told you my story, I can understand it if you never want to see me again."

I said, "Jill, don't get me wrong—I wished you never told me, but I did ask and I appreciate your honesty. I am sure it wasn't easy to tell me what is happening and has happened. But since you did, maybe I can point you in the right direction. The fact, Jill, that you talked about it might mean you want to change the unpleasantness in your life, and that is positive. I still feel you need a councilor—and don't underestimate religious officials. Their job," I chuckled, "is saving souls. You might want to consider that option." With that last statement I let her face go and both of us headed back to the club.

I now knew why boaters drank. We all lived too close to one another on these slips. We all shared too much information about each other. We all had such very different personalities, and like the saying went, sometimes familiarity bred contempt. No sooner was I in my boat than a double scotch was in my hand. What in God's name had I gotten myself into? I was no psychiatrist. And as for Paul Adler, I would never look at him the same way again, that rodent. George was no better, making a woman prostitute herself for his shenanigans. Then there was Jill, so weak and with such a low esteem of herself. I guessed some of us were lucky. We were either brought up or dragged up in life. She was dragged in more ways than one. I had a lot of thinking to do.

Chapter 13

The Storm

LIVING IN THE NEW ENGLAND AREA could be difficult weather wise. They said just wait a few minutes and the weather would change. Hurricane season was usually late August to early September. However, New England weather changed its mind more often than a woman. It was forecasted to be a tropical storm, just a lot of wind and rain. The forecast had to be pretty bad to create a mass exodus of boats escaping to Briar Ridge for refuge. A lot of boats from different clubs in the area used our club when storms or severe hurricanes were predicted, the reason being we were in an inlet that protected them from the oncoming winds that could destroy a harbor. As I mentioned, no such storm was predicted. It was mid-July, not a real rainy season, but Mother Nature had a mind of her own.

The rain was predicted to start early that Saturday morning. Tony had rented the hall for a wedding that was to take place around three o'clock. It was one of the members' sons. The hall was set up to serve one hundred and fifty people. The bride was only having her reception at the hall, and the actual ceremony would take place in a nearby church. Tony and I were not formally invited. The parents did, however, ask Tony and I to stop by later to toast the happy couple. Tony was an elected officer, and I was sure this was an act of respect extended to a Vice Commodore. Tony had worked diligently making sure that the table, hall, dance floor, and bar were in perfect order. He also made sure there were plenty of waiters and waitresses to accommodate the large wedding. Tony would oversee the wedding during the ceremony to make sure everything went smoothly. I had some errands to do and told Tony I would return around seven that evening. Around five that same day, I noticed that the sky was getting very dark. In fact, it was so dark that if I didn't know better I would have thought we were getting a tornado. Tornados were very rare in New England, but on occasion they did show up. I decided to head back to the club before I got caught up in the rainstorm. When I approached the club, bolts of lightening decorated the darkened sky. It was extremely frightening. One of the bolts must have hit an electric pole, because the next thing I noticed was that all the street and store lights went out. The joyous wedding that was taking place was now in total darkness. While I sat in the car, I could see that backup lights were starting to come on in the club area, thanks to the club's generators. The club had purchased generators just for moments like this. I also noticed as I got closer that candles were quickly being lit. The rain came down in buckets, but worse of all the wind picked up. The wind seemed to be coming from all directions. I got out of the car, and naturally my umbrella blew inside out. I threw it angrily back into the car. At this point I just wanted refuge. As I ran towards the entrance of the club, I heard someone yelling for help from down on the floats. I ran into the reception area and found the room slightly lit. Some guests noticed me. I was drenched and puddles were forming wherever I stepped. I spotted a few members and told them that there seemed to be a crisis down on the docks. As nonchalantly as they could without causing any more chaos, some of the members at the wedding departed for the floats. I tried to find Tony. I was told that he was helping the Rear Commodore in the galley.

When Tony saw the expression on my face and the condition I was in, he smiled and said, "Hon, you look like a drowned rat."

I said, "Thank you very much, but there is a crisis down at the floats."

Tony said, "Relax, everything is under control. The generators are on."

I looked at him and mentioned again, "Did you hear me? There is a problem on the floats. Listen, Tony, the wind has come up in all direction, and it is unbelievably strong." Tony immediately went out through the galley exit. No one at the reception saw him.

Within minutes he was back, yelling to everyone in the galley and reception area, "I need more help! It's a disaster on the floats!" Tony then went on to say, "The wind is so strong it is tearing the boats from their slips. One boat in particular is crashing into another with such force that it is causing it to flood and sink. A tug of war is taking place!" With Tony's pleas, members started to leave the wedding and head down to the floats. I ran down too. I witnessed a crew of men and nature. Some of our men were in tuxedos, and they all were working so hard against nature. Nature was winning. All our male guests and members were holding onto ropes to try and bring some of the boats to safety. I don't know how they could even see. The wind and saltwater splashing vigorously had to be burning their eyes. The lightening was not letting up, and the thunder was so loud that it sounded like we were being bombed. Nature was at war. Nature was our enemy! How could we fight nature? I heard a scream—it was Tony. I could barely recognize him. His hair was plastered over his face. His uniform was stuck to him like someone had taken an iron and decided to press certain parts of the uniform right onto his body. He looked like he was holding onto life more than the floats. I was frightened. Then Tony yelled, "Watch out! Part of the dock is splitting in two!" Everyone on the dock managed to escape to a safer place. Fortunately no one got hurt, but it was only a matter of time before someone would.

Finally the worst thing happened. In order to save the majority of boats, some had to be sacrificed. The part of the float that was damaged had been supporting some huge yachts. The ropes were untied to free up the weight, and like a horror flick we watched Mother Nature encompass our club. That night eight boats sank. It was the worst disaster in yachting I could ever remember. The only positive thing was no one died. There were a few cracked ribs and cuts, one that required stitches. There was a broken wrist and lots of small cuts and bruises. Some of the men's hands had huge rope burns. Some of us then acted like Florence Nightingale and helped soothe the wounds of our injured heroes. There was no way we could soothe our minds. It was not easy to make the decision to cut the ropes. I was glad Tony was not Rear Commodore that year, but officers stuck together, and everyone abided by Peter Flanagan's command. One of the boats cut loose was Peter's, so we all knew how hard it was to make that decision. In the long run it was the smartest decision that could be made. The hard part would be trying to put it all back together again. So much for thinking that Mother Nature would respect Briar Ridge's inlet. Other clubs in the area also had their share of damage, but none as bad as Briar Ridge. I guess it was our turn to deal with the many moods of nature. It was called a hurricane. It was a surprise. And all the king's horses couldn't keep her away.

Chapter 14

The Repair

WELL, I SAID WE WERE A family. Those of us whose boats were left unscathed took care of the boats that were not so lucky. We had meals on certain boats to provide food for all the working crew. We still had to keep spirits up. Sometimes we would all pile into one of the surviving boats and take a cruise on a hot day or night. This helped keep the courage up for the crews working on rebuilding the docks or collecting the remains of the yachts that went to sea. It was hard keeping up the morale. So much paraphernalia washed up onshore in the following weeks. As soon as we tried to put aside the anguish of the hurricane, something else would wash up, reminding us of nature's cruelty. Tony said to me one day, "Hon, imagine how difficult it must be when someone loses their entire home. All their belongings are destroyed and all their memories and hard work. What do they do?"

I said, "Rebuild just like we are doing."

Tony said, "That is easier said than done."

I laughed, "Tony, what choice do we have?"

He smiled at me and said, "You know this is hard for me?"

I said, "Why?"

Tony said, "I feel guilt because my boat is fine. I feel that Nature picked and chose who she wanted to hurt." I thought about what Tony said. Was nature that powerful?

Then I said, "Tony, everyone in life cannot escape a crisis. We have no idea what is waiting for us. The most important thing we have is each other. Our job right now is to help our friends rebuild. I think we should get the children involved."

Tony frowned at me in a sad, hopeless way and just said, "I lost my bearings. I thought all us guys could overcome that disaster. I feel like a failure." At that point Jim came over and needed Tony for something.

I just brushed Tony's hand and smiled. "It's okay to feel." My mom cooked and sent lots of pastries down to the floats, and the children did help with the days of cleanup, and there were many. Of course we tried to keep a sense of humor, but the only real chuckle we got was when Rocco burst into hysterics. It seemed that his fishing boat, one of those to go down, had an old sofa on it. Now, no matter how hard he tried to get the fish smell off the sofa, he failed. Rocco was seriously considering getting rid of this sofa.

When the catastrophe took place, Rocco's only remark was, "Well, I guess I got rid of that smelly sofa at the cost of my boat." Well, wouldn't you know, that gosh darn sofa floated up on shore. We all couldn't help but laugh. We called Rocco and told him that there just wasn't any way that damn sofa would go away. It was our first chuckle in weeks. Someone actually wanted to reupholster it and place it in the upstairs hall as a reminder of the tragedy that took place. Then someone wanted a plaque to be placed above it naming the yachts that went down. In the end each idea was scratched. One thing that was on my mind was whether one's wedding day symbolized one's life. I thought about that couple and the fact that their wedding day produced such an awful memory. The worst part was that their marriage was fated. The couple had a stormy relationship that later ended in a horrific divorce. I suppose that should have been on a plaque along with the sofa and the boats that sank.

Chapter 15

The Surprise Party

TONY'S BIRTHDAY WAS APPROACHING. IT WAS one of those landmark birthdays that some people wished would just slip by unnoticed. But the children wanted to do something, and so did I. Ironically, Tony seemed to look better middle aged. He had just started to gray at the temples, and with his Italian complexion enhanced with an ocean tan, he looked damn good. We decided that it should be a surprise otherwise he probably would not show up. I called a few of his closer friends, and they thought a float party was in order. The floats were back in order after many tedious weeks. Some of the members offered to go out, check their traps, and bring back lobsters. I would supply hamburgers, hot dogs, and sausages. Everyone would probably come down to see what was going on, but at least fifty to seventy-five were invited to the gala event. Most of my gal pals offered to bring salads of various kinds. It was a wrap, and the plans were set. Late July was one of the most hot and humid months in New England. It would be nice to be on the ocean.

The time passed quickly. Tony just assumed we were having a July bash and welcomed the future event. He thought this would be great for morale and would be like a celebration of the hard work of rebuilding the floats. He promised to transport all the liquor down to the floats in large coolers and set up a bar. We let him think he needed to do this, but every boat on the floats had its own bar, and for parties no one bought a drink.

Well, hot was not the word for the day of the party. It was 97 degrees in New England. The wind was southwest, which was a warm breeze and not too refreshing. Two of the teenagers, along with my children, decided to bring in some blow-up pools to set up along the floats. This added a bit of humor, as they placed rubber duckies in them. The pools were no more than eight or twelve inches deep. Probably six to eight people could sit in them. There were three pools filled with miniature yellow rubber duckies. Then my daughter decided to get more involved and took plastic barrels placed them near the pools and filled them with water balloons. At that point I knew we were in for a wild time. I was ready!

We decided that four o'clock was a good starting time; the club fishermen had left early in the morning to check their traps. They would soon be approaching with an ample supply of our favorite crustacean. A smaller group of children ten and under was busy shucking corn that would be steamed with the lobster. There was nothing better than a New England lobster fest.

The Rear Commodore sent Tony out on a fool's errand. Peter asked Tony if he could pick up one of his sons from baseball practice. Peter said that he thought his son was an excellent player, but he wanted Tony's opinion. Tony was surprised by Peter's request. Everyone knew Peter's son was a great player. Tony said to me, "I guess Peter knows I love baseball and values my opinion. He must want me to see his son play. I am glad to do this for Peter, and I will bring the boy back to the club. I think I'll take our boys if they want to come."

I said, "Fine." Peter estimated the trip would take enough time that Tony would return around five. Peter's son knew of the plan and promised to involve Tony in a few questions about baseball. One of our sons went. The others stayed behind to help with the party. The bartenders told Tony they would bring the liquor down to the floats, which would truly never take place, but they wanted Tony to know that the Vice Commodore's end was covered. Every boat was full to the brim in honor of the celebration, but the most surprising boat was George's. Jill came over and asked me to come to the *Rusty Scupper* to see something. Lo and behold, Jill had made a giant sheet cake with our boat pictured on it. Underneath the boat was written, "Happy Birthday Vice Commodore." I was overwhelmed. I had forgotten about a cake in all my excitement and I never even consulted with my children to see if they had purchased a cake. I never asked my mom. I was so busy planning everything I forgot one of the most important parts of a birthday party. Amazingly, Jill took the time to make such a perfect cake. I gave her such a hug that I surprised myself.

She looked up with those doe eyes and said, "You have been so nice, it is the least I can do to show how much I respect you both."

I said, "Well, it worked. Thanks."

It was four, and the music from one of the boats was already blaring. Pat came over with a nice, cold Sea Breeze (cranberry, grapefruit, and vodka on ice). Pat knew what could cool me down. I looked over at the floats, and they looked so pretty. Tables were set with red-checkered paper tablecloths and tons of napkins held down by large containers of condiments. Lobsters were messy crustaceans, and sometimes the men used hammers to break the claws rather than those dainty metal crackers. Why let us girls struggle with those hard lobster claws when a hammer could do the job? Of course these hammers had been cleaned. I thought I saw hammers already sitting in hot water. The pools with the ducks did add a touch of humor, but out in the water were Mary and Jim on a blow-up dragon, just waiting to take on passengers for a special ride around the floats. The dragon could accommodate five people, and it looked like a version of the Loch Ness Monster.

The time had come, and Tony's car was spotted. We all tried to act casual. Jim and Mary had brought a radio with a tape that had a kid's song on it that sang, *"Hey, Tony, it's your birthday!"* As Tony approached the stairway to come down to the floats, our daughter blasted the birthday song. Tony just looked. He turned around to go back up the stairs, shaking his head in dismay, when our son who went with him to the baseball game grabbed him.

"Come on, Dad, we planned this party just for you." He started to laugh and realized there was no way he was escaping this party. As he walked through the floats towards me, he was greeted and cheered and comically booed by all. I handed him a beer, gave him a kiss, and said, "Happy Birthday, Baby." And that was just what it was.

The pools proved to be the topic of discussion. As the night progressed, people began sitting in them. Some had bathing suits on, and others opted for their casual clothing, but the highlight was when the Rear Commodore entered a pool with a face mask, a snorkel, and fins. We all just sat there and cracked up. The fins hung over the plastic edge of the pool and caused it to collapse. This, in turn, got poor Peter booed, and then of course a water balloon fight erupted, leading to more hysteria. Was it hot? Not on these floats. They said laughter was the best medicine. It was, but without other people it would be a quiet silence. The combination of many people laughing was so special. As I looked back on this party I realized that this was the best party Tony ever had. We were with our friends and family, and we were having the time of our lives. The last scene of that night involved Tony and I being thrown gently into one of the pools with a rubber ducky, and a birthday hat was placed on his head. It was a picture I would treasure forever. We were young, had our health and our friends, and took it all for granted as we do at those times in our life. Thank goodness for memories.

The next day reality set in again. The Commodore informed us that the club's electrician felt it was dangerous to have pools on the floats. All pools on the floats were banned. When I looked back on it, it was a very good idea and we were very fortunate that nothing occurred during that party.

Chapter 16

The Invasion

WE WERE ALL LOOKING FORWARD TO the upcoming invasion. It was the first social interaction with another club since the hurricane. The night before the invasion, we were all so excited. Tony had ordered chilled buckets of champagne for the burgee hanging. One would have thought we were launching the *Queen Mary*. I had added to the festivities by making a shrimp quiche. Betty and Peter were just as receptive with their platters of mini sandwiches; enough, I might say, to feed all the boaters on the floats. Tony was hoping that Peter would go Thru the Chairs and be the next Vice Commodore.

The ceremony started with a brief description of the history of the club, presented by the Commodore. Then Jim and Mary presented the burgee to the Commodore, who in turn asked his Vice Commodore and Rear Commodore to assist him in the hanging of this exquisite piece of work by Mary. That was the decision the Commodore made when Tony talked to him previously about Mary's desire regarding her burgee. The Commodore said all three officers would take part in the ceremony. They were a unit, and Tony agreed. Someone in the background played "Anchors Away" as we all saluted our officers and each other. We all toasted to the club and our friends. I then thought of Jill—maybe there was a way out for her. I had been so busy I hadn't really had time to think of how I could help her. I was hoping she was visiting religious organizations these days, but I was sure that this was wishful thinking. On my part, I believed good triumphed over bad, and if someone really wanted to change badly enough we should be supportive of them. I thought of the lovely cake she made for Tony, and I knew I really had to pay her a visit.

This club was like family. Family didn't always have to be biologi-cal. Granted we could not discuss Jill's past escapades, but maybe we could end them. I toasted to all the good in the world and prayed it would follow in Jill's world.

The morning of the invasion was wild. We were glad we had a pre-invasion celebration the night before with the burgee. We wanted all the different yacht clubs that were visiting to see this beautiful burgee Mary made. And what a sight it was. It stood over the top of the clubhouse, reminding us that all of us were a unit. Members and friends, we stood side by side. It also reminded us of how we united together and helped all the victims in need during that horrific hurricane. The Rear Commodore, Peter, was busy greeting and situ-ating all the visiting clubs along with the Fleet Captain. Betty was busy arranging the menu for the evening dinner, and I offered to help along with Pat. We set up the raffle table, and Pat brought a Basket of Comfort as a donation. It was all about *feet*—bathe them in sea salt, wrap them in sea oil, and sip a huge mug of sea grape tea while performing this foot adventure. I truly felt it was an appropri-ate donation. I just couldn't see the rough-and-tough guys at our club rubbing sea oil on their feet and sipping tea.

Jill approached with the most beautiful white christening dress with little lambs embroidered on it. It was so delicate she had it in a box with a piece of white satin she had found at a yard sale. Jill looked at me and her eyes actually were twinkling. Her face had a sweet glow, almost like she was reincarnated. Then she said the nicest thing. "This dress represents new beginnings." Jill went on to say, "It is like when a soul is cleansed from all sin." I inhaled a deep breath; maybe, just maybe, things could work favorably for Jill. I thought to myself that maybe she had sought out religious counseling. In my opinion, the fact that she had such symbolism in the beautiful christening dress meant she wanted a clean, new start.

Pat made a tremendous fuss over Jill's donation and then said, "Jill, could you make another christening outfit? One a little more masculine for my daughter's new baby?"

Jill said, "That is possible, Pat. Can I ask you a favor? Would you give me an opinion on my afghan?"

Pat said, "I am sure your colors are perfect, but I would love to see it." I thought to myself that this was a start in the right direction. We all had worth, and Jill was about to realize her worth. Other donations arrived, and Pat asked Jill if she would help at the donation booth. We decided that two-hour rotations would be sufficient. We placed fresh flowers and raffle tickets next to Jill and told her one of us would relieve her in two hours. She looked elated that we gave her the responsibility, and I prayed it would go well.

Then I had a sudden ill feeling. For one second I thought, *Please keep your hands out of the till, Jill.* I was ashamed for my thoughts. I had no real proof that Jill would be untrustworthy; I was angry at myself for letting negative thoughts come into play. We were giving Jill a chance to show her worth. I had to stay positive.

Peter had set up two huge grills for preparing lunch. The sausages were taking on a favorable aroma, along with the hotdogs and peppers and onions. The sausages were made a few days earlier at a secret sausage party. It was true,you took a vow of secrecy not to reveal the ingredients in the sausage making. According to hearsay, at least, as I never partook in the makings or the ceremony; one of the older Italian members of our club had a great-grandfather from Italy who brought the recipe from the old country. It had been passed down to only a few, chosen members of his family. This story got even better. Before makers entered the room they had to sign a statement saying they would not use the recipe unless they had permission from the president of the Secret Society of Sausage Makers. All I knew was that I put the delicious sausage between two slices of bread covered it with peppers and onions and it worked for me. So hats off to the Secret Society of Sausage Makers.

I just remember that it was time I relieve Jill at the raffle table. As I approached, lo and behold, Paul Adler was standing there in front of Jill's table. I greeted him with a question. "How many raffles are you purchasing, Paul?"

He quickly cleared his throat, reached into his pocket, produced a five-dollar bill, and said, "Give me five bucks worth, Jill." Jill tried not to laugh, took the money, and gave him the tickets. With that, Paul left. He was shaking his head in dismay, and God knows what he was mumbling under his breath.

I looked at Jill and said, "I am sure he is not too happy with my quick approach towards him." Jill laughed. "Your timing was perfect. He was starting to make me nervous. Fortunately he did not have a chance to really speak to me." Jill had customers and did well selling raffles. She had marked everything down and had about fifty dollars worth of stubs to be entered. I hoped I would do as well. As Jill left to get a cold drink, she said, "Hey, thanks."

"What for?" I asked.

"Just perfect timing," she said.

I smiled and said, "That's what friends are for." I thought to myself, *The less said about Paul Adler the better.*

BY EVENING THE PLACE WAS JUMPING with activity. Jim had set up some great activities for the kids. He bought some crabs and painted the shells different colors. There were six of them, and the kids were betting on the crab races. It was a penny a race, and the winner got a candy bar. The crabs raced about three feet from yardstick to yardstick. When my children were younger they loved this, but now they were older and the mad magician doing card tricks had their attention. Paul Adler was watching the magician too. He was all alone. Maybe the magician would make Paul disappear.

I loved these invasions. After I was done manning the raffle table, I saw all the lobsters our fishermen had brought in from their traps. We were truly spoiled. There are people in the world who have never experienced a New England lobster. At the club we ate them like candy. We were very overindulged. Tonight was surf and turf, but it was the surf that was so great. Right out of the ocean in front of us—how much fresher could it get? I loved seeing all the officers at night in their uniforms—so sexy. A man in a uniform turned women on. Don't kid yourselves, men, I know very few women who don't go gaga over it. I fell in love all over again when Tony put his whites or blacks on. I loved the hat especially. We were having a nice band tonight, and I was excited. I loved to dance. These were the times I would remember along with the feeling of belonging and being in a great comfort zone.

The night came and went with fun and a lot of reminiscing of times gone by and of times to come. Jill and George were there, and they danced and seemed to have a good time. Jill dressed very conservatively in a white frock with white pumps and a very prim white dress similar to a christening dress. I felt the conversation I had with Jill was worth it.

The next morning there was a huge crowd gathered at the club-house. The conversation consisted of yelling, abusive words, and almost a drag-down fight. I awoke Tony and told him something was wrong. I could barley hear what the problem was from our position on the floats. We had decided to sleep on our boat, but so many boats were tied to one another that we were in a different location. The Fleet Captain approached our boat. It seemed someone had stolen Mary's burgee in the middle of the night. Some people said it was a joke, and others said it was retaliation over the episode at the dart game; all in all it was not a good thing. There were jokes, but this was terrible—it wasn't funny at all. We had finally gotten Mary and Jim to feel comfortable. Not that one could be comfortable after a tragic death, but Mary and Jim seemed to be having less of the lion's paw in their life. Don't get me wrong, the lion's paw was there. But the club was helping them recover.

Mary got up and pleaded with a group of people to please stop arguing and return the burgee she worked so hard to make. Of course no one came forth, and the bottom line was Mary's burgee was *gone*. Some of the officers from the visiting clubs expressed concern and said that it definitely was not one of their members. Our club's con-sensus of opinion was it was a joke gone badly and that there was a culprit or probably more than one. Someone wanted to search the boats, but that suggestion was quickly axed. So a night of fun ended in a quandary: *who stole the burgee?*

One month passed and still no burgee. It was the talk of all the yacht clubs. Our club even offered a bonus or suggested that someone mail it to us with no questions asked. The missing burgee was not being returned too quickly.

Labor Day was approaching. The Commodore's wife was planning some type of fundraiser. She was having a meeting with all the officers' wives to discuss the matter, and she asked me to be involved. I was more than willing to accommodate her wishes. We left our conversa-tion with the Commodore's wife informing me of the date and time of the meeting. I wondered what type of fundraiser it would be.

Chapter 17

The Commodore's Wife's Casino Night

I HAD ALWAYS LIKED TO GAMBLE, and that went without saying when it came to Tony. The Commodore's wife could not have made a better decision when she decided to plan a casino night for charity. She hired a professional company to assist her. Then she decided what members and guests would do. Tony and I were dealers for the blackjack tables. This was quite a switch, as I had always been on the other side of a blackjack table. However, I thought that I was going to love my odds. We had a quick lesson for those who had never really gambled, and a few changes were made regarding doubling down situations. Otherwise it sounded pretty simple. The gamblers would be playing with chips purchased for twenty dollars. They would receive five hundred dollars worth of chips. There were various prizes donated for the first five winners, the best being a twenty-seven-inch TV. All proceeds would then go to the Christmas party for the orphanage.

The casino night was an event that attracted many participants. The Commodore's wife at any time could choose to run any charity function. As a courtesy, she and the Rear Commodore's wife consulted each other. The Commodore's wife did not have to run anything if she didn't want too. If her husband had gone Thru the Chairs, then she had done a lot during his Rear Commodore year. However, every once in a while the Commodore's wife made a statement. This year the Commodore's wife wanted to increase the amount of invitations sent to the orphanage. She wanted more children to attend the Christmas party this year.

I was dressed in black pants, a white blouse, and a necktie. This was how we distinguished ourselves from the gamblers. I had confiscated one of Tony's ties. It was safe to say I picked one that he would never wear. It had large calla lilies on it, and to Tony this was not a representation of a manly tie. Nor was it a yacht club tie either, but this tie was perfect for my attire. The first groups were members from the club, so the first few hours went smoothly, and naturally the house won. Then I took a break. When I returned there was a different group of people. This particular occasion was also open to the public. I now had a group of unfamiliar faces sitting across from me except for this one odd face. At first I couldn't quite place where I had seen this face before, but then all of a sudden the hairs on the back of my neck started to cringe. I started to actually hear my heart beat. My palms began to get sweaty. It was Andy Bower.

He might have been blackballed from joining the club, but there were no reinforcements to keep him out of this function. He immediately noticed how uncomfortable I had become. I could sense the pleasure in him knowing how uneasy he was making me feel. I continued to perform the best I could under these unpleasant circumstances. Now I needed cannonballs, I thought to myself. The blackballs didn't execute enough strength to keep him out. A cannonball could blow Andy Bower away. I started to regain my composure, but it ended quickly when I dealt Andy a blackjack; he snickered, gave me a sleazy smile, and pressed his bet. The next round Andy Bower got another blackjack and gave me a seething grin. This was too much pressure for me. No one at the table understood my predicament. They did, however, sense my uneasiness. I knew it would be another half hour before my replacement came. I kept hoping that a member or a friend might notice my uneasiness. My prayer was soon answered. Jill was wandering around observing the different tables. She stopped by our table and also sensed how uncomfortable I was. Jill saw how obnoxious Andy was acting as he continued to win. Instead of being joyful, Andy was almost vengeful as he filled his pockets with winning chips. Jill wasn't familiar with Andy Bower, but she was intelligent enough to know he was getting on my nerves. Jill gave me a quick wink, and the next thing I knew George showed up at the table. Not exactly what I had hopped for. Naturally, George appeared to be three sheets to the wind. But beggars couldn't be choosers. I was glad he had appeared. Just as George arrived, another player at the table got up from his seat. George immediately took this seat and gave me a wink. George made his bet and then looked at Andy and said, "Mr. Lucky Pants, why don't you increase that bet? I can see by the huge bulge in your pocket you have plenty of chips. You should press when you win."

Andy agrees and said, "Why not? I am in the lucky seat. This dealer does not have a chance with me." He then looked at me with piercing eyes. If those eyes could have shot daggers at me, they would have. Mr. Lucky continued to be lucky. It seemed no matter what I dealt him he kept winning. George continued to play him.

George said, "If that was me, I would realize that Lady Luck comes once in a great while. I would put half my money up on the next bet."

Andy looked at George and said, "Well, it ain't half your money and mind your own business." Now the table was starting to complain that the two men were destroying the gambling aura that supposedly existed. Andy looked at me and said, "This dealer and I go back a long way. That is why she is dealing me such great hands. She would hate to see me leave." I want to vomit, especially when he grins disgustingly at me. I tried to keep my composure and prayed my revenge would come in the cards. Finally Andy said, "Come on, Lady Luck, I have faith in you." Then he put half of his chips on the line. I dealt Andy an eight and a nine, and the house had the blackjack and the last laugh.

George looked at him and said, "Hey, pal, come on, let me buy you a drink for that bad advice." Andy looked at me disgustingly, picked up his remaining chips, and mumbled something under his breath. I yell, "What did you say?"

He says "Nothing."

I repeat louder, purposely to attract attention, which I did very nicely, "What did you say?" Soon I was being questioned by one of the members on why I was yelling at Andy Bower. I didn't know this particular member personally, but I did recognize him from the work I had seen him do on the floats. Tony often referred to him as the Moose. When I asked Tony why he called him that, Tony would say,

"Just look at him. He can do more work and lift more supplies than any young man I know." Those words rang in my mind.

I immediately said to the Moose, "I have been talked to rudely."

"Who talked to you rudely?" Mr. Moose asked. I then pointed to Andy Bower. Andy was trying to make a quick exit toward the door. However, he was not as quick as the Moose. The Moose, which I hated to refer to him as but didn't at this point know his name and we really didn't have time for an introduction, said to Andy, "Why don't you repeat to me what you said to the dealer." I was trying not to laugh. The Moose didn't know my name either, so now I was "the dealer."

Andy sneered at me and said to the Moose, "I said nothing to her; I was referring to someone else." Andy departed with the few chips he had. The Moose followed him to the exit door.

The Moose then said, "Do me a favor—don't test my patience. The dealer was very upset. You had to say something to her to make her that angry." Andy yelled back at him, but I could not hear what he said. If I had to guess it wasn't pleasant. I thanked the Moose, who introduced himself as Al Butcher. He then said, "Anything else I can do for the Vice Commodore's wife?"

I said, "No thanks, but thanks." As Al Butcher departed, George appeared and we both smile at each other. George seemed to be sober. I guessed that he was putting on an act to get attention from Andy at the blackjack table.

The evening continued with a lot of fun and laughter. Pat had made a bunch of lobster sandwiches, and she sold them for fifty cents apiece. The money was donated to the Christmas fund. The bartenders donated their tips, and so did the dealers. I probably made more money on tips that I would have done actually playing blackjack. No wonder people like to deal at Las Vegas. The twenty-seven-inch TV went to a nonmember, a little old gray haired lady. She was so sharp, with that little old Grandma Moses face. She reminded me of those Bingo players who came with dobbies in different colors. They would buy three to four cards. They would see everything, including their neighbor's cards. They sat at the benches at the Bingo hall. These ladies actually were in such control that they could observe other players' cards that were three seats down from them. If you try and get in their way, you get dobbed too.

Well, that was our winner. She stood up and announced her name. Mrs. S.T. Smithers. Then she said, "Could someone be so kind as to deliver this TV to me?" We all realized that Mrs. Smithers couldn't lift this TV, and naturally she had plenty of volunteers. The club was very respectful of the elderly. When the volunteers heard it would be delivered to a fifth-floor apartment, she was left with only a few strong men. Al Butcher decided to help her out. The Moose would deliver the TV. The second prize was a microwave. A member got it and gave it to their son for college. The other prizes were in the form of gift certificates. The Commodore's wife was happy that her function had created a great donation for a worthy cause.

The next day on the floats, lots of people came over to discuss my mishap with Andy Bower and the way it was handled. I did not comment too much as it was not a good discussion and one I would rather forget about. Instead, I changed the subject to the fun time that was had and the famous Mrs. S.T. Smithers. And then we all wondered what the S.T. stood for.

Mary commented, "Maybe it stands for smart and tenacious."

I laughed and said, "When we get to be her age we should remember her as a role model." We were just having a few laughs. The weather was pleasant. In the background we could hear some of the fishermen talking about large schools of blue fish that had been spotted a few miles out to sea. Mary volunteered to us her favorite blue fish recipe. In the middle of Mary describing the ingredients that she used on this fish, Pat came over and interrupted her. Mary was rather put off by this, but when she saw the expression of concern on Pat's face she realized something was wrong.

Pat said, "Please tell me how you liked the lobster sandwiches I made?"

"Pat," I said, "I can't help you. I did not have any. They were all gone when I went to get one." Mary said, "Gee, Pat, I thought they were great."

Pat said, "Well, I overheard them say in the galley that the club had received a call that someone got quite sick on them."

I said, "Pat, who complained?"

She said, "I don't know."

I said, "Look, let me make some cold drinks and let's talk about this." The weather was getting hazy and humid, and iced tea was in order. When the weather got hazy on the floats it was like a wet, moist fog had rolled in. It felt like we were talking through a smoke screen. The only difference was that it didn't smell like smoke—it smelled like salt and it felt clean on our skin. However, it made our throats dry. Iced tea was definitely in order. Once we quenched our thirst, we started the conversation about the lobster sandwiches.

Mary said, "Pat, you need more information. You should get a name and try to determine if in fact it was actually your sandwich that caused the tummy ache." Pat agreed. She seemed to have calmed down. Pat was a proud lady. She took pride, as I said before, in what she did. It was upsetting for her to think her sandwiches were the cause of someone's sickness. Pat went up to the clubhouse to get the facts.

I then looked at Mary and said, "So what was the final ingredient in that blue fish recipe?"

"Sage," she said as she laughed. I then had the strangest thought. Could it be Andy, retaliating? Could he be using Pat's sandwiches? Was he that clever? Maybe!

Pat returned to the floats. By now Mary and I were on our fourth iced tea. It was cocktail hour. Pat looked extremely frustrated. Pat sat in the boat and said to Mary and me, "Are you sitting down?"

I said, "Pat, look at us. What is wrong?"

Pat said, "You are not going to believe this. It was Mrs. S.T. Smithers."

I said, "You have to be kidding."

"No," Pat snickered. "My sandwiches made her very ill. Our S.T. Smithers went to the doctor this morning, and he diagnosed her with a touch of poisoning."

I then said, "Mary was right, I believe, that the T does stand for tenacious. And she is no longer our role model."

Pat continued, "The club offered to pay the doctor bill, but she felt she needed compensation for the unnecessary distress."

I sounded like a parrot and again replied, "You have to be kidding." I paused and then said, "Who is handling this, Pat?"

Pat said, "I think the Rear and Vice Commodore."

"Pat," I said, "let them handle it."

Mary made a good point, saying, "The doctor should have a name and the club should see a bill."

Pat said, "She, being Mrs. S.T. Smithers, did not want to involve the doctor."

I said, "That is simple enough. There is no proof." I knew Pat was right that this predicament would fall under either Tony or Peter. They were the officers who would have to resolve this problem.

Pat said, "This is the worst part—that sweet, little old lady threatened us. Mrs. S.T. Smithers said that an article would appear in the paper if this was not taken care of."

I said, "I bet there is more to this than meets the eye. Who is this lady? What is she looking for? How much money is she after? I am sure the two officers of the club will handle it."

Mary said, "If this isn't handled right, there goes all the profit from our charity event."

Pat reminded us, "This is why the club has insurance."

THE REAR AND VICE COMMODORE DEMANDED to see a copy of the bill from the doctor. A bill never came, but calls from Mrs. S.T. Smithers did. In fact, an attorney called and left a threatening message, but he failed to leave his name. Tony and Peter decided to ignore the whole thing and said someone was trying to just ruffle feathers.

After three weeks of being badgered by Mrs. S.T. Smithers, the mystery was solved. It seemed when Al Butcher delivered the TV to Mrs. S.T. Smithers, he noticed a family picture, and who was in it but her nephew, Andy Bower. Al did not pay too much attention to this matter at the time, but when he heard what was happening with the lobster sandwiches he remembered that this was the man who had been harassing me on casino night. He informed Tony and Peter about the picture of Andy Bower. The two officers put two and two together and had the club lawyer call Mrs. S.T. Smithers to inform her that with one more harassment she would be prosecuted along with her nephew. She asked if she could keep the TV. The club let her have it with the firm understanding that she and her nephew were barred from the club. This incident was over. So much for my Grandma Moses image—more like the daughter of Grazilla and the nephew of Godzilla.

Labor Day was soon approaching, and along with it cooler temperatures and hurricanes. We had just experienced one, and even though they called it a tropical storm, we knew what it was. I was hoping for a peaceful weekend, but again a giant invasion was scheduled. It would not be at our club, though. I wondered if Valley Crest would welcome some of our members. Some of the members did accuse them of stealing Mary's burgee. I wondered if they did take it and if it would be returned at the invasion. Maybe it would be mysteriously put into one of our boats.

Chapter 18

Jill

I<small>T HAD BEEN A WHILE SINCE</small> Jill had confided in me about her sordid situation. I had tried to come up with a solution, but in all honesty this was not something I was good at dealing with. I decided to call on her. I waited till George left for his job and went over to the sailboat. Jill was just getting ready to go to one of her cleaning jobs when she saw me approaching. "Jill," I said "I would like to meet you, maybe for lunch today. Any chance that you could fit me into your schedule?"

"Gee, maybe," she unexcitedly replied. "I guess I can take a break between jobs. I have two jobs today." Jill finally agreed to meet me at a little hole-in-the-wall cafe called Vicks.

And so we met. Jill looked tired and out of breath. She sat down and released the barrette that was holding her hair back. She said, "I hate pulling my hair back so tight. If I keep doing this I could go bald."

I laughed, "Jill, you're way too young to worry about losing your hair." Jill's face look tired. Her eyes were back to being doe like. Her freckles blended into her skin. Jill had a sallow complexion today—she looked washed out. Her hair, with its slight blond streaks, fell to her neck like thin strings on a used-up mop. I ordered two ginger ales from the over-enthused waitress.

Jill looked up at me and said, "I hate doing floors. This house has three levels. One level was dirtier than the other. But the owner I work for pays me well." And with that she took a huge gulp of ginger ale.

I wanted to cut through the formality, so I said, "So, Jill, how are things going?"

Jill looked at me like we never had any conversation before. "Why do you ask?" she said.

"Why do I ask? Why do I ask? You have to be kidding. Jill, you told me some very bad episodes in your life."

Jill looked frazzled, and then she firmly stated, "I am fine, things couldn't be better. I have a job. George has a job. I am enjoying the club. What more do you want from me?" My jaw dropped.

"Jill, I don't want anything from you. In fact, I am one of the few people in your life who cares about you." She looked at me, baffled.

"I have a lot of people who care. Just the other day, George told me he really wants me to be with him, and my employer that I clean for gave me an extra ten dollars because I work so hard."

Well, I thought to myself, *what a turnaround.* Either I was missing something in this conversation or Jill was a schizophrenic. My time was precious. I had my own family to consider, and obviously Jill did not want my help. I got up. "Jill, I am glad you are doing well. Thanks for meeting me."

Jill looked at me and said, "I was glad I could help you with the cake and with getting rid of Andy Bower."

I said, "Thank you," and told her I was glad she was on the straight and narrow, even though I didn't believe it for one moment. She had gulped her ginger ale, but I noticed she barely ate her salad. She poked and rearranged her food on her dish until it formed a wreath around her platter. I felt she was covering up more than before. Besides her unhealthy appearance, Jill barely lifted her head or looked at me when she spoke. Her head just kept hanging over her emaciated salad. At one point I reached over and tried to pick up her face, making a comment like, "Jill, your head is going to fall into your lunch. Maybe you smelled too much floor polish." I was trying to keep it light or maybe create a smile. I had edged my chair closer to her so I could balance the weight of her head in case I needed to pick it up. My hands were now extremely close to her.

She just replied with her head still defying my touch, "I have been working hard and I am tired." She started to get up, so I edged my chair back and got up too and we both left. All I could do was keep an open door. This conversation had not gone well, or maybe it had. Why was I trying to help someone who was in such denial? I was not a psychiatrist, but this girl needed one. She needed professional help.

When I returned to the club, Tony was programming the loran. This was the mistress of the waters. He asked me where I had gone. I lied. Just like that it came out. I told a lie. Why?

I looked at Tony and said, "I tried to find some yarn for Pat." Thank goodness he didn't question any further, especially since Pat didn't knit.

Tony then mentioned, "Hey, hon, I saw Paul Adler. You know, his wife is extremely ill. In fact, she is so ill that the doctors are not very hopeful."

I asked Tony, "Do you want a cocktail?"

He laughed and replied, "It is only three o'clock in the afternoon."

I said, "Tony, it is six o'clock somewhere else in the world, and I would just like to pretend I was there. Are you with me?" I needed to sit on the bow of the boat and get my head together. I just didn't want to deal with any more problems.

Tony looked at me and said, "First, you didn't even comment on Paul's wife. Second, you are extremely uptight. What is going on?" Tony must have seen my expression. He raised his voice, something he rarely did. He repeated with force, "I said, what is going on?"

I said, "Tony, I can't talk about it now. I have to get my head together, but it has nothing to do with you or the family."

"That is just great," he said. "Then who the hell does it have to do with?"

Tony was getting angry, and my responses were not helping the situation. I had lied, and in the back of my mind I was angry at myself. I didn't know how to get out of the web I was slowly spinning. Tony came over and put his arms around me. "Hon, please tell me what is going on. It is very obvious to me you are avoiding something."

I wanted to cry, but I just said, "Tony, it was just a discrepancy with one of my girlfriends."

"Which one are you having problems with?"

"I would rather not say at this point. Maybe I can work it out. I hate to bring the men into it." Tony just said, "Hon, you have Pat and

Mary. They are great friends. Please work it out." I swallowed with a lump in my throat.

I said, "Tony, I will." I felt I wasn't lying at that point; Tony just assumed it was Pat or Mary.

Then Tony said, "How about I fix you and me a cocktail?" I agreed. We talked about Paul Adler's wife. I didn't know which was worse—the fact that she was married to Paul or the fact that she was very sick. Maybe it was both.

Chapter 19

The Wrong Club

A VISITATION WAS BEING PLANNED. WE were going back to Valley Crest Yacht Club. This club was under heavy suspicion regarding the missing burgee, as I mentioned before. Mary was still stunned over the abduction of her hard work. We were all going with mixed emotions. We had no proof that they were the culprits, but they were one of the newer clubs in the loop, so they were targeted. This was the first time that something this serious had happened to the club.

We were leaving on a Friday night around dusk, and the Fleet Captain had charted the route. There were about fifteen boats making the journey. It was a beautiful, warm late September night. Basking sharks were spotted nearby, and we enjoyed watching their floppy fins in the water. Valley Crest was about an hour's ride south of our club.

On our arrival we were cordially greeted. In fact, we kind of walked into a luau. There was Hawaiian music playing, and all of us girls got leis. They were actually fresh-flowered ones. This was a very nice touch. Some of the members and their wives were dressed in grass skirts and wildly flowered shirts. There was a giant pig on a spit that created such an aroma that my mouth watered. There were huge bowls of rum drinks with flowers floating in them. This was going to be fun. I knew from past experiences that a lot of work went into this, and they were trying hard to make us feel very welcome.

As officers and officers' wives, we were seated at the head of this elaborate luau. We were given head attire. Mine had fresh flowers, and between the lei around my neck and the crown of gardenias I was ready to sneeze. Tony and the other officers were given wreaths made out of palms. *God, I hope we are not getting sacrificed.* We only think they took the burgee, we really don't know. Some hula dancers entertained us, but then, of course, we were beckoned to participate. Tony had a hard time with this. Maybe a rock-and-roll dance, but the hula? I didn't think so. I, on the other hand, was ready, and so were Jill, Pat, and Mary. We just loved it—we truly became exhibitionists. They said there was strength in numbers. It must have been the fact that the four of us were all on the dance floor at the same time. We just blended to the beat of the drums and music. We got lost in the dance, or the rum, but we had fun. Then the meal was served, and it was great. If one was not into pork, there was so much more to choose from. Some fun speeches and jokes were said, and all and all it was a nice night. We retired early as the ride over was tiring.

THE NEXT MORNING A NICE BUFFET was prepared. The room was pleasant, and as we entered we saw a huge mermaid, probably taken from the hull of a huge ship designed years ago. Someone had touched her up and made her even more remarkable. They had named her Camellia. The morning was spent socializing. We were familiar with many of the people there, and it was nice to catch up on different experiences that we all shared in yachting. Of course, the story of the lobster trap attaching to the motor was the topic at our table.. The Fleet Captain always made sure that his fleet of boats stayed together, the reason being that if there was a problem with one of the yachts we were all able to assist. One time one of the boats hit a lobster trap, and it took some time to clear the strong netting and part of the rope that was wrapped around the motor. It had wrapped itself around so tightly that it took a lot of patience and skill to unfurl the tangled motor. Some of the men had to steady the boat while others tried to repair it. Not a big problem, but a frustrating one.

After breakfast we found ourselves confined to the docks. Unfortunately, the geographical location of this club was not supplying us with a nice southwest wind. It became sticky and hot. We managed to occupy ourselves with plenty of cold drinks and great conversation. As we sat and talked, I noticed a couple of our members heading toward the Camellia room, and I wondered why they were going up there because after breakfast it was supposedly off limits. Everything that was needed for our hospitality was set up on the docks. I gave it no further attention until we were leaving. As we were pulling out, I heard a huge scream. One of their officers was yelling "Halt!" At first we thought it was a joke, but the officer continued yelling, "Stop the boats from leaving!"

Tony and I were still partially on the dock. Tony pulled in, tied up the boat, and went to see what all the commotion was about. When Tony finally came back to the boat, he said, "Guess what? Camellia is gone. The mermaid has been lifted off her pedestal, and she has been confiscated."

I said, "Tony, is this joke?"

He said, "I am afraid not." With that explanation, Tony went back to where the officer who was yelling stood.

My mind flashed to the two men from our club that I had seen earlier entering the sanctuary where Camellia resided. Could it be those men? I thought, *Can this really be happening?* Was this retaliation for the burgee? Was my mind running wild? Was I falsely accusing those men without proof? I had to stop imagining such a prank. Just because I saw two men didn't mean they were doing anything wrong. We still had no proof that Valley Crest took the burgee.

Tony and I just stood there on the docks. We were dumbfounded over this whole matter. The officer who was yelling happened to be the treasurer. I think he realized by Tony and my expression that we certainly did not abduct Camellia. Some of the boats were out in the water, and only a few were close enough to hear the yells and return to the dock. The frustrated treasurer and Fleet Captain of Valley Crest asked permission to come aboard the returning boats and search. Our members were so shocked at what was happening that they just nodded yes over and over again. It was a quick eye search as Camellia was quite large and not easy to stow away.

Peter Flanagan apologized for what was happening. He promised the treasure from Valley Crest that as soon as he returned he would check all the boats that were on the docks and were unable to return. Peter felt that it was probably a children's game of hide-and-seek. Teenagers at parties sometimes had a habit of taking a souvenir. Peter explained firmly, "How many times do you see street signs or flags that teenagers have stolen and displayed in their rooms?" Peter then continued to say, "I think that these accusations, silent as they may be, are beginning to get out of hand. Some members at our club think that your club took the burgee, and some members of your club think our club took the mermaid. Until we have some proof on both matters I suggest we stay coolheaded." With those words of wisdom from Peter Flanagan, our Rear Commodore, we departed from Valley Crest.

When we got back to Briar Ridge the Fleet Captain told Tony he had questioned everyone. The Fleet Captain came up with a different scenario. He felt that someone from their own club might have stolen it to make us look bad. I had never thought of that. I just remembered the two men entering the room where the mermaid resided. When we returned to the club, we saw two members blatantly remove Camellia from their boat. When questioned, the two guilty members replied in unison, "They took our burgee, and when they return it, Camellia will be given back. In the meantime she is our hostage."

Tony was furious. He walked over to the two thieves and said, "What in God's name are you talking about? What proof do you have that they took the burgee?"

One of the men, who mainly lived on his fishing boat, spoke up. This man had huge green rubber boots that smelled of fish. His hair stuck out in every direction. His clothes looked like something that he had slept in for weeks, and he had a stubby beard. I guessed he was about fifty, but his haggard appearance made him appear older. I knew by the quickness in his walk and the way he approached Tony that he still had a lot of life in him. "Listen," this gruff pillager said, "they are the new guys on the block. We have never had any problems till they came to our club." The Commodore was now aware of the problem and approached the docks. He was a large, distinguished officer. He was in full uniform, as he had just returned from a naval function.

Everyone on the docks stepped aside and let the Commodore address the situation. His first words were, "I have received a very unpleasant call from the Commodore of Valley Crest Yacht Club. I have been informed that a mermaid carved from a very old schooner has been stolen. Of course during this conversation I was surprised to think anyone from our club would be involved in this type of behavior. However, I am witnessing two members and a mermaid on the floats. What do you have to say for yourselves, gentlemen?" This was funny because the Commodore looked so regal and the other two members looked like scallywags, almost like a scene from an old English movie where the captain punished some of the crew members.

The same man with the green boots said, "Mr. Commodore, when I go fishing in the morning and meet up with different fishing boats, I hear things."

"What kind of things do you hear, James?"

So his name is James, I thought.

"I hear, Mr. Commodore, that Valley Crest was angry over the dart tournament with the ladies and they thought it would be funny to take the burgee."

"James," said the Commodore, "I need names, not hearsay."

James then said, "It was a joke gone badly, and now the person that took the burgee is afraid he will be in a lot of trouble. I think that is why he didn't bring it back."

The Commodore then said, "James, you have been a good member. It seems to me you know more than you are saying. Here is my proposal. I will call Valley Crest and let them know we have the mermaid. That is all I will say regarding the mermaid. I will then tell them, 'One of our members has a strong feeling that your club has our burgee. If that be the case, please mail it to our club, no questions asked, and the mermaid will be returned. In the meantime it is in safe quarters and I will personally be responsible for it.'" Then the Commodore looked at James and said, "You'd better be right."

James then said, "Thank you, Mr. Commodore."

TWO DAYS HAD PASSED SINCE THE Commodore's call to Valley Crest. Valley Crest had employed an attorney who called the club and demanded the return of Camellia. He informed our Commodore that the officers of Valley Crest swore up and down that they never took Mary's burgee. Our Commodore held a meeting for which Tony was present. Tony later informed me that the decision to return the mermaid was made. The two members who took Camellia were to return her and apologize. If they refused, then they were to lose their slips at our club. Amazingly they agreed! The day they left with the stolen property, we all held up signs reading, "Free Camellia." Even Mary had a strong feeling that Valley Crest was not the culprit. The culprit still remained anonymous.

The end of the season also brought the end of Paul Adler's wife. She lost her battle with the sickness that had riddled her body. The wake was to be held on a Wednesday night. It was customary that the officers of the club meet prior to a wake and attend in full uniform. This was done out of respect for club members. I definitely was not looking forward to this; actually, I didn't know anyone who couldn't wait to attend a wake or funeral. There was no such thing as a good funeral, but I guess when someone suffered as Paul's wife had, then at least one can feel they were at peace. That was how Paul seemed to address his wife's passing. The hard part was that Paul and his wife never had any children, and now Paul was alone. Paul had a brother, however, who flew in from out of town. As soon as his brother paid his respect to Paul, he made a quick exodus. It was sad to think how when we needed our family the most, so many of them were absent or, even worse, incoherent to how we feel. Sometimes family just went through the motions of robots. They think, "We had to go, we had to do or else people would talk about us." Did they never realize that they had to feel? It was unfair of me to judge Paul's brother. My own opinion of Paul was low. I guessed I was there out of respect for his wife. Paul was really all alone. Of course, he had the members of the club. In my mind I had selfish feelings. My feelings were those that Jill had influenced. As far as I was concerned, he was not a nice person. I felt he preyed on a young and naïve girl.

The year finally came to an end, and I knew without a doubt that Tony would make Commodore. After all, he was going Thru the Chairs, and handling his responsibilities quite well, so I looked forward to the coming year as Mrs. Commodore! Ha!!!

Book 3

The Commodore

Chapter 1

The Grand Umpa Makes His Claim to Fame

TONY WAS IN, AND AS A young girl anticipated her first big date, Tony had anticipated this moment for a long time. It was finally here, and my hope was that it would be exactly what he wanted and more. Of course, in the back of my mind, like all women with instinct, I hoped it would not be like the letdowns that occurred on first dates, but I remained positive toward this new adventure. Along with Tony's election, Peter Flanagan made Vice Commodore and Sam made Rear Commodore. I was thrilled for Sam. He had worked hard and it paid off. His wife was now getting involved with the club as well. The best part was that Sam and his wife were getting involved with each other. The two of them were boating. His wife told us of her new discovery. It was a small pill called Dramamine, a pill that helped control motion sickness. This was going to be a great year, and in a small way I was able to take the ride with Tony.

The spring Opening ceremony at the club was wonderful. It was the official swearing in of the three officers and their appointed staff. Tony had made arrangements for Joe Pissano to have a short leave from the nursing home; Tony felt he would like Joe to be a representative in this special inauguration of officers. Tony had always liked Joe and thought this might be the last time everyone would be able to see him in this fashion. It was also nice for Joe to be able to wear his uniform and have one last grand memory. I hoped it still would fit him. He was so excited to be involved once again in the club. The first part of the ceremony was very serious—the swearing in of officers. Strong commitments of leadership and honor were being made. Then the seriousness turned to humor, and it was almost like a roasting. The past officers brought up all the experiences that Tony and his crew had endeavored through the last couple of years. Everyone laughed, especially over the dissection of the chandelier. All in all it was a special night for Tony. He looked so handsome all dressed in black and wearing the famous Commodore's hat. The emblem on the hat signified his dream and seemed to shine fluorescently as the ceiling lights shone down. Our children and I were setting sail on a new adventure.

Chapter 2

The Planning of the First Event Under the Commodore

ONE OF THE NICEST EVENTS THAT took place at the club was the Palm Sunday Dinner. This particular religious holiday was hosted for the elderly people in the community. The planning and arranging took place through the Commodore and the mayor. The two had a meeting to decide on which nursing homes would be invited. This decision was based on the different types of facilities. Some nursing homes or elder facilities catered to extremely ill people. In reality there were a lot of people in nursing homes or homes for the elderly that really did not have to be there. Usually they were there because no one wanted them or they truly had nowhere to go. Joe Pissano was a perfect example of someone with nowhere to go. So this affair was based on this type of elderly housing with nursing home facilities. The arrangement was that four hundred guests would partake in the Sunday celebration. They would be brought over by buses that the city would provide through the generosity of the mayor.

The new Rear Commodore, Sam, would be in the galley. He would assemble a crew to prepare several large hams accompanied by potatoes, carrots, and a raisin sauce. Tony would oversee all of this, but his main job was to give a speech and introduce the mayor. Politics were now in play. One member of the club, usually the Commodore, met with the city officials. This occurred when decisions regarding the club had to be made. Tony's position now involved handling all the politics and real estate of the club. If there were any decisions or problems regarding this area, it was Tony's responsibility to solve it.

Sam asked me to waitress. I had never been great at this, but I did accept. I always had a problem when it came to getting the tray up and over my shoulder. I would just come out with the tray right in front of me, and I always felt like I was going to drop it at any minute.

I don't think people realize the movement and strength it takes a waitress or waiter to accomplish this task. If you don't believe me, try it. However, do yourself a favor. Do not put food that can stain on the tray while you experiment.

But this was a charity event, so I figured I would give it my best. I truly wanted to help Sam. Sam put his galley together for the event. He was excited. It was quite a task to serve a sit-down dinner for almost four hundred people. One of the members Sam chose was a past Commodore named Charles. Charles had one of those personalities that made people feel calm and relaxed. He was middle aged and had a rock-solid shape. He was a veteran, and I think that no matter how serious the problems at the club could be, Charles had experienced far more in the war. Not that Charles ever discussed his days in Vietnam, but after watching the horrors on TV for so many years, one could just imagine. Charles had a son about fourteen who had inherited his dad's personality. Charles asked the Rear Commodore if his son could also help in the galley. This young boy was often seen spending a lot of time with his dad, so it was apropos for Charles to bring his son, Teddy, along. Teddy asked if he could be in charge of desserts. This project involved opening cans of chocolate or vanilla pudding. Teddy would have to put them in small dishes and squirt whipped cream on top. Teddy loved this assignment.

Sam's wife was going to organize all the waitresses. This would be good for her, as she was used to helping Sam at the deli. Each guest was allowed two glasses of wine or beer. The guests would receive a stamp on their hand, and this helped the bartenders. It was a way to show which guests were still allowed to drink, as many were on medication. Believe me, this would be monitored closely by Betty and Peter. The table decorations would be white linen table clothes with Easter baskets full of colored eggs. The eggs would be plastic, the reason being that in case we volunteer waitresses crashed into anything with our trays, which we hoped we would not, there would not be a mess of broken hard-boiled eggs.

Chapter 3

Palm Sunday

IT WAS A DREARY DAY, AND the April showers lived up to their name. The good news was that the spirits of everyone involved were up. All of the volunteers got to the club by ten in the morning. The event was scheduled for 12:30. Of course, the chefs in the galley were there much earlier preparing the giant hams. There were three members just peeling potatoes and scrapping carrots. Sam's wife had a friend who made the waitresses cute little red, white, and blue aprons. It was a nice gesture. She asked us to dress in black pants and white shirts so with our new aprons we would be recognized easily in our new profession. I laughed over this new recognition as the guests were all elderly and decided to do a double take the next time I looked in the mirror.

There were twenty of us, including Jill. I was glad to see her. She looked well, and I hoped for the best for her. I decided to peek into the galley and see how the chefs were doing. Too my surprise, there was one of the members with an actual drill used in the street. He was mashing the potatoes with it. I immediately questioned the cleanliness of this giant mashing process, but he told me it had never been used in the street and had been purchased a long time ago just for occasions like this. He had borrowed it from another yacht club. At this point I felt it best not to ask another question. Sometimes the less I knew the better, and this was one of those times. Then I noticed a large cauldron on the stove. Sam stood on a stool beside it with a canoeing paddle. Sam was stirring the raisin sauce. I said, "I suppose, Sam, that this also has never been used for its sole purpose and that it is brand new."

"Absolutely" was Sam's one-word response.

Then all the men in the galley echoed, "Absolutely."

"Okay," I stated, and I then decided my services were needed elsewhere. But just as I was leaving, I noticed Charles's son Teddy. He had pudding around his mouth and whipped cream all over him. Teddy had all the dessert dishes lined up to perfection. Teddy must have measured the proportions because they were all the perfect amount of pudding and whipped cream. I guessed Teddy felt he needed a reward so in between he sampled the desserts to make sure they tasted the same. I said a quick prayer to the god of cleanliness and hoped for the best—maybe this went on in all restaurants.

One of the younger members was doing DJ work on the side, so he decided to come and play some music during the dinner. While he was setting up, the guests began to arrive. Mostly ladies—it seemed we lived longer. They looked so cute in their Sunday best and so excited to be invited out. They sat at tables set with rolls and butter and admired the centerpieces, which would be given to one of the lucky guests seated at each table at the end of the day.

Tony entered, dressed in full uniform, along with the mayor and a pastor. Tony's speech was short, warm, and welcoming. He thanked everyone for coming. I noticed that Tony was a little bashful in front of so many people. Tony never was bashful with the members, but this was a different stage with different players. Tony even seemed a little uncomfortable in the presence of the mayor. I realized that Tony felt awkward in this type of limelight. This was an aspect of this position he might have thought would come naturally, but he would have to work at this. I thought that was why he quickly introduced the mayor. The mayor, a true politician, gave a beautiful speech about how many of these people gave so much of their time to this community. The mayor, on the other hand, loved the limelight. I was sure he had lessons on elocution, for his speech was impeccable. He even knew when to stop and smile at his audience. He was trained in capturing his observers to a T.

He then went to the different tables and spoke to many of the guests who were familiar to him. He shook hands with the men and gave the ladies a hug. They responded by saying the mayor made them feel special. The mayor responded and said, "You are special.

You are the backbone of this community." Then Tony introduced the pastor, who was a much more serious personality. However, he was still a politician of the church and also well versed in sermons. He said grace and spoke about the holiday, but most of all he spoke about being thankful that we lived in a community where people cared about each other. He kept his sermon light and short, but he reminded us of the trials and tribulations that occurred thousands of years ago on Palm Sunday.

The first table I was assigned to was very nice. The ladies were great and not too demanding—there were no men at this table. My second table was not as easy. It would become a challenge. It was a mixture of men and women who were very demanding. More bread, more butter, a cup of tea, some lemon, etc, etc. But I managed. The waitresses served no liquor. It was up to the guests to go to the bar and deal with Peter and Betty. The music began with the best of the best. Frank Sinatra, Tony Bennett, and Andy Williams crooned during dinner. A few dishes could be heard crashing in the background, but all in all it was going quite smoothly. The best part was I hadn't broken a dish even though I had a unique way of serving.

A few more officers in uniform came in, and a couple of the little ladies at the tables asked if they cold dance with them. It was such a sight to see these ladies holding onto these young officers like they would have held onto their husbands had they been there. I actually filled up with tears. When we were young we took so much for granted. Husbands and wives, brothers and sisters, and family and friends all assumed we would always have each other. We never thought that we could end up all alone, in a home, and without the ones we loved. Yet there were four hundred people in this room doing just that. The room became very quite as we all watched a few ladies hold onto lost memories as they danced. Some had closed eyes, as if they were back in their husband's arms. They all shared some kind of memory; it was seen in their faces and felt in their silence.

One woman grabbed our Fleet Captain, who was extremely attractive in his full uniform. She looked at him and said, "I want to dance with the most handsome man here." Of course he was one of them. He smiled with those pearly white teeth. His tanned complexion added to his comeliness. His vibrant blue eyes cast a spell, and he knew when he looked at her that he would accommodate her wishes. She reached up, looked in his face, and was mesmerized at what she saw. She said, "Thank you," and then collapsed onto the floor. I ran over immediately. Everyone was so frightened. They certainly were familiar with the smell of death. Immediately 911 was called. I thought she might be having a diabetic attack. I had seen one before, and this looked similar. It was only a guess. One of the waitresses was a nurse, and seeing all the commotion she immediately came over and did what she could. She knelt down and observed the poor, fallen victim. She then got up and tried to form a forced smile. This nurse did not want to upset the tables of frightened elderly. She motioned to one of the officers. The officer sensed by her expression that the woman on the floor had expired. However, we tried everything possible to create the illusion that she had just fainted. However, these people lived in homes where death was a common visitor. They learned to sense death and smell death, but most of all they feared death. Finally the ambulance arrived and the woman was removed. They were cautious to not cover her face in front of the questioning faces of the other elderly guests. In time they would know what fate met their fallen friend.

The music picked up as a means of distraction. I started dancing with some of the men, and before anyone knew it, waitresses, officers, and galley crews were all participating in changing the mood. It started to work, and some smiles appeared. However, no one dared dance with the Fleet Captain. He was upstairs in the members' lounge, recuperating from that awful experience. Sometimes it wasn't so good to be so handsome. His wife was one of the waitresses, and we sent her to console him. They said if you fell off a horse you had to get back on. Well, his wife followed that tale. She brought him back down and had the DJ play "It's a Wonderful World." The two of them danced, and then they went around to the different tables and involved the guests in their dance. A calmness settled in the room, and the rest of the day went smoothly.

The woman who died was once a large investor in motorcycles. So, needless to say, when her fate reached the media it was a funeral filled with a motorcycle processions. It was then attested that she died doing what she wanted. She was always a nonconformist, and to live her life any less was not her style. She drank, danced, and was merry right up to her last *kiss*.

Chapter 4

Disappointment Sets In

I WAS BEGINNING TO FEEL A little let down now that Tony was Commodore. He was more involved in the politics of the club and city and less involved in the everyday routine that created so much fun on the floats and in the galley. Maybe I was just jealous—after all, I had felt a strong part of the events of the past two years, and now here I was just sitting on the sidelines. I was quite bored. My children were more into their friends than their parents. This was very normal with teenagers.

Tonight the children were going in different directions. My daughter was attending a sleep over. My boys were going to a basketball game. My mom was at bingo. Tony was at a meeting. It was early evening in the middle of the week. I decided to go down to the boat, thinking maybe I would run into Pat or Mary.

I went up to the clubhouse to get some ice, and I heard noise in the galley. I decided to take a peek and see who was working diligently after hours. There was my old friend and past Commodore working on some concoction. I said, "Hi, what are you doing here all by yourself?"

He said, "I come here sometimes and cook for some of the members who are working after hours. I give the Rear Commodore a break. Plus, you know that this is my therapy, and I think Sam knows it and lets me do this." I laughed. He then said, "You look sad—anything wrong?"

I said, "You sensed it?"

"What is wrong?" he asked. "You should be so happy! Everything that you and Tony wanted to achieve here at the club is happening."

I pulled up a stool and said, "Can I bend your ear?"

He laughed and said, "Shoot."

I then had a long conversation with my old friend. I told him of how bored and left out I felt and told him that I thought that Tony, who was a hands-on man, was also missing the physical involvement he had at the club. Tony was never a pencil pusher; he liked the action in the galley or on the floats. This position as Commodore required a lot of negotiating on decisions of real estate and new events that would benefit the club.

Before I continued my tale of woe, my friend interrupted me. "Excuse me," he replied, "but wasn't this what Tony strived for? Sitting back and letting others do the hard labor? Tony has done his share of hard work for the club. This is the reward that you reap."

I said, "Yes, but I don't think this is what really makes him happy. Tony likes his pals at the club. This was his comfort zone. Tony is out of it, and I am too."

My friend was wise and was a great mentor. He came over to me, put his hands on my shoulders, and said, "It is you who are unhappy. It is you who feels left out. Has Tony expressed his feelings to you?"

I replied, "Call it woman's intuition—I feel he is unhappy, but because he has finally reached his goal, he doesn't want me or the children or the members of the club to think he is not appreciative of the opportunity. I know Tony; he will give it his best."

Then my friend said, "What are you going to do?"

I said, "Take the ride, I guess."

Chapter 5

The Wedding

SPRING WAS IN THE AIR, AND it was wedding season. We had received
an invitation to our niece's wedding. Tony, being Commodore, had
lots of benefits. One was that every yacht club in the area opened its
doors to him. He and his family and boat were welcomed in their
marina at all times. Tony decided that on Saturday, the day before our
niece's wedding, we would stay at an exclusive yacht club across the
street from the hotel where the magical event was taking place.

That Saturday morning was particularly hot for late May, and
in fact the forecast was for almost 80 degrees, one of those freak hot
days that settled in early, one of those days when it was impossible to
figure out what to wear. I was in between wardrobes, not to mention
wedding attire. The only advantage we had was we were going by
boat. This would make the ride pleasant, with cool winds against
our back as we rode the small rollercoaster waves. It was about an
hour's ride. The ride over was beautiful. The smell of the saltwater
was so refreshing, and occasionally a splash from a nearby boat was
welcomed. There was a regatta of sailboats with multi-colored sails
spraying the sea. It was like a hundred rainbows were crashing into
one another to make one huge arch over the sea. It was a great boating
day. Tony and I hadn't had an alone day in a while, and we were
finding a lot of comfort in it. We were now about to reap one of the
benefits of going Thru the Chairs.

We finally arrived at our destination. We were greeted by the
Fleet Captain and the Rear Commodore. They helped us get settled
and invited us to partake in a luncheon upstairs in a room overlooking the skyscrapers of the busy city. The view was magnificent, totally

different from the view from Briar Ridge. This was a bustling, busy area, which became a novelty full of excitement for us. It was fun to see planes, trains, and huge freighters all in one gigantic area. This city had a pulse, not one I could enjoy every day, but certainly one that was fun to experience now and then. We chatted through lunch about the family and our friends, and then we met some different people who came to our table and greeted us. We then decided to depart to the comfort of our boat, and with the afternoon heat so heavy upon us, we sat in the harbor and read. We spent a quiet afternoon reacquainting ourselves with each other. It felt good. Nighttime sleeping on a boat had its rewards as well. We were gently rocked to sleep with the sea as our cradle, and the busy sounds of the city faded in and out of our dreams; it truly was a great experience.

Chapter 6

Early Morning

T HE FOLLOWING MORNING WAS SO BEAUTIFUL. The city was asleep. It was Sunday. The mist on the ocean looked like a soft white cloud had landed, and once in a while a foghorn could be heard in the distance. It was seven o'clock, and the coffee was permeating the air from the different boats. Tony and I sat enjoying the nice taste and aroma that this delicious brew created. *What better atmosphere to have coffee in?* I thought. The wedding was at two, so the morning belonged to us. It was still predicted by the weatherman that the temperature would be warmer than normal, another 80-degree day. I decided we could not have been in a better place. I was savoring the moments alone with Tony. My friend was right—I was having a hard time adjusting to my husband's journey. I did still feel Tony was a little bit out of his element, however. Time would tell. The cards were dealt, and this was a hand that Tony would play out. I guess I had to play it out with him. I had to change my attitude. If I wanted to be with Tony, then I had to take the ride.

It wasn't easy getting dressed on the boat. After all, we had a small bathroom. However, trying to blow-dry my hair and put on my makeup with Tony in my way was a small price to pay for the lovely time we were having. Eventually we got into a rhythm so we could get dressed. It worked and we were off to the wedding. The hotel was lovely. It was one of those old, antiquated places that made me feel I was entering a different time in history. I was almost afraid to sit on the chairs in case they were not as strong as they appeared. The paintings made me feel like a number of guests from a different period in time had also been invited.

Tony and I were enjoying our new surroundings, or should I say old. The room was to accommodate about 150 guests. The ceremony would take place in the garden room, and then we would be escorted to the reception area. There we would find engraved cards with our names on them placed in front of seats at flowered tables. I was looking forward to seeing some of the cousins and catching up on old times.

The bride was beautiful; she was the sweetest of nieces. She was wearing a pure silk wedding gown encrusted with pearls. She had fresh flowers in mini-white rosettes cascading down one side of her head. She was a vision to behold, and when she smiled it appeared all the pictures on the walls were smiling back. That was how radiant she was. The groom was very stately and dressed in a formal black tuxedo, and he had eyes only for his beloved bride. My husband's brother and wife were some of our favorites, and we were welcomed with open arms. Everything was perfect, right down to the band. The afternoon and evening went smoothly. I could tell we were having a pleasant time because Tony and I didn't want it to end. When it was time to depart, Tony mentioned that we were staying across the street in the marina, so if someone wanted to stop by for a nightcap, they were more than welcome.

Surprise!! With the weather being so hot, the city had become sticky and uncomfortable. When we got back to our boat, we had an entourage of about twenty people. I remembered that earlier the Fleet Captain had said, "At this club we keep quiet hours after eleven."

"Certainly not like our club," Tony had said after the man had left. "I think we are at a very prissy place." Tony was right. It was about nine, and I told Tony that by eleven everyone had to leave—after all, we were guests here. I must say we were having a great time. It was a hot night, and it was so refreshing for everyone to be on the floats. One thing led to another, and then Tony decided to take the boat out. We had enough life jackets, but I was against it. People were drinking, it had been a long day, and truthfully I was tired. The majority ruled, however, and Tony's decision was upheld. The boat would be departing. There was one serious problem. Everyone was drinking more. Tony knew at this point that he could not go back to that marina. It was past eleven, and the voices on our boat were at a high octave. Fortunately, Tony did not operate boats under the influence of liquor, but if we had to depend on anyone else, we were in trouble because the crew was bombed. It was like a booze cruise out of control. Tony stayed cool. He radioed to our club for assistance. We had no idea what we were going to do with all these people. We took the crew back to our yacht club, where our friends were waiting for us.

One problem was that our guests' cars were parked on the other side of the city. This was a dilemma. It did have its advantages, as no one was driving home. Everyone passed out on our boat or on some very charitable yachters' boats who knew Tony needed assistance. Let me tell you, the next morning the floats at Briar Ridge looked like the aftermath of a pajama party gone wrong. The funniest part was that there were people there Tony and I didn't even know. He had thought I knew them and visa-versa. We gathered whomever we could up and gave out tons of coffee. Tony, accompanied by Jim, then drove all our evening guests back to the city to reclaim their cars—hopefully they had not been towed away. The city's ordinance on all-night parking was very questionable.

I cleaned the boat; to this day I have never found one of my shoes that I wore to that wedding. Tony said he remembered someone drinking from it because we were out of glasses. We were out of everything, including cough medicine. I said to Tony, "What a tough crowd. The only one remotely close to us was a distant nephew." I then began to laugh. "Who were those people, Tony?"

Fortunately for us no one got hurt, but maybe they got a lot of parking tickets and towing. The city was not so forgiving. We sent a lovely thank-you note to the Prissy Yacht Club, and to this day they wondered why we left. We just said personal problems at home. If they only knew, they would have thanked us for being respectful.

Chapter 7

The Fog in June

TONY HAD BEEN INVITED TO HIS first Commodores of America event. He decided that because the weather had been so hot even in early June that we should take the boat. Of course this special occasion was limited to the new Commodores their wives or girl-friends. I was used to traveling in a fleet, always feeling secure in the safety of numbers; this would be a new experience. We would be cruising in unfamiliar territory. The forecast was for hot, humid weather with occasional showers, but it was nothing to stop Tony from taking command of his boat. So off we went. The ride was smooth, and it was a little over two hours toward Cape Cod by boat. This was an afternoon event. It was a welcoming party, a social gathering to introduce and acquaint all the newly elected Com-modores. Each club from the various surrounding yacht clubs sent their newest Commodore. When we reached our destination, as usual we were welcomed by past Commodores. The usual beautiful corsages and boutonnieres were on a table nearby. The corsages and boutonnieres were to distinguish the new officers and their wives from the past Commodores. Introductions and speeches were given, and Tony seemed to be more relaxed than his first social event on Palm Sunday. I observed my husband from a distance and could not help noticing how he attached himself so nicely to the crowd of new Commodores. He was among his own. His opinions, work, and future ideas were being shared with men he had something in common with. I hoped he would take with him this positive feeling of understanding and camaraderie that he was now sharing with his fellow officers.

At one point he looked up to see if I was standing near him. When he realized I had moved further away, he moved away from his comrades to search for me. I watched him eagerly eye the area, and when our eyes finally met I gave him thumbs up and a huge smile. He smiled back and resumed his position in the Commodores' circle of men. Then and then alone I finally felt that Tony had finally achieved his quest. He was Commodore.

I joined a small circle of new Commodores' wives, and we all shared our excitement for the new year ahead. It was a little plastic. By plastic I meant we were smiling constantly to be polite even though we might not agree with parts of the conversation taking place. My mouth formed a mouthpiece that was a perpetual smile. Everyone has experienced these moments.

After the luncheon we departed to a very large board room. Pictures were about to be taken of all the new Commodores. Each Commodore's picture would be displayed on the wall of the club he represents.

This certainly was not like a visitation; this was extremely formal. It was even a little judgmental; I felt that we were being judged on every word we said. Tony felt I was over reacting. When I told him how difficult it was at times to smile and not voice my opinion, he said, "Welcome to the world of politics."

Once we were settled in the boat and headed towards Briar Ridge, we looked at each other. "What are you thinking about now?" Tony asked.

"I think this is what you wanted. I think you are making a better adjustment than I am. I also think you miss, more than you realize, your friends from the past two years." Tony paused for a second. The waters were calm, and he lowered the throttle on the boat to an almost coasting speed. He still had his uniform on and from the profile of his face he really looked like a Commodore. He would have fit the role perfectly in a movie. However, this was not acting—this was for real. He then broke his silence by saying how much he loved the boat. I agreed, but in the distance I noticed clouds building up in a block-by-block pattern.

Before I could give it any further attention, Tony brought our original subject back. In a mellow sort of humble voice he said, "You're right." That was it. He then pushed the throttle higher to gain more speed. I assumed he also saw the approaching clouds.

In my heart I felt that this was one of those times I really did not want to be right. I said, "Tony, give it a chance."

He said, "It is lonely at the top, but I am going to give it a chance. I am taking this position to the end. I want you to take the ride with me. It is you, hon, who has to give it a chance." I thought about what my husband said and felt bad that he didn't understand that even though woman were not considered members, it was hard to live in someone else's shadow. I loved Tony, and because of that I would take the ride. As we continued to cruise home I noticed that the fog was now rolling in. Fog on the ocean could be frightening. Our visibility was soon less than four feet. First of all, we had no radar. We did have a loran, but it was very scary to not know if a large object was in front of us. How it rolled in so fast was a mystery to us, but it did. I was up on the bow, like a Cyclopes, and my eyes were focused. We were in unfamiliar waters, and the loran was guiding us from point to point on marked buoys. The loran could not anticipate objects in front of these buoys. In the distance, foghorns and motor sounds were heard. Tony was using his radio to try and contact an area that was safe to moor our boat. The fog was getting thicker, almost like someone had just wrapped Tony, me, and the boat in a cloud. This cloud had no boundaries—just blankets and blankets of white netting that had been covered by thick spider webs. With every move we anticipated being eaten up by a larger vessel or, worse, the deep waters of the ocean. I was very scared. If Tony was, he certainly did not show it. Suddenly right in front of us was a huge pier that we were headed for. It looked like a small roller coaster on a track. I screamed!

Tony was sweating profusely. He had taken off his Commodore's hat, and his hair was plastered to his face. His arms were moving in so many directions that the steering wheel on the boat was spinning. The muscles in his forearms were flexing in such a rapid movement that he looked like some bionic creature ready to attack the next thing that came in his direction. In this case it was the huge pier. Tony kept maneuvering the boat. We were close to shore, and the thought of going onto rocks was even a more dangerous concern. My heart was beating so rapidly it sounded like I was holding onto an alarm clock.

Tony had to execute an extreme amount of calmness and fortitude to turn the boat in a different direction. Tony usually kept cool in these situations, but he knew how scared I was. I was trying my best to be brave, but by now my knees were trembling, my palms were sweaty, and my eyes were almost falling out of my head. Tony kept reinforcing me by saying that he had radioed for help and someone would find us. He said the most important thing was to stay focused on the problem. That, my friends, was easier said than done. To our surprise and maybe my prayers, a coast guard boat was nearby. They heard Tony on the radio and guided us through the fog to safety. It took four hours to get back to Briar Ridge; I was physically and mentally spent. If Tony for one minute was scared, he never showed it. He also never admitted it. I knew my husband was brave, but we were all human and it was frightening out in the ocean that day. He was extremely tired when we got back and admitted strongly to that. His arms were sore from all that maneuvering. This was one of the more terrifying experiences I had encountered in yachting. We were very lucky we did not crash into that pier. We were also fortunate that we did not hit another boat or rocks. We were glad to be back at Briar Ridge.

When we got back to the club, the last thing I wanted was to stay on the boat. I just wanted to be on land. It was about eight in the evening. I decided to go up to our car that was in the Briar Ridge parking lot and crash in the back seat. It was a van with tinted glass, so no one would ever know I was there. Tony understood my desire for land, and so with my puffy pillow I departed.

I must have gone into a coma, because when I awoke my watch said it was about four-thirty in the morning. I was about to get up when I heard voices outside by my car. I knew one was Jill. I hadn't really talked with her since the Palm Sunday dinner. Our conversation then had been limited to the death of one of the guests. Jill wanted to know why the woman was drinking if she was a diabetic, which was a good question. Betty informed us that the woman was drinking other people's drinks when they weren't looking. This news was given to Betty after the fact. But one thing I couldn't forget was Jill's little girlish, sad voice. The person outside my car was definitely Jill.

The other voice was not so easy to identify, maybe because I was still so groggy it didn't click in. Then I realized it was Paul Adler. It was hard to make out the conversation, but it sounded like Paul was pleading with her to be with him because he had lost everything, including the baby. *What baby?* I thought. His wife and he had no children. Jill kept calling him names, saying he was an old fart and she would never leave George for him. Paul kept telling her he would send her to school or help her get a better job. Jill was cruelly ridiculing him; it was like I was hearing a role reversal. Jill was acting like the Paul she had told me about, and Paul was acting like the Jill I thought I knew. I was starting to breathe heavily like I was in a movie and the script had changed for the worse. I was so afraid that I would be found out. I actually put my hand over my mouth to prevent any sound. I then took my puffy pillow and sunk deep into it.

Finally they departed, but not on friendly terms. I waited for about ten minutes and then peeked out the window. The coast was clear. It must be times like this that made that saying "The coast is clear" popular. I did have to be careful for there was a full moon. The light of it reflected on the water and lit up the floats like a giant beacon. I did not want anyone to see me. I headed toward our boat. I was tiptoeing and ducking between different slips to avoid any contact. I finally approached my boat. I was so glad to be there that it actually looked comforting. It certainly was better sleeping accommodations than the car. I accidentally woke Tony up when I entered. He asked if I had a nice rest. I commented, "I had a nightmare."

He said, "Do you want to talk about it?"

I said, "Not really," so we both went back to sleep. I, however, tossed the Jill and Paul confrontation back and forth in my mind. The issue magnified itself the more I thought about it and just kept me awake. I spent my night tossing and turning and thinking over and over again about the opposite roles that Jill and Paul were playing.

THE NEXT MORNING OVER A CUP of coffee I tried to put the pieces of Jill's puzzle together. The more I tried the more confused I was. I then made a great decision mind my own business. And that was it. I would stay clear away.

Chapter 8

Lonely

AGAIN I FOUND MYSELF MORE AND more alone. During the summer most of our friends were so busy with family or trips that it was difficult to all get together. Tony's activities were taking him more and more away from the club, especially the floats. Lately I had found myself on the boat in seclusion. I often asked the children to come to the boat, but they had summer jobs. When they did have free time they chose to spend it with their peers. They loved us, but it just wasn't cool to hang with parents. Therefore I decided to stay home more, enjoying my mom. Sometimes my friends, knowing I was alone, would call and invite me down to the floats. They were involved with their husbands, and I was starting to feel like a fifth wheel. I found myself making excuses on why I couldn't visit with them. I wanted to be involved in any plans the Rear Commodore's wife had regarding charity events, and in her defense she had her crew. She had people she felt comfortable with. I barely knew Sam's wife. All my friends assumed that I wanted a rest—that the last two years were hard work and this was relax time. So, thinking they were doing me a favor, they didn't include me in any of the club activities that needed work. I certainly hinted at wanting to help, but they took my words as just being kind. I had to think of a way to get back in the fun of things. I missed being *me*!

Chapter 9

The Walk Out

IT WAS FLAG DAY, AND THERE was a special evening planned by the Rear Commodore. We usually did not have a large function on this day other than commemorating the American flag, but this was a change and change was good. It was just for officers of the club, and of course their lovely wives or significant others. I was so looking forward to this. The flag was hung high over our club, but still *no burgee*. However, in our hearts it was still there. The night was great, and I really enjoyed being with some of the women. I again iterated that I was willing to help in any upcoming events. Then trouble started as a loud echo of angry words coming from the galley was heard, and it soon erupted into a yelling match. It was difficult to understand what the problem was because everyone was yelling at once. Then I thought I heard the sound of dishes being thrown. At this point everyone's eyes were riveted on the galley door.

In a bold statement, a group of cleaners that were friends of one of the newer members of the club made a quick exodus from the galley. Our new Rear Commodore, Sam, came out of the galley and in a frustrated motion signaled to Tony. It seemed that the newer member had offered to donate his time and put a crew together to help clean in the galley. This selection of men were not members, though they were friends of this new member. The Rear Commodore assumed that the new member had explained to his crew that they were volunteering their services. These services would be rewarded by different means. For example a boat ride, lobsters from fresh traps, a bottle of wine, etc, etc. There would be no money exchanged. If the new member wanted to pay them out of his pocket, then that was a private arrangement separate from the club.

Unfortunately, there was a lot of misunderstanding. The new member thought he was the only one not getting paid. He thought the club was paying for his friends. When everything was explained by Sam, one of the cleaners angrily spoke up, "You have to be kidding me. I am not getting paid for cleaning up after all these people?" Then it seemed the other cleaners broke out in unison.

Sam said, "Please don't quit now. We can barter on the subject." The angry cleaners responded by throwing a few dishes against a wall. The newer member pleaded with them to no avail. Finally, in desperation Sam asked them to leave. This left the newer member and Sam alone in the galley. When Tony came back from his conversation with Sam and explained what happened, the table we were seated at became very sympathetic to Sam's crisis.

Tony then stood up and announced, "I know that this is a private function and many are all dressed up, but I need some dish washers." Everyone started to laugh.

I then got up and said, "I will be happy to help Sam in the galley."

Then Betty got up and said, "Peter and I will be happy to help Sam too." Remember I said I wished someone would ask me to help? Be careful of what you wish for. I, along with others, rolled up my sleeves and helped Sam clean the galley till it sparkled. We laughed, joked, mopped, and swept, and once again we were a family sticking together. The new member appreciated our services and apologized over and over again for his ignorance on club policies. I knew after that I would be asked to do anything because that was the messiest job of all, especially on my new shoes, which went to the same place my missing shoe, went—overboard! Oh, by the way, Sam's wife, who was sitting at a different table, also joined in the cleanup. It was not easy to take the bitter with the sweet, but we all did that night and actually had fun.

A FEW WEEKS LATER A GROUP of us were gathered on the floats. It was nice to have Tony with us. We all got an instant urge for something to eat. We were fished out, and the sound of a pizza was in the making. Across the street from the club was a Greek pizza place. The man who owned it also worked out at a local gym and was known for his physical strength along with his cooking skills. He was very amicable with his customers. It meant nothing for him to drop what he was doing and sit and have some pizza with customers. His pizza was fabulous—thin crust, lots of olive oil, plenty of cheese, the best quality pepperoni, and a light marinara sauce. The best part was we could just walk over. That night we decided that we were going to Kafla's—that was the owner's name. It was ten in the evening; the place was partially full with a small area of about fifteen people, including the cook and our friend Kafla.

When we entered, Kafla came over as always and grabbed Tony in a bear hug. "What's ya say, we play a little la motta?" This was a game better known in the streets as buck up. It was played by two people, and each put one hand behind their back. Each person yelled a number at the same time and exposed one hand. That hand either has one, two, three, four, or five fingers showing. However, numbers up to ten could be called. If, for example, a player yelled seven and their opponent had two fingers showing and they had five fingers showing, then the seven would win. If the opponent yelled six during the same game, he would loose. It was repeated until one player won ten games. It was a very loud, emotional game, and sometimes fingers popped up after they were called. Tony did not enjoy playing this game with Kafla because Kafla was one of those players whose fingers popped up after the call. But was Tony going to question Mr. Muscles? I didn't think so. But I, on the other hand, was a buck up expert.

When I was a child, we played softball in the city park. We would buck up to pick kids on our team. Both captains would engage in this, and I always wanted the best team so I learned the odds from my grandfather. However, this is a family secret, so I will proceed with the story.

Tony said, "Kafla, ask my wife—she is good at this." And so Kafla and I went at this game. I quickly won five games in a row; the cheering was unbelievable, especially in my favor. This was not acceptable to Kafla, and I was almost ready to lose just to keep peace. Unfortunately his assistant was making the pizzas. I wanted Kafla to make the pizza, but these crowds of onlookers were not allowing me to quit. I ended up beating him ten times in a row, and the pizza paid the price. It was terrible. Kafla said he let me win but demanded a challenge game at a different time. We decided to go while the going was good, but Kafla grabbed Tony and decided to prove his manhood in a game of arm wrestling. Of course Tony refused as he knew he had no chance against Mr. Muscles. Then Tony rethought his decision. Maybe it would be a good chance for Kafla to get his dignity back. After all, the pizza there was *really good* if Kafla made it.

Kafla was gentle at first, but by the third time of bringing Tony's arm to the table, Kafla got a little rambunctious. Tony was in pain, and as a simple reaction he grabbed Kafla by the hair and said, "Hey, man, let up." Everyone was surprised when Tony was holding Kafla's hair in his hands. Kafla went out of his mind.

He looked at Tony and angrily said, "You did that on purpose to embarrass me." Tony was shocked and just stood there with the toupee in his hand, dumfounded.

Tony could only say, "Hey, pal, I am sorry. I had no idea." Kafla was furious. He could hear laughter in the background from some of the customers, and that only infuriated him more. Tony was standing still holding the small hair piece when Kafla grabbed it out of his hands. Tony again repeated, "Hey, pal, you have to believe me—none of us realized you had a toupee." Kafla was uncontrollable at this point, so we did the fastest exit stage right possible. We didn't walk—we ran as fast as we could back to the main bar at Briar Ridge. This was safe ground in case we needed protection. The bartenders were strong like Kafla. This incident went down in the books. First for the innocence of it, but most of all anyone from our club was warned not to order pizza or have it delivered to the boats until things quieted down with Kafla. If they did it was at their own expense. Tony did try calling Kafla several times to explain his innocence, but Kafla never came to the phone or called us back. I guess his image of Mr. Muscles lost some spark that night. Too bad. We liked him and missed the pizza.

ONE EVENING WHEN TONY AND I were having a late dinner he said, "I have to tell you something." He became very formal. At first I got scared because Tony very rarely addressed me that way.

I said, "What is it?"

He laughed and said, "It is not about us. It is about the club."

I said, "Are you sure you want to discuss conversations that take place behind closed doors?"

He smiled at me, knowing I was giving him a zing. "You might be involved in the solution," he said.

"Well," I said, "I can't stand the suspense. What is it?"

He then looked at me and said, "The club is about to have some financial problems. It seems the assessment has doubled. Of course the land is extremely valuable, and there are condo associates that would love to get their hands on this prime property." This made no sense to me. I felt they should have a lot of money, and I questioned the financial situation. Tony continued to say, "The club does have some money, but the added expenses on improvements through the years have dipped into a lot of the savings." He then told me, "This is not a problem this year, but by next year with the new assessment coming into play, there definitely will be a financial issue.

I asked him, "How is this your problem?"

He says, "It is everyone's problem who is involved with the club. The club brings pleasure to a lot of families. It is a landmark, and it would be catastrophic if condos were built in its place. We need to prevent this by raising a lot of money."

I looked up at him and asked, "Tony, how do you propose to do this? And how am I about to be one of the solutions to this problem?" Tony took a deep breath, and then he looked at me. I knew this face. I had seen it before. It was the face of someone who desperately wanted something. His eyes became wide open, and his head began to tilt to one side. A pleading look a child might give to get what they wanted came to his face. He then proceeded to tell me what the recent meetings were all about.

"There are a couple of fights in professional boxing coming up. If the club could bring in satellite TV and have a few screens set up in the large function hall, we could raise some decent money. The galley could do sausage-and-pepper subs. The bar would limit drinking to beer and wine at a reasonable price. The club could easily accommodate four to five hundred people if they extended a couple more TVs in the members' lounge and back deck, which in case of inclement weather could be closed in."

I looked up at Tony and said, "Well, you seem to have come up with some ideas. So what is the problem?"

Tony decided to refresh our wine glasses. We were still at the dinner table. The dirty dishes from our late-evening meal were starting to permeate the kitchen with a garlicky smell. However, I liked garlic and did not want to stop now and start cleaning. I wanted to stay focused on this subject—I wanted to know how I was a part of this solution. After all, I was not considered a member. Tony addressed the topic again. "The problem, hon, is that we need initial investors from the club to front the money to bring the fights to the club." My ears and eyes perked up. I now knew why Tony was so willing to tell me the behind-the-door plan.

"Are we one of the investors, Tony?" I asked. Tony became silent. He took a sip of wine before he answered, "Of course. hon, it is entirely up to you." I knew when I was being played, so I went a step further.

"How much, Tony?"

Tony took another sip of wine and blurted out, "Five thousand." (Remember this is the eighties.) I gasped. He quickly informed me, "Listen, hon, there are four investors, each putting up five thousand. It will cost twenty thousand dollars to bring in the two fights. At fifty dollars a ticket, that is almost fifty thousand for the two fights, plus food and beer. After paying back the investors, the club should see at least twenty-five to thirty thousand. If this is so, the club will be able to ward off any problems until they can settle on a fair assessment or have the club attorney fight for a lower assessment. As Commodore I feel I should get involved personally, but I need you to agree."

"Tony, I have been waiting for a formal dining room set for two years now. Every time I bring up the situation, it's the same old thing. This child needs this; the roof needs to be replaced, etc, etc. Now even my dining room set is being put on hold for this assessment issue involving the club." I let loose! I went berserk and actually yelled, "How, Tony, can you justify this over our own personal needs?" I took a huge gulp of wine. Tony stayed very calm, which was one of his attributes, not mine.

He said, "We all get a great deal of pleasure from the club. It has been a safe haven for our family, and look at the support it gave Jim and Mary during their crisis." He then proceeded to tell me, "Jim has also offered to be one of the investors." I became quiet and started fingering my napkin. Tony then looked at me and said, "I promise no matter what that after these two fights you will have your formal dining room set."

I dropped my napkin and immediately asked, "What are the dates that these fights are taking place?" Tony knew he had struck a positive chord with me.

So, relaxed he said, "One fight is in mid August, and the other fight is the first weekend after Labor Day." I decided not to be too obvious and told him I will give him an answer in the morning.

I then turned around to face him and asked, "Who are the other two investors?" He said Sam was willing but had not made a firm commitment.

Then Tony paused before saying, "We are still looking for one more." Somehow I did not believe him about the one more, but after being a Calamity Jane I decided not to push it. I left the room and went to bed. Tony did the dishes.

The following morning I gave him a wink and a smile. Tony knew the answer was positive. He gave me a kiss, and we never brought up the fights. It was the beginning of July, and I was looking forward to the Fourth. The officers had asked the Rear Commodore and the Fleet Captain to plan a trip to Boston Harbor to see the firework display and listen to Pops perform. Anyone interested was to sign up and the Rear and Fleet Captain would make the necessary arrangements. I was ready and Tony was too! No more fights over the fights!

Chapter 10

Jill's Departure

IT WAS JULY 2 AND I was sitting on the boat. I saw the *Rusty Scupper* docked way down on the opposite side of our slip, and I decided to go over and visit. I hadn't conversed with either George or Jill since Palm Sunday in April. The episode outside my car was still a puzzle to me, and I knew Jill never suspected that I was listening to the conversation while hiding in my car. Even though I wanted to mind my own business, I could honestly say I was curious on this subject. Jill had become distant; there had been no serious communication. I was beginning to feel bad because there was a brief period where Jill was starting to get along with some of us girls. Jill had made the beautiful christening attire for Pat, and Pat couldn't thank her enough. The girls had liked her in the dart league. I figured I would try one more time to have a conversation with Jill. As I approached the *Rusty Scupper* I noticed that George was busy fixing something, but what? Well, those who owned boats were always fixing something. "Hi," I said. He looked up, kind of surprised!

"What's going on?" he replied.

"I was about to ask you," I said.

"Well," George said, "if it's about Jill, we are through."

"Well," I commented, "I haven't seen her around and I was just hoping she was feeling okay." "Oh, she's fine," George says, "since she doesn't need me anymore, Miss Independence decided to go back to Texas. Listen to this—she conned Paul Adler into getting her a one-way ticket back to wherever the hell she came from. So I say good riddance to her." And with that he accelerated his working to full throttle. I thought if George hammered any harder, the hammer would go through the teak wood into the cabin. I could tell by George's expression that he was bitter. I gave him a shrug and left. I hoped it was for the best that Jill left and prayed she would find a life better than the one she had been living. I was hurt that Jill didn't take the time to say goodbye to me. I thought she could have at least sent me a note. All I could think of were those doe eyes conning Paul into buying her a one-way ticket. I guessed Jill used me. Maybe when one was dragged through life one became so cunning. This must have been one of the survival tools needed to get through a tough childhood.

On the Fourth of July, we were all lined up for the journey to Boston Harbor. My last trip there was for the wedding of Tony's and my niece. Ironically, the same fancy yacht club was allowing us to tie up at their floats and participate with them in the gala firework event. Fortunately, Tony and I had left before all the chaos took place the last time we stayed at their club; I think they felt we left because we were not having a good time. They truly wanted us to come. I was glad because this way we could concentrate on enjoying our newfound friends and officers. This event would also let our members and officers intermingle with theirs. Maybe they were not so prissy after all. I had a newfound respect for them. I had misjudged them.

Chapter 11

The Fireworks and the Music

IF YOU HAVE NEVER SPENT THE Fourth of July on the Charles River with the Boston Symphony Pops performing, then I don't think you could ever even imagine the enchanting feeling of being there. We were left breathless. Each firework fired into the sky had its own melody attached to it. For example, bursts of yellow and white rays that erupted as sparkles dripping from the center of the firework vibrated to the symphony's majestic sound of "It's a Beautiful World." Each sparkle reached out over the sky and felt like it was reaching down and touching everyone. The music was so overpowering that at times it drowned out the huge explosions. The orchestra's different instruments all found their own individual firework to compliment its uniqueness. "Bombs bursting in air" were in red, white, and blue cascading over the skies with rocket-shaped extrusions falling and spinning in different directions. The drums and symbols were in perfect harmony with each explosion of color. My body felt like I was on some mystical ride through space, floating through the sky with a million colored Milky Ways passing by. The finale was an endless display across the sky. All the skyscrapers were lit in fusions of color. Music introduced our freedom by bellowing out all our patriotic tunes. The Charles River acted as a giant mirror reflecting all the colors of the sky. This phenomenal display truly left everyone *breathless!* When all was said and done, every yacht's man and woman honked their horn to display their gratitude for this fabulous extravaganza. At this point, we were sitting in a fog from all the smoke that covered the water. We were in America, sipping champagne and toasting our freedom, and for that moment we all reflected on how lucky we were to have our freedom. It certainly was a night that I will never forget; it was and probably will be the best Fourth of July I ever had.

After a few hours, the fog caused by the extreme firework smoke cleared and all the boats started departing. We decided to stay where we were because it was pretty hectic. Boats were moving in all directions. Tony decided it would be more intelligent if we left first thing in the early morning. We were glad that our visit was such a memorable time, and the hospitality of this yacht club turned out to be a nice way to cement our relationship with them. We left this club on a good note, which was appropriate in a Pops way!

FOR THE NEXT FEW WEEKS THINGS were relatively quiet for Tony and me. He was still involved in the backroom financing and legal aspects of the club, and I was still left out of the loop. I knew this was something he thought he wanted. I was concentrating on the dining room. I was going to turn it into a project to keep me busy.

Chapter 12

Dot's Fundraiser

SAM'S WIFE HAD DECIDED TO HAVE a fundraiser and called for my help. This was great—I loved being included. She also included Mary and Pat. It was old times again. At an informal meeting, Sam properly introduced his wife, Dot. Dot had decided to plan a scavenger hunt. This was the first time she actually got involved with Pat, Mary, and me. The aprons that she gave all the waitresses on Palm Sunday were a very nice gesture. However, actually having a conversation with Dot had never taken place. We were finally going to learn about Dot, the Rear Commodore's wife. Dot was planning a function that would take place at the end of July. She wanted it in the late afternoon. It was amazing to hear this woman talk.

Dot was a short lady with sharp eyes and a very affirmative attitude. Dot knew what she wanted. She didn't ask us for our opinion—she just told us what she needed. I was hoping that she and Pat would get along since Pat had authoritarian ways too. I know Dot helped Sam at the deli, and I guessed she was used to giving orders. She was standing in front of the three of us girls and giving different commands. I think if she had delegated them to us, our attitude toward her would have been extremely responsive. Dot never asked us. She just told us what she thought we should do. Did she realize that we were not on her payroll? Did she forget we were volunteers? Mary said to me, "Dot is going to have to change fast and drop her superior attitude if she wants to have people work with her." Did Dot realize that "you get more out of honey than you do vinegar?"

I said, "Mary, let's give her a chance. This is new territory for her."

Mary said, "You are right. I will give her a try." Pat agreed as well, even though she had a deep frown on her face. Pat shrugged her shoulders as if she was motioning an "I don't care" attitude.

Dot decided that she would like to combine the event with a lobster feast at the club. Our job, Pat, Mary, and I, would be finding products to hide. The other team of girls Dot asked were all associated with the newer members of the club. We were unfamiliar with some of these ladies. I felt this would be a good chance to make new friends. Their job would be finding locations to hide these products for the hunt. Dot informed us she would be doing the clues and the directions for the treasure hunt. Dot also informed us that she was a computer expert and had a copy machine at the deli. Dot felt this was a perfect position for her. None of us said a word. The Rear Commodore was, naturally, in charge of the food. This, I kept telling myself, was going to be a fun project. For thirty dollars a couple, people could participate in a scavenger hunt, win a prize if they were lucky, and have lobster. This sounded good to me. Lobsters would be provided, as usual, by the fishermen of the club. We always welcomed their donations. So Pat, Mary, and I were going to go hunting for treasures. I just hoped I would not have another bee episode, but I would load my pocketbook with meat tenderizer just in case!

Chapter 13

Collecting the Stuff

YARD SALES SEEMED TO BE WHERE we had luck providing items for the auction, so it was unanimously decided that we would start there. We needed six items no larger than a bread box. We picked a gorgeous day and a great neighborhood. The first home we visited was lovely. The owners were moving to the southern part of the country. I guessed they didn't need skis, poles, boots, and a snow blower for South Carolina. A lot of the items displayed were extremely expensive.

Pat was the first to find a treasure. It was a Buddha smaller than a bread box (just barely). It was made of some metal, and had a big, fat tummy that looked like it had been rubbed a lot. I asked the person running the yard sale if she wanted to part with this. She said, "This Buddha brought me a lot of luck, but luck should be spread around."

Pat said, "I agree with your philosophy, and I knew I liked this lucky Buddha the minute I saw it." So Lucky Buddha was the first item that we purchased for the scavenger hunt.

We picked through the rest of the items, and then Mary said, "Girls, I think we should move on. We have a lot of territory to cover." So we did. It was nice to have most of the old Mary back, but now and then the lion's paw appeared. The loss of her child would never escape her memory. Thank goodness for the birth of her niece's little girl. I was so glad she named her after Mary's daughter. Mary and Jim spoiled that little girl terribly, and that was a good thing. Mary and Jim loved to babysit for their niece's child. Every time they looked at that little girl, it was like a part of their daughter was reborn.

Our next stop was a different experience. It was a small novelty store full of little knickknacks, and it was going out of business. We tried for a donation, but that didn't work. Sometimes stores or restaurants donated gift certificates for charity. This person needed every cent, however; they were going out of business so we knew we had no bargaining power. Pat reminded us, "These prices have been drastically reduced. I feel that whatever they are asking is a great deal." Mary must have had an intuition. There it was—a small traffic post that lit up red, green, or yellow. In this case red meant no drinks, green meant "I am ready," and yellow meant "I am contemplating." The post with the lights stood about a foot high, bread-box size, and batteries were included. We liked Mary's pick. We all agreed it was a fun choice. As I was leaving I saw a ceramic beehive, and I immediately exited. Just the thought of a bee sting made me panic. The girls decided to take my attention elsewhere. We decided to take a break and do lunch. We would continue our search later.

PAT WAS READING THE PAPER AT lunch and found one more yard sale in a high-priced neighborhood. Pat read aloud, "Sacrifice sale—mostly estate items. Owner can't afford upkeep."

Mary said, "Pat, are you sure you want to go to something that sounds depressing?"

"Why is it depressing?" Pat asked.

Mary replied, "Because it sounds like they are losing everything."

"Mary," Pat informed her, "we just came from a store that was going out of business. By purchasing different items we might be helping them. That is why they run ads."

Mary shrugged. "I guess I didn't look at it that way."

I intervened, saying, "Let's give it a shot, girls. It happens to be on our route back toward home."

The neighborhood reeked of money, but would we really find a sacrifice? Often people with means were very generous, and this was one of those occasions. The woman was quite elderly and had no problem informing us that she had never married. This was probably why she had lived so long. Her frailty scared me. I was afraid that if a gust of wind came it would blow her away. She was dressed in a white lace dress. The dress looked like an old-fashioned wedding gown. In the center of her neck, where the dress collar encompassed her throat, was a beautiful cameo. She kept her hands clasped for fear that we would notice the obvious shake, but to her dismay it was very perceivable. Her hair was snow white. It was wrapped in a huge bun that sat on the top of her head like a lid. Running through the bun was a small spear that resembled a chopstick. This stick was painted with small, black and white flowers.

This little old lady informed us that she had inherited her gorgeous, brick Tudor house from her parents and now was forced to sell it. "You know," she said, "I can barely take care of myself, never mind this huge house. I have been advised by my doctor to consider assisted living. My premises will now consist of three small rooms." This was a far cry from this ten-room estate. She then said, "I am not sad about my new living quarters. I had a good life, and I am actually looking forward to some companionship. The nights and days are very lonely roaming around this silent home, and it is time to have it ring again with a new family." I liked the way she accepted her fate. Change was hard, especially when habits were strong. It took a lot of courage to close the door on one part of her life and open another door that she hoped would be welcoming.

We continued to poke around, trying desperately to find something that would fit into the scavenger hunt. Everything was old and huge. The silver pieces were great, but we couldn't use them in the scavenger hunt. Pat commented, "These beautiful silver pieces would probably be stolen before anyone in the hunt could find them." We found a decoy way over in one of the many crannies of the house. It was a duck that had been used in hunting. It was in decent condition, but it was a little bit larger than a bread box. We needed a meeting of the minds on this one. We decided to take it and hoped that Dot would not object.

When we tried to purchase the decoy, our gracious host said, "I insist on donating it." Her charity did not go unnoticed. On the way out I saw a beautiful silver frame sized 8x10. I thought someday when the time came I could put a wedding picture in it of my daughter. It had bells and roses filigreed on all four sides. I bought it at a mere twenty dollars. I told this classy older lady my intention, and that caused her to give me a smile. I figured she hadn't done that in a while, and it made me feel good. I took her hand. It was so small and fragile in mine. I was afraid if I squeezed it too hard her fingers would fall to the ground. I decided I would hug her instead. There was more of her that way. She looked into my eyes and thanked me for coming, and I wished her well in her new surroundings. We were done for the day. We had the Buddha, traffic bar light, and decoy in hand. Our adventure would continue next weekend, which Dot had given us as our deadline. Maybe it was a command. Ha!

Chapter 14

The Deadline

THE NEXT WEEKEND ARRIVED; WE WERE now, as the saying went, under the gun. We had to find three more items. The other team had already started working on hiding places. Dot had agreed on our first three items and was now busy writing coded directions for the hiding places. Dot really wanted to create the perfect execution of a scavenger hunt.

Pat had again circled places in the paper that were having flea markets or yard sales. We thought we would try a flea market again. Mary felt there would be so many tables to choose from. The flea market was out of our area, in a parking lot that had once housed a huge lumber yard. We approached the scene like dedicated buyers on a mission. After about a half hour, I heard Mary laughing; I turned to see her holding a large washboard used in prehistoric days. Although, when I was in New Orleans it was used as an instrument, and quite effectively I had to say. Mary yelled out, "Bigger than bread box? Longer, I think, but not wider." Pat and I laughed. Mary pleaded, "We have to take it," and so we did.

I said, "This item isn't going to be easy to get by Dot." Then we giggled more. Two more items were needed. It then became easy. We saw a pair of jumper cables.

Pat screamed with enthusiasm, "I have a great idea! The problem with my idea might be convincing Dot to let us do it."

"Let's hear your idea, Pat." I said.

"It would be a jumper cable caper," Pat said, and then with such zest Pat started describing her idea. "We would put wigs on; we would be dressed in crazy getups. We would be ladies in distress. We would be in the Stop and Buy parking lot with car problems. We could be part of the scavenger hunt. I think Dot would get a kick out of it." Pat was so excited over her brainstorm that her mouth was going faster than we could keep up with.

Finally Mary said, "Pat, hold on, let me play this back. You want us to disguise ourselves as ladies in distress and park at the food store pretending that our car broke down. Am I right so far?" Pat nodded a yes. Mary then continued, "Pat, where do the jumper cables come in?" Pat had not lost any of her gusto.

She explained, "One of us stands holding the cable pretending we don't know how to attach it to the car."

Mary looked at me and laughed; she then said, "I don't know how to use jumper cables." I looked at Mary and burst out laughing.

"Neither do I," Pat said with a little less gusto and a little bit of disappointment towards our lack of cable knowledge. "Well, then I guess I have two people who can really play the part." Mary and I looked at each other and tried not to snicker too loud. Now with girlish laughter that was so good for the soul, we agreed to buy the jumper cables. It was amazing how grown women could get lost in the shuffle of life and forget how girlish they really were. It took good friendships to bring the girl part out. It took good friendships to make a woman laugh and sometimes forget the seriousness and responsibility that life could throw at her. Pat, so thrilled at her idea being accepted by us, announced, "We are not finished yet. We have a deadline." We plowed along through the many tables at the flea market. Pat yelled again, "I found it!" She placed around her neck a fake diamond dog leash, or maybe it was something used in S&M. I preferred to think it was dog leash. Now we had our products. We just had to deliver them to Dot. We hoped Dot would agree. The dog leash was questionable in my mind, and I also hoped she would go along with Pat's jumper cable caper.

Dot was ecstatic about our plan to be in the parking lot at the supermarket with jumper cables. Dot was one step ahead of Pat's plan. Pat had forgotten that most people knew what kind of cars we all drove. Dot had no trouble addressing the question to Pat, saying, "But what car will you use?" Dot asked.

Mary interrupted and said, "I will ask my niece if we can borrow her car or switch off cars."

Dot then said, "I have my end to do regarding this event. You have your end and I have to trust you to do your part."

Pat said, "Trust us, Dot? Don't you trust us?"

Dot stood her ground. "Trust you? Of course I do otherwise I would nix the whole idea." I knew it was just a matter of time before Pat and Dot, two strong personalities, would confront each other.

Pat said, "Let me remind you, Dot, that all the women who are helping you are dedicating their time. We are not on your payroll, and I feel you have a tendency to command rather than ask." Dot took her time in responding to Pat's remark. I felt Pat was out of line. I felt that when Dot made that comment on trust she said it as we would say to our own family and children, "I trust you will do the right thing."

Dot looked up at Pat and replied, "If I appear to you to be in charge it is because I am. I know my responsibility to my husband's role at this club. If you are having a problem with the way I handle things, then you do not have to be a part of it. I don't think I did anything wrong. The items are fine and the caper is fine. I don't think anyone is on my payroll. I do think that organization is important, and that is how I work. Take it or leave it." With that answer Dot excused herself and left.

Pat looked at me and said, "What?"

I said, "Pat, I think you were out of line. You took a common remark and blew it out of proportion. Of course this is just my opinion."

Mary blurted out, "Ditto."

I then put my arms around Pat and said, "Let's talk about the jumper cable caper." Pat was glad we changed the subject. She didn't want to not be a part of her idea. It wasn't easy for Pat to admit she had been a little aggressive towards Dot's remark. Mary and I did not expect her to admit it; we knew that Pat regretted her actions because she didn't quit—she stayed. Our next discussion was how to disguise the three of us. I liked this part best. We would get wigs, lots of crazy makeup, and funky clothes. Dot said before her exit that she would have a meeting in three days, and all the plans would be laid out there. I believed Dot. One thing I was learning about Dot was that she would go along with what we wanted. However, Dot expected us to run with our decision. I understood Dot now that I was getting to know her. Sam had waited a long time to be Rear Commodore, and Dot was not going to be the reason he didn't make Vice Commodore. She was going to do her best as I had tried to do when Tony was Rear Commodore. I guess I wasn't so authoritarian because I wasn't in the workforce. At home with children I learned to use more convincing understanding tones when I spoke.

The other girls involved in the scavenger hunt were busy finding hiding places. Dot was directing. Dot was making clues to where these items were to be found. Tony was laughing at how happy and excited I was. Tony said, "You girls have so much fun together. Hon, don't ever take that fun for granted."

I laughed at Tony and said, "I won't." Tony mentioned that the day of the scavenger hunt he would find something else to do. He knew too much about the hunt. Tony agreed he would meet me later for the lobster feast. However, he might hide at Stop and Buy and take some pictures of us girls incognito.

THE END OF JULY CAME QUICKLY. Dot's elected teams for the scavenger hunt had completed most of their missions. The hiding places were great! The Buddha was in a garden in front of a Chinese restaurant. The owner was very happy to get the recognition from our club. The red, green, and yellow light was to be on a bar top in a local tavern patronized by the members of our club. The decoy was to be placed in a pond, and that was something we really could not get permission for. We decided that one of the girls would sit inconspicuously on a nearby bench and try to prevent the wrong people from taking it. The washboard would be left at a local Laundromat. Again a girl would sit there guarding this treasure until she noticed a few people with Dot's printed directions in their hand. Pat, Mary, and I had our jumper cable caper project to concentrate on. The funniest would be a girl from the placement team. She owned a dog and would be walking her dog in the designated area. She would make sure the fake diamond collar was flashing. Dot had all the clues typed out on index cards. She would distribute them when she officially started the scavenger hunt or treasure hunt. Remember: "one man's junk is another man's treasure."

Chapter 15

The Jumper Cable Caper

HAVE YOU EVER BEEN ON A treasure or scavenger hunt? It is basically the same thing. If not, you have no idea what you are missing. Think about this for your next party.

The scavenger hunt was on! There were four teams of ten people and two teams of eleven people. We had sixty-two participants searching for buried treasure. Dot handed each participant clues and directions to the hidden treasures. There was no restriction on which clue or direction people could go first. Whichever team found the object first would take it and leave a note saying, "Beat you to the treasure!" There was a time frame, and Dot was very strict with this rule. If people were not back by 6:00 PM, they were *out*! If they had a treasure and were not back by six their team was still disqualified. Dot's rules. This was to keep everything on schedule. Pat never commented on this rule.

There were many people partaking in this event, but not in the scavenger hunt. A lot of the older members just wanted to enjoy the food and see how the teams went. Tony made a suggestion that to raise more money we could bet on which team would have the most treasures. So Sam set up two girls to take fifty-cent bets, and no more than five bets per person. The house would take twenty-five cents on the dollar.

Mary, Pat, and I were posted at the supermarket. Mary's niece had let us use her Dodge. We were acting as damsels in distress. I had a blond wig and a miniskirt. My eyes were done like Cleopatra, and I had knee socks with a pair of old blue Keds sneakers. I looked more like I was going to a Halloween party than a scavenger hunt. Pat had a curly red mane. Pat also had a bra stuffed so much that she looked like she would fall over. Pat had go-go boots that were left over from the sixties. I think the two of us looked extremely ridiculous. Mary took a different approach. She was the mother of these two wild and funky daughters. Mary was camouflaged as an elderly woman with a gray wig and spectacles. Mary had stuffed her tummy with a pillow and was wearing an old pair of Red Cross shoes owned by her departed mother. This was too funny for words. Our only concern was that someone not from the scavenger hunt would offer to assist us.

I looked at my watch, the only thing still familiar to me. It had been about twenty minutes since the teams departed for treasures. I got out the jumper cables, pretending that I didn't know which end went where, which I didn't. I hemmed and hawed until a car pulled up. The man behind the wheel was definitely a member of the club. I recognized him immediately. I hoped he didn't recognize us. He said, "Missy, may I help?" Then he stared at me for a long time.

I noticed that he was getting suspicious, so I immediately replied, "You certainly can. I don't know which end is which." Then he looked in the backseat, where we had left Mary.

He motioned to the rest of his team and said, "Team, take a look at the girls, especially Mary."

I said, "How did you know?"

He said, "The clue was three hot chicks in trouble trying to buy groceries at SOS or SB. We guessed that SB stood for Stop and Buy but somehow the legs on Granny looked to young to go with the gray hair."

I said, "Mary is sitting down."

He laughed and said, "Ya, but the dress is way up over her knees."

I guessed the pillow she used pulled the dress way up. I knew Mary should have worn those old lady stockings. When I told her to wear them, she had said, "It's too hot for those Ruth Buzzy hose." Pat had wished her caper would have lasted longer, but we did agree we had fun. Team two left the premises with the jumper cables. Tony pulled up with a Polaroid picture of Pat and me leaning over the car. Then he took one of Mary when she finally emerged from the backseat.

His only comment was, "Girls, you really worked hard at making yourself obvious."

I said, "Tony, what do you mean?"

He grimaced. "Well, let's just say that it was overkill on the disguise."

I said, "Tony, we really tried."

He said, "I know you did, but look at you—who dresses like that in July?"

"Oh," I said, "maybe we should have worn bathing suits."

"You know, that wouldn't have been a bad idea," Tony snickered. "The only problem being I would have had to stop all those young men from fighting to see who could get your engine started. I guess after all, ladies, you picked the right disguise."

"'Sure," Pat said, "you are just trying to make us feel good."

Tony said, "I am proud of all of you, and I have the pictures to prove it. A lot of people would not have the courage to do something like this. Your girls were not afraid to have people laugh at you and with you. I love you all for it." We then left the premises for a shower and a new set of clothes—our job was finished. Next to the return-cart stand in the parking lot was left a "Beat you to the treasure" sign.

Chapter 16

The Results

THE WINNER WAS TEAM TWO. WHILE we were being stripped of our jumper cables, the rest of team two were following, "Rub my tummy and read a fortune that will be granted." There were only three Chinese restaurants, and they got lucky on the first one. Team one found the decoy, but they wasted most of their time recovering it from the pond as the lead weights didn't do their job effectively and it floated further out into the center of the pond. The team, however, showed their bravery when they all arrived in wet clothing. Thank goodness it was July? Team three came back empty-handed. Team five had the bar light but partook in some spirits while they were there and forgot the rest of the hunt. Team six found the dog, "something sparkles on this main canine beauty." They rode around the beginning of Main Street and had another car posted at the end of Main Street. They had team members walking both ways. They were very determined. In the middle of the road one of the members saw the dog and the necklace. Up close he saw that it was one of the members' girlfriends under her dark black pigtail wig. One item was not retrieved. The washboard was not found in time, and our spy returned it. When it was held up, a younger member asked if he could by it. It seemed he also had been in New Orleans and was prone to washboard music. Dot agreed, and the young member made a great donation for the washboard.

Other than team one, who was soaked to the skin, everyone came back having a lot of fun and ready to party. This was a super day. By the way, team two was a long shot and paid out a lot, but not too many people were confident enough to bet on that team. Dot raised over $1,800 toward her gift for the club.

When we arrived home later that evening, Tony asked me, "Hey, hon, what is your gift going to be this year for the club?"

I said, "Tony, our gift will be presented when it comes time for you to step down from the chairs after completing your run as Commodore. I am working on it. My group of girls and all the officers that helped has allowed me to accumulate almost $3,000. This money is being held by the secretary of the club. I have an idea, Tony. I think I know where this gift might be needed. I just want my team that helped me through the years to give me their input before I make my final decision."

Chapter 17

Summer Days

AUGUST WAS COMPARATIVELY QUIET. I WAS very involved with my family. A lot of my cousins from faraway places came up. We had a huge family reunion, and naturally Tony cooked. Sam donated some fabulous briskets that Tony cooked and sliced. Tony then enhanced them with mustard and sauerkraut. Tony took some of the younger family members out on the boat. He took them fishing, and they were introduced to Tony's outstanding blue fish.

While Tony was fishing, I went down to the club to have lunch with Pat and Mary. I ran into Paul Adler in the parking lot. Paul had aged quickly since the last time I saw him. He had deep frown lines on his forehead, and I noticed that his hands were shaky and he seemed despondent. I knew what stress could do to a person. I went over to him and asked him if he had heard from Jill. He said that he had heard from her and mentioned that Jill was crocheting unbelievably and delivering her wares to a local consignment store. She had purchased a ten-speed bike with a basket attached to the front steering bar. This was her means of transportation and delivery. She was happy being with part of her so-called family. I questioned Paul about her so-called family.

Paul looked right into my eyes and said very seriously, "I figure that maybe when she was in the foster homes, she just might have had a pleasant experience with one of the foster guardians. I feel by the letter she sent me that she is content."

I said, "Paul, what made you help her out? I know it is none of my business, but I can't help asking."

He put his head down and said, "I owed her." When Paul made

that comment to me, I was surprised. I figured I would let it go there. I was so afraid that I would burst out with the blow job information and smack him. Things were working out for Jill, and if I betrayed her confidence he might get angry at her for giving me that personal information. Paul was a sorry sight; he had lost his wife after years of sickness, never had any children, and was truly alone aside from a few friends at the club. He lost George over Jill's departure, but George was a fair-weather friend. I doubted Paul really missed his friendship with George. I saw Pat and Mary approaching and knew this was a good opportunity to say my farewell to Paul.

Pat and Mary immediately wanted to know about my conversation with Paul. They had no idea about Jill. I just said, "Paul misses what he had." We all agreed that Paul looked like a beaten man.

LATE AUGUST WAS APPROACHING, WHICH MEANT that many meetings were being planned for the fights that Tony and his crew were planning. I was still kept out of the loop, and when I brought the subject up regarding fight night, Tony soon changed the subject towards something else. "Don't worry, hon, you'll get your dining room set. I guarantee it!" I knew Tony had dipped into our savings account, but I had agreed to let him use the money for fronting the fights.

I said, "Tony, I want the dining room set before our children start going in different directions with all of the activities they're involved in. It is bad enough that their friends monopolize most of their time. I still, however, have manged a Sunday family dinner twice a month. I want the Sunday family dinner back on a weekly basis. This is very important to me, Tony. I like the times we sit around the table and discuss everyone's activities. It gives us a chance to know what is going on in our children's lives beyond the walls of our home. Also, Tony, the holidays are coming up in the fall and I want my set."

He laughed. "Hon, listen to me—do you really think teenagers like to sit around a table with ten people talking?"

I said, "Our kids *will*."

He said, "Well, you soon will find out. I promise you will have your dining room set by Christmas."

I said, "Great, there goes the fall. I am going shopping tomorrow just to see what's new and exciting in furniture for the dining room."

"No problem," he said. "Hon, the funds will be deposited back into our account as soon as the fights are over." I was thrilled by this news. No more sitting around a six-table dining room table with extensions and folding chairs. At each meal I prayed that someone's glass wouldn't spill because each table had a space and a different level where the two tables met.

The next day I was at every furniture store in town. When I got to the last one, I saw it. I went over and sat in one of the seats, ran my hands over the beautiful oak wood, and gasped. I guess that was how Tony felt when he bought the boat. The table smelled of lemons—the store must have just polished this beautiful wood. The salesman saw my passionate behavior. I was a dead giveaway. He approached me, smiled, and said "It is beautiful, isn't it?" I looked at him and smiled. His tie was overpowering, He must have noticed my expression when I looked at it. I told him curtly that I just wanted to sit alone and picture how great this set would be in my home. In other words, I told him to leave me alone with my thoughts.

He was extremely accommodating, and that made me look at him and say, "Look, if I purchase this it will be through you. Leave me your card. I know I will have some questions. I am very interested." He handed me his card and left. I continued to look over the set. I was so impressed with the china cabinet. I had stored my grandmother's dishes in cardboard boxes for so long, and now I would have the opportunity to display them along with all the other things I had tenderly saved. I could finally unpack the Wedgewood pieces Tony had bought me throughout the years. I had a small china cabinet now, and this china cabinet would take up a whole wall in the dining room, allowing me to display so many pretty things. I wanted this. Finally I approached the salesman and told him I was very interested. I asked a few questions and then asked if I could put a deposit on the set. I told him I would need it delivered before Christmas. I wanted my husband's opinion, but I also wanted to secure this set. I knew in my heart I would be so disappointed if someone else purchased it. I didn't want to lose it. I gave him a one-hundred-dollar deposit, and he told me I had one week to make my decision. I left the store. I got a huge coffee at a little cafe and danced my way towards the car. It was amazing how good I felt when I shopped.

When I got home, I told Tony that I wanted him to stop by the furniture store and give me his opinion. "No problem," he said, "I'll go look at it."

I said, "I want to go with you."

He said, "I think I would rather like to talk to the salesman alone. Look, if this is what you want, and the price is reasonable, you can have it."

Oh my God, I thought, *the price, I never asked the price. What a ditz! What is the matter with me?* I was being punished for all the times I had made fun of men and their love affairs with their boats. I had to call the salesman and ask the price, but I had given the card to Tony. I waited till Tony left and then nervously called the store. A very pleasant voice answered on the other end. I told her my dilemma. I described the salesman. I said, "The man I spoke to was about five feet, eight inches tall. He had horn-rimmed glasses and wore a very vibrant tie."

The lady on the other end of the phone laughed. "What kind of a tie was it?"

I said, "A large, purple moon against stars. I am not making fun of the tie, but I found it rather gaudy. Please don't relate that to him, though." The person laughed again and told me she knew who it was and that he was known for his statements with ties. She mentioned that she also had a record of my deposit. Next to the deposit was a description of the dining room set and the salesman's name. She informed me that his name was Al Furber. Al came to the phone and asked if he could help me. I said, "Excuse me, but I was so taken aback by the dining room set that I forget to ask the price." He laughed and told me there was a tag on the table displaying the price of the table, chairs, buffet, and china cabinet. The whole set was five thousand dollars. However, if I wanted two additional chairs it would cost more. The set was priced for eight chairs.

I replied, "Thank you, Mr. Furber." I hung up the phone. I then said a prayer for the saint that represented furniture to grant me this wish. I wanted the set and the eight chairs. I think the saint was St. Joseph; after all he was a carpenter.

Chapter 18

A Disturbing Lunch

I RECEIVED A CALL FROM PAT. "Let's do lunch at the club," she said.

"Pat, I can't wait to tell you about the new dining room set I am getting."

Pat said, "Does this mean lunch?"

I laughed—I was just so excited. "Yes, it means lunch."

"Okay," Pat said, "see you soon." As I drove towards the club, I couldn't stop thinking about how I would arrange the new set in my dining room. I couldn't wait to describe the new set to Pat. I hoped I was not counting my chickens before they hatched. When I arrived at the club, Pat is sitting at a nice table outside overlooking the ocean.

"Pat," I blurted out, "I am finally going to have a new dining room set."

Pat laughed. "Let's hear all about it. I have never seen you so excited over furniture."

"Pat, it is not just furniture. It is creating an environment that places many different people around a table, and that table induces conversation. Remember, Pat, I told you if I ever opened up a restaurant I would call it 'La Tabbala.' It would mean friends and family around a table, conversing."

Pat started to laugh harder. "I love you, and I love your enthusiasm, so tell me all about your new set." I didn't tell Pat about the circumstances surrounding the dining room set. I left out Tony's desire to put up fight money that he borrowed from our savings. I didn't even know if Pat was aware of the upcoming fights. I just concentrated on that beautiful oak set.

"Pat," I rambled on, "the china cabinet fits on one whole wall. I can put all the things I have been saving along with my grandmother's dishes into it. I can sit eight people around the table and even more without an extension." I just kept going on and on until I realized that Pat was absorbing my words like a sponge but wasn't commenting or asking any questions. I felt that I had become overbearing, so I decided to take a pause. Pat was very quiet. I said, "Pat, am I boring you?"

"No," she replied, "don't be silly. It is just that I have something to show you, and I am having a tough time with it. I feel like I am raining on your parade by showing you this."

"Pat, nothing can rain on my parade." Then she handed me an article. It was a newspaper clipping. I read it and immediately felt woozy. My eyes became all watery, and I felt like someone had lifted my head off and let everything that held me together pour out. I had now become a rag mop, something one could sweep the floor with. I didn't think it was possible to go from ecstatic to deep depression in only a few minutes. But it was possible. I reread the article out loud. "A young girl was killed, struck down by a truck driver. She was on a ten-speed bike delivering crochet goods to a consignment store. No one knows her real name. The woman who owned the trailer where this young girl lived reported her missing. The woman was asked to identify the body. The woman identified the body as 'Jill.' She gave her first name only. If anyone has any information regarding 'Jill,' please contact Sergeant Berry." I stopped reading and dropped the clipping to the table. A waitress approached us, and before she had a chance to ask us for our order I told her I had changed my mind on lunch and that a glass of water would be appreciated. Pat agreed with me. We had lost our appetite.

I said, "Pat, where did you get this article?"

Pat said, "It was sent to Paul Adler. The woman in the trailer park found Paul's address and sent it to him, hoping he could shed some light on the subject. It seems Jill was taking care of this woman, who is a paraplegic; in turn she had a place to stay. The woman said Jill was so sweet and meticulous that she never asked her too many questions for fear of losing her. The woman mentioned how hard it had been to get someone who would care for a paraplegic. The woman also told Paul that she assumed Jill was a runaway. This poor woman was just so happy to have some companionship that she accepted Jill with open arms."

I choked up a question, "Why did Paul give it to you, Pat?"

Pat said, "Because Paul knew you liked her. He knew you tried to help her. He also feels you hate him. Paul feels you blame him for interfering with Jill and George. At least, that is what he related to me." Then Pat looked at me and asked, "Is Paul right? Is that how you feel? Paul also thought maybe you knew more about Jill's past."

I said, "Excuse me; I have to go to the ladies room." I barely made it to the ladies room, where I entered one of the stalls and broke down in tears. Maybe if I had minded my own business Jill would be alive. I didn't want to move from the ladies room. I must have been in there awhile, lost in my thoughts, because Pat started banging on the door.

"Please come out," she kept saying, but I didn't want to. I just thought of those doe eyes and the fate that met her. Finally I merged from the bathroom. I gave Pat no explanation. I just told her I was tired and sad. I also told her I needed to get home to make dinner. I mentioned my mom was coming over. Pat just stood there stupefied. She then looked at me and said, "No problem." I left.

When I got back, Tony was sitting in our kitchen. "Hi, hon. I went to see the salesman regarding the dining room set. I approve— it is super, and for Christmas it will be yours." I guessed we all had priorities. If I could bring Jill back, screw the dining room set. So therefore the excitement that Tony expected was instead a half-assed smile. I then proceeded to tell him the news that Pat had brought me. His reaction was awful. "Well, what do you expect?" he said. "She ran around with undesirables; she was a whore. If you live by the sword you die by the sword."

I looked at him with all the anger I could muster up. I said, "You didn't even know her."

He said, "And you did?"

"More than you," I replied.

He said, "I just came home with good news about something that you have wanted for a long time, and this tramp, which unfortu-nately had a terrible fate, is ruining it."

I said "Tramp, Tony?"

He said, "Yes, tramp." I then turned around and went out for a walk. All of a sudden I needed some fresh air.

I walked about two blocks, and then I headed back toward home. There was nothing I could do—Jill was dead. Tony was right in one small way. I really did not know that much about her. I did know that there was a lot of good in her. Someone had to bring it out in her. She had been on the road to a better life. I had to believe that. I believed in second chances. Not everyone in life was born in a loving environment. Jill was dragged up. Tony was brought up. Tony disappointed me in his thinking. I had thought better of my husband.

On my way back, I noticed a man with his head down holding a peace sign. It was Tony. "I am so sorry, hon. I know you liked her. Pat called to see how you were, and she read me the article. I feel like such a fool. Maybe you're right, and she was trying to turn her life around. Maybe you helped her in a way."

I said, "Tony, I need you to believe that. I thought all these years that you were sensitive towards people. What made you say such harsh, burning words about her? I didn't even think you knew her well.

"Gossip," he said.

"You believe in gossip, Tony?"

He looked at me and said, "The source was pretty reliable.

"Oh, Paul Adler?" I said.

Tony looked at me and said, "Paul Adler never said a word about Jill. In fact, rumor had it he was in love with her."

I said, "Paul Adler in love with Jill?"

Tony said, "Hon, that's why he gave her money to go back home. Paul really wanted Jill to stay here. He even offered to help her. He asked her if she wanted to go back to school. He even asked her if she wanted to take classes in something that could improve her career, but she wanted to go back to Texas. She kept saying she wanted a fresh, clean start like a white christening dress. When Paul told me this I was surprised. I told him she was not his answer. First, she was too young for him. Second, he was used to a different type of woman, and Jill was far from the likes of Paul's wife. Anyway I left it with him.

He is a big boy and he has to make his decision on what is best for him."

I looked at Tony and said, "How come you never told me any of this?"

He commented simply, "Paul told me and I didn't think it was open for discussion. I also had the gossip from a couple of other members about Jill that was rattling in my brain. I just didn't think it was worth talking about." He then said, "I promise I will never speak of anyone so harshly again until I have all the facts." Then he looked at me. "Truce? I need a second chance."

I smiled and said, "I believe in second chances."

Chapter 19

Labor Day Came and Went

THE REAR COMMODORE HAD A GREAT float party, and a lot of children were there to celebrate their last free weekend before school started. Our children and all the older teenagers were heavily involved in themselves. I found that they needed me less, listened to me less, and felt the less I was around the better. So just to spite them I hung around more, talked more, and showed up more. Let's face it—teenage years were serious years. If teenagers made it to twenty-one without a drugs, drinking, or sexual endeavors that led to problems, there might be a chance. So I *demanded* they come for this weekend. "Bring a friend," I told them, so of course they brought many. But I didn't care—I knew where they were. The boys liked to play pool, so that was great, and the girls, well, they liked to sit up on the bow of the boat and catch the last rays of summer. Besides, the children were proud of their dad's promotion Thru the Chairs, and he was quite impressive in his Commodore's uniform. It was nice to show him off to their friends.

The big topic opened for a lot of discussion on the floats was the upcoming fights. Both these fights would now be in September. Tony and his officers announced to the members at the last meeting what their intentions were regarding bringing the fights via satellite to the club. Tony told me after the meeting that there had been a positive response from the majority of members. The Rear Commodore, Sam, got a professional printing company to create flyers that would be distributed all around the club, city, and neighboring areas to promote this spectacular event.

I didn't know much about fighting. I particularly didn't enjoy watching people getting themselves beaten up. But I was a small minority, and when it came to this sport Tony was excited. Judging by the hype down on the floats, these fights were going to be sold out. That made me happy, for after all I had already spent the returned money. I lifted my glass of wine and toasted to Tony. "To the fights."

He smiled back at me and said, "You mean to the dining room set."

I laughed. "Whatever!"

THE WEEK PROCEEDED, AND SOME OF the boats were removed from the floats and shrink wrapped for the winter. A lot of people, though, boated into early November. We called them the brave ones. They were fearless of hurricanes and early snow storms that could cripple a city, never mind a yacht club. Our boat was among the boats that were destined for an early retirement because other than sitting on the boat while it was docked, I was not anxious at all to go out on the high sea after our experience in the fog. That episode left me frightened. Tony thought it would pass, but up till now I was still apprehensive when it came to traveling by boat. This was hurricane season and I wanted to be on land. I guessed I had just lost my desire. This was probably why Tony had the boat pulled. He figured that in the spring I would be ready for the high seas again.

I hadn't seen much of Pat recently. I thought she was confused over my over reaction to Jill's death. We were close friends, and maybe she felt I was holding back something. I guessed we were close friends because she was right—I was. I just felt that at this point nothing good could come of what Jill had told me. Jill was dead, and may she rest in peace. My real reason for not calling Pat was, to be honest, that I was really throwing myself into a dining room makeover. Remember the story about the woman who purchased a new lamp for her bedroom? When she placed it on the table, the table looked shabby so she purchased a new table. The lamp and table looked so great, but the rug underneath looked so worn that it just wouldn't do, etc, etc. The color of my dining room was wrong; it would never match the new set. I decided to get some paint that I thought might uplift the room.

I took the paint chip to the furniture store to see how the fabric on the chairs would look with this new color. The fabric looked great. I now had a new dilemma; the drapes would never go along with my new paint makeover. This was becoming a project. I now fully understood the story of the lady and the lamp. I was, I had to admit, truly enjoying my new project, so I kind of slipped out of the yacht club rostra of information. I was redecorating!

Chapter 20

The Fights

ALL I COULD SAY ON THE subject of the fights was that I stayed away from the club on both occasions. Tony's description of these events was described in one word: "Dynamic!" He was so excited over the response that when he described it to me he was rambling the same way I rambled to Pat about my set. So I listened as he said, "Hon, the place was sold out, even the standing-room only section. If the club was larger we could have sold more tickets. Sam was unbelievable. He worked so hard trying to accommodate the barrage of orders. The galley could not cook enough sausages, hamburgers, or hot dogs to feed the crowds of people there. Sam summoned his wife, and Dot quickly arrived with platters of cold cuts. Dot had to replenish these platters ten times over. I have to tell you, hon—Dot is a real professional. The way she handled the crowd was great. You know how boisterous people can get in these situations. Dot had a way about her that calmed people down."

I said, "It must be her dictatorship ways."

Tony smiled. "That's not fair. I just think that she has a way of demanding respect, and she does know how to work a crowd. Dot is a businessperson."

I smiled back. "Yes, she is, and I am glad it all worked out." There was a profit. I was not to be privy to the amount though. If I or any of the ladies ran a function, we knew the profit. This function and its detailed expenses were privy only to the officers. I had to remember I was not a member. However, the club was in a positive rather than negative position if the upcoming assessment went through. I asked Tony, "Tell me—where there any problems?"

He laughed and said, "Just one small adventure that involved George. George decided to climb the flagpole."

"Well," I said, "that's not so bad."

Tony chuckled, "Hon, he stripped down to his skivvies There he stood hanging on to the top of the flagpole singing, 'God Bless America.'"

"Tony, what did you do? How did you get him to come down?"

Tony said, "Are you ready for this? One of the firemen attending the fight had a small engine come over. They put the ladder up toward the flagpole and one of the firemen grabbed George. The funny part was in the process George's skivvies dropped. The crowd burst out laughing. George didn't care, he just kept singing."

I said, "Well, at least he is happy and over Jill."

Tony said, "Who knows whether he is happy or not? He was drunk. Maybe he was crying in his beer."

"What happened to him when they brought him down from the flagpole?"

Tony smirked. "George was disposed of in his sailboat. From what I heard, the boat was filthy with debris."

I interrupted, "That boat would never be in that condition if Jill was around."

Then Tony went on to say, "At one point I was told one of the members wanted to cut the sailboat loose and send George adrift. Naturally I quickly axed this idea, not because I didn't want to get rid of George but because of the consequences it would create. I told some of these members that in a month or so the *Rusty Scupper* would be gone, and George with it."

I laughed. "There is always drama at the club."

Tony said, "Hon, every club, no matter what kind, has drama as long as it has people. Life is drama. Children are drama. Anyone who doesn't experience drama isn't experiencing life."

THAT WEEK I WAS SO BUSY involved in my dining room makeover that I was really oblivious to everything Tony and the club was involved with. Then I got a call from Dot asking if I would help out at the Halloween dance. It was a few weeks away, and she was having a meeting to discuss the event. I agreed and checked off the date. I then anxiously went back to my project. Tony had pushed up the delivery of the dining room set to November so we could celebrate Thanksgiving in our new, renovated dining room. *Yes,* I thought, *what a day to celebrate my new set. A day to be thankful is very appropriate.*

Chapter 21

Dot's Meeting

THE MEETING WAS GREAT. IT WAS more like a reunion. Pat and Mary were there, and it was so nice to be with my friends. I had really forgotten how much fun we had when we were all together. Dot kept the plans simple for the upcoming dance. Dried leaves would be put in ceramic pumpkins for the centerpieces. Pat said to me, "Do you think Dot is afraid of another stabbing?"

I laughed, "Well, I think Dot is smart to eliminate carving utensils." We both chuckled silently. Dot continued with her plan. Instead of a band, a DJ from the club had volunteered his service. Colors would be orange and black—how appropriate. However, guests had to be in costume. This, in my opinion, could create a problem. We had a lot of macho men who hated to dress up. They would either come in their officer's attire or fisherman attire. Anyway, it was Dot's call. She wanted to raffle off a fruit basket, and my and Pat's job would be to sell raffle tickets. This was Dot's command. Dot knew what she wanted and was also very convincing in getting her way, as Tony had reminded me when we discussed the fights and how she had handled herself. She was the Rear Commodore's wife, and this was her opportunity to handle this affair her way. The plan was set. We all agreed, as if we had a choice.

For the rest of the evening we just gabbed and gossiped like groups of ladies do. Pat asked me, "Have you heard from Paul Adler?"

I said, "Why?"

"Well," Pat wondered, "I was just curious if Paul had found out any more information on Jill."

I said, "Pat, Jill is dead. I feel awful about it, but life goes on. Jill was on a crash course, a real train wreck. The sad part was she finally was trying to change. Jill was looking for that second chance. Unfortunately for her she never achieved it. I hope she is happier in the next life. Paul Adler certainly didn't add to her happiness."

Pat said, "Why would you say that?" I then realized I had said too much. Pat continued, "I thought Paul helped get her a ticket back to Texas. Or did he help her to go back to someone in her past that she might have been close with? Maybe he helped her to be with whoever took care of her when she was young?"

I said, "Pat, look, I really don't want to go into this, but I just never took to Paul, it is as simple as that." But Pat wouldn't stop with the questions.

"Listen," Pat said, "Paul had a tough time with his wife being so sick all those years, and I think it was very noble of him to help Jill. Paul has no one really, other than a distant brother."

"Fine, Pat," I said, "Paul Adler is noble. Now do you feel better that I agree with you?" Pat gave me such a painstaking expression. Her eyes were almost watering. Understand that Pat and I rarely had arguments. This conversation, I was beginning to realize, was about to turn into an argument if I wasn't careful on how I handled Pat's inquisition.

"Don't you dare placate me," Pat roared. Then Pat looked me straight in the face and firmly replied, "Something has your Irish up with Paul. I have been your friend for a long time, and I know when you're not telling me something. I just know."

"Pat, please let it rest." I tried to stay calm as I spoke. "First, Pat, I am not Irish. Second, I want to answer your questions but in doing so I might break a confidence." I realized when I looked up at Pat that she had a hurt look. I then tried as best I could to explain as little as possible. "You see, you and I have been close friends for years. One of the main reasons we are so close is that we try very hard not to betray each other. We have confided in each other for years. I know, Pat, if I ask you not to repeat something that you will go to your grave with that information. Therefore just try to understand that if I am not giving you the information you want it is because I have been confided in." Pat smiled, which surprised me, and then she came over to me and gave me a big hug. I needed this hug.

She looked at me and said sincerely, "Forgive me for not realizing why you are my friend. I am sure if you could tell me why you don't care for Paul you would. Let's just drop this conversation."

"Good idea," I said. "I don't know about you, but I am ready for a nice glass of chardonnay." We both ordered a glass of wine and toasted to friendship.

Mary came over and said, "What was going on with the two of you?"

I said, "What do you mean?"

Mary laughed and replied, "Well, it was obvious to the rest of us girls at the meeting that you two were in a heated conversation. I thought it best to not interrupt you. Actually, I was afraid for a moment that one of you would storm out of the building."

Pat laughed. "Whatever gave you that impression, Mary?"

"Well, first of all, girls," Mary said, "don't try to kid me. Pat looked like she lost her best friend, and you," she said as she pointed to me, "looked like you were in a predicament you couldn't handle."

"Mary, Mary," I commented. "You have great insight. Pat and I are friends and we worked it out."

Mary said, "It is a good thing you did because that is what I told Dot when she questioned me. She asked me what you two ladies were up to. I told the inquiring mind not to worry and that you were good friends solving a problem. So, my friends, did you solve the problem?"

Pat said, "Let's just say we put it to rest."

Chapter 22

The Halloween Dance

I FINALLY CONVINCED TONY TO DRESS up in costume, but he said he would agree only if he could pick the costume. He went as Dracula. I went as a Playboy Bunny. However, I had pink, footed pajamas, a large cotton tail, and the fluffiest long ears imaginable. Pat painted my face with huge white circles on each cheek. Then she took black eye pencil and made little dots on the white circles. My whiskers were thin black pieces of pipe cleaners stuck on with glue, which Pat assured me would eventually come off. I hope so, otherwise I was circus material. I was told I looked more like the Energizer battery bunny on the TV ads. That was a far cry from a Playboy Bunny.

Pat was a gypsy. She had found a Spanish purple gown at a used vintage store. Then clever Pat bought a piece of black lace and made a mantilla for her head. Pat's husband Bob, who rarely came to the club, decided that he would make an appearance as a pirate. Bob was a very shy, quiet man who socialized on occasion with Tony and I. Tony and I often commented on how lucky Bob was to marry Pat. Pat was the total opposite of her husband. Pat accompanied Tony, Mary, Jim, and I many times without Bob. Bob loved curling up in his den and watching TV. We were overjoyed when Pat told us he was coming to the Halloween party.

We were now all having a great time, sitting together and laughing. The table looked so festive with the fall leaves cascading over the bright orange ceramic pumpkin that sat directly in the center of all of us. The party seemed to be going smoothly. Mary and I sold some raffle tickets as promised. The DJ played Frank Sinatra and Tony Bennett tunes. It was quite comical to see devils, angels, movie stars, and other people dressed up in fun costumes performing on the dance floor. Tony and I snuck in a dance. I had to say I actually enjoyed getting bitten on the neck by Dracula. The only drawback was that when Tony kissed my face, or should I say *bit* my face, he ended up with my whiskers. We enjoyed our friends, but in all honesty the costumes were starting to irritate us and we opted for an early night. Both Tony and I couldn't wait to go home and take the silly attire off. We said our farewells and departed for the parking lot.

At first we thought we heard a whimper like someone was crying, but then it got louder and louder with the sounds of trash cans falling over. Tony then ran ahead of me towards the noise in the parking lot. I finally caught up to Tony, and we found Paul Adler and George in a brawl. They were rolling around together, with George yelling at Paul. George's voice was loud, and it was hard to understand him. I sensed he had been drinking because his words were blending into one another. George kept repeating, "You got rid a did of her you got rid a did of Jill a Jill." Paul could barely be heard. George was getting the best of Paul in his wrestling.

Paul kept mumbling, "The reason she left was over you George. You were a bastard, George, face it." With that Tony intervened.

"Look," Tony said, "I don't know what you are fighting over but if you want to kill each other do it off the club premises. Now both of you get the hell out of here." I had never seen Tony so impatient. Tony was so belligerent towards both of them. Paul headed back to his car with a swollen mouth. Paul turned around before he got into his car and looked at Tony quizzically. I then wondered if he realized that Tony was Dracula. George was more defiant than ever. Tony said, "You keep it up, and I'll get the police here in one second, George." George was already inebriated; Tony advised George to head down to his sailboat and sleep it off. George was limping, but it was hard to tell if it was from the skirmish with Paul or from the condition his condition was in. A couple of members were departing from the dance, and they saw that Tony was all flustered. They asked what the problem was. Tony just looked at George and said it was nothing. Tony then addressed a couple of members standing by, saying, "George had too much to drink. Maybe some of you can give me a hand and get him back to his boat." George, at this point knowing he was outnumbered, succumbed to Tony's wishes.

When Tony and I finally got in the car to head home, I said "Gee, Tony, I have never seen you so angry."

He said, "Hon, I waited a long time to be Commodore. No one is getting killed on my watch." Then he said, "I wanted this position so bad, but you know what? Now that I am here it is not all it was cracked up to be."

I said, "what do you mean?"

"Well," he said, "Part of the fun was working so hard to get here. You and I and our friends working hard together on the floats was so much fun. All our pals from other clubs working along with us during all those visitations were such special times. I guess what I am trying to say is that I'm a hands-on man, and this Commodore position is the pencil-pushing part of the chairs. It's behind the scenes with political aspirations of getting into town politics. I guess I am just a working man who loves his wife, family, and friends. Hon, I am sorry I dragged you through this."

"Tony, I would not have missed being a part of your life for one minute. I will agree this year was not as great as the past two, but the fact that you have worked hard with the club to secure the future of the club means a lot. Our time will pass, but the younger generations will continue to have the fun that we had, and that is all we can really ask for. I will agree that at first I felt left out at times. I guess that is natural for anyone who has a wife or husband in office; however, when all is said and done, some of my best memories will be of my friends and me planning some of the most memorable events. Next year you will be retired from your position here, Tony. Do you intend to carry on with the Commodores of America?"

He took awhile to answer, and then he said, "I guess I'll have to think about it, hon. I know one thing—I love you—and maybe three years is enough. In the meantime I am trying to figure out what the hell Paul and George were fighting about. Do you have any idea?"

I took a deep breath and said, "We have had enough talk tonight. Let's just call it a night."

"Fine with me," Tony said.

Chapter 23

Time for Me to Make a Decision

AFTER THE OTHER NIGHT, I REALIZED that Tony's position as Commodore of the club was slowly coming to an end. I now had to decide what gift I would present to the club. I would have to have a meeting with the gals who helped me throughout the three years. I had money saved for a gift to the club, and I needed some feedback on what gift would be appropriate. I was pretty sure we were getting a canopy for the front entrance, something in navy canvas with the club's name lettered in white and the burgee painted in red, white, and blue. Of course this would never replace the burgee Mary had made, which by the way was still unaccounted for. I thought that with all the weddings and gala events that a canopy would be nice to have. That way when people pulled up to the front door they would be protected from some of New England's nasty weather. The winds blowing offshore in the fall sometimes were of hurricane force, and ironically fall was a big time for weddings. I could picture a red carpet being rolled out to the limousine for the new bride and bridal party to walk on. How elegant this would all look.

I called Pat and ran this idea by her. We had talked about doing something like this prior. Pat was in total agreement, but any excuse to get all the girls together was something we all loved, and naturally their opinion was very important to me. So Pat said she would call them for me because she knew I was busy with the completion of the dining room. All that was needed was the furniture. It would be arriving any day now.

Chapter 24

The Meeting and the Furniture All in One Day

WE WERE MEETING AT THE CLUB for lunch, and the furniture store called the night before to arrange delivery. Of course, as with all deliveries they told me, "We will be there between ten and four." I begged them to be more specific, but it was useless. Tony had recently taken a foreman's position down in the area of Cape Cod. Tony was staying over a few days during the middle of the week because the drive was horrendous with evening traffic. The children were in school. The only one who could meet the furniture truck was me. My mom was getting on in age, and strangers frightened her. I didn't dare ask her to help me on this occasion, so I would have to be the designated furniture greeter. Then I had a brainstorm—I would call Pat and have her pick up lunch at a cute restaurant I liked. This would be my treat. This way I could kill two birds with one stone, as the saying went. My house would have to be the place for lunch and the meeting.

When the girls finally arrived, they were so impressed with the color of the dining room and the drapes. Naturally, the furniture arrived exactly when we decided to have lunch, but no one complained. My friends were just as anxious as I to see it all together. They truly were happy for me, and they helped arrange and fix everything until the room was a showpiece. I looked at them and realized that this was what Tony missed; he put himself in a position that eliminated a lot of the people who had helped him achieve his dream.

I went downstairs and got a bottle of champagne. I was going to celebrate my first time in the new dining room with my friends. And if Tony called to see if the furniture had arrived, he would hear champagne bubbleheads celebrating and laughing. This was exactly what a dining room was supposed to do.

We toasted the dining room, friendship, and family. I then figured I should bring up the subject of the canopy for the front entrance of the club, but before I could complete the sentence Pat seconded the motion and Mary completed the decision. The other gals must have had some idea through Pat because they just toasted their champagne glasses in agreement. It was a wrap. Before they left, they presented me with two gorgeous brass candlesticks. I was very surprised. They said that when I lit them I would remember them and all the good times we shared. It was important that when I blew out the candles that I made a wish for our friendship to continue throughout the years. I was taken aback; I actually felt a few tears start to form in my eyes. We had three years of close camaraderie Thru the Chairs even though we were not members. We were all friends and hoped we would be till the end.

TONY RETURNED AT THE END OF the week, and we had a romantic dinner in, you guessed it, the dining room. Tony was very impressed with our new surroundings. He looked at me and said, "Thanks for believing in me," and then he laughed. He said, "Hon, if anything had gone wrong with the fights I was afraid you would put an anchor around my neck and drop me in the ocean."

I said, "Tony, you did a good thing for the club. You and your friends invested in the club's future. I only hope it is appreciated." Then Tony told me how he was very into his new job on the Cape. He said that it might be time for us to buy a little place there where we could summer.

I said, "What about the club?"

He said "Hon, we can always go to the club, but this is an investment for our future." Tony seemed very excited as he explained where he was working and how nice the area was away from the bustling city. I promised that I would take a look at the area and have an open mind. I was a city girl. I was used to stores, movies, and restaurants all at my fingertips; the Cape sounded to me like another country. I did not want to rain on Tony's excitement, especially since he was working there. I was glad he liked his working conditions. I wasn't so sure about making the Cape a permanent home. We didn't talk about it any further, and I just rambled on and on about the luncheon with the girls and how much fun they all were. I thought to myself that if I went to the Cape I would be giving up my friends in the summer.

Chapter 25

The Cape Trip

IT WAS A COLD DAY IN November. Tony was scheduled to do a one-day stay on the Cape. The working crew that Tony was in charge of was in the process of closing in the condos for the winter. The project was all framed, and the windows were in. The project would not resume until the electrical work was complete. New England weather during this time of year made it impossible to work unless workers had access to heat. Once the electricians completed the electrical work and the building inspector approved it, then Tony and his crew could continue with the project. Until then the weather was getting cold, and working conditions were hard. The nights were dark now, and electricity was badly needed just to see what one was doing. In New England it started to get dark between four and four-thirty. Tony decided that since he was only spending one night at the cape, it would be a good idea for me to join him and keep him company during the ride down. I knew Tony wanted to show me the area that he was getting attached to.

When he saw the expression on my face, he quickly said, "Hey, hon, there is a small mall in the area where you could go shopping and get a start on Christmas. Then at night I would like to take you for dinner to this cute bistro I saw in the area. What do you think?"

I thought to myself, *Talk about brownnosing me*, but I just said, "I promised you I would have an open mind, so I will go with you." I looked at my husband and knew just by the expression on his face that this was the start of convincing me that it was time for us to change our summer quarters. The ride down to the Cape would be nothing but Tony persuading me to agree to what he wanted. I knew Tony wanted Cape Cod. I just said nonchalantly, "Okay."

The ride was about an hour and a half long. It was a cold, clear day, and I could see all the cranberries waiting to be picked for the big turkey-day celebrations. There were many bogs and cranberry pickers frantically filling containers. It was a scene sometimes us New Englanders took for granted. The bright, vibrant, dark red cranberries sat straight up like shiny red marbles waiting to be plucked. This scene was contrasted by patches of frost—it looked like someone took a giant salt shaker and sprinkled all the bogs. Picture this setting against a silver gray sky. It was a sight to behold. I was glad I had brought my camera and said, "Tony, you have to pull over so I can capture this fabulous scene." I knew he would agree. Let's face it—today I could get anything I wanted as long as I kept a positive attitude towards Tony's desire for the Cape.

He immediately pulled the car off the highway into the break down lane and said, "Take your time, hon, this is a beautiful cape scene." I made a mental note on how he emphasized the word "Cape." I got out of the car. There were acres and acres of berries against the blue winter sky. When the sun shone on them they looked like bright red ruby crystals. My hands could not stop taking one picture after another. I must have shot a half a roll of film.

When I got back in the car, Tony was laughing. I said, "What is so funny?"

He said, "It is nice to see you so excited about that scene. You couldn't take your hands off the camera. I was afraid that the cold air had made your fingers stick to the click button." I laughed too.

"You're right," I said. "Scenes like these should never be taken for granted. Thank goodness I decided to take my camera."

We finally arrived at the project Tony was working on. I stayed in the car because the air was a different cold. It was a damp cold that went through my bones and took my breath away. I was still cold from all my photography, and the heat of the car gave me great comfort. Tony spent about a half hour at the project. He then came back and said, "Hon, I am going to drop you off at a nearby mall. I have to spend a little more time here than planned."

"Tony," I said "I hope the mall is enclosed."

He laughed. "Hon, it is still modernized here on the Cape." I asked him how the project was going and he replied, "Well, there is one more electrician I have to talk to, but it shouldn't take long. You have about an hour to do some holiday shopping." We arrived at a small, enclosed mall. There were a few specialty stores and a well-known food chain on the premises. I did notice a bookstore, and at that point I knew I could get lost in the mystery section. When Tony dropped me off he said, "Do you need any money?" This was my day to get what I wanted.

I said, "I can always use a bit extra." Tony handed me more than expected, and like any normal wife I took it. We agreed on meeting in an hour in front of the bookstore. I approached a few specialty stores and did find a couple of cute kitchen gadgets that would be nice holiday gifts. I loved the bookstore and decided it was where I wanted to concentrate my efforts. I definitely got lost in all the different novels and must have forgotten the time, for when I looked up Tony was standing in front of me. "Having fun on the Cape?" he asked. I made the second mental note on Tony sneaking the word Cape into his remarks.

"Tony, you know I love bookstores." With that I made my purchases and we left. That night we enjoyed the bistro, and Tony and I limited our conversation to our family.

The next morning we returned for a short time to Tony's project. Once he felt everything was going smoothly, we embarked on the real mission. This was what Tony couldn't wait to show me. When our car pulled up to a vacant lot, Tony jumped out of the car and said, "This is a special parcel of land." I got out of the car. I was breathless, partially because it was cold and partially because I knew Tony had a new mistress. It was not the loran anymore but this piece of land on the water in this small bay completely surrounded by oak and beech trees. It was like a mermaid had come up from the ocean and mesmerized my husband. I knew no matter what I said Tony was going to buy this property. He looked deep into my frozen face and asked, "What do you think, hon?"

I said, "I'm breathless." What else could I say? Of course I meant from the cold.

He grabbed me and said, "I knew you would like it; I put a deposit on it."

I said, "*What?*"

He said, "Don't you like it?" I held back my first impulse, which was murder. I was trying to understand why Tony would put a deposit on this property without discussing it with me. I decided not to use the panic approach.

"Of course I like it," I said through gritted teeth, "but I think we should discuss it."

"What's there to discuss?" he said. Now, I was trying to be logical, although we were in no-man's land and I might have a chance to get away with murder. However, the logical approach might be best, and I tried to recall the fact that I myself put a deposit down on furniture. However, we had agreed that a dining room set would be purchased. Tony and I had no agreement or conversation about a Cape lot.

I got my composure back and said, "Well, first of all we have one child entering college and two in high school. I certainly do not want to start pinching pennies at our age."

Tony's voice raised two octaves higher as he said, "This is our dream! We have to do it while I am still working and active and in the business of building. I have connections in the building material business today, and I don't know if I will have those connections tomorrow." Let me tell you, as a wife I could have come up with a million reasons, but I knew Tony's rebuttal would go on and on. The bottom line was Tony was going to do this; this was not something I was going to overcome. Tony was shaking his head like a child who just found out he lost the race.

I switched gears and said, "Listen, why don't we talk about it somewhere warm." A new strategy now was about to take place. Tony then took my hand and led me to the edge of the bay. The water was an icy blue, white peaks showed on each wave as they approached the shoreline. There were broken pieces of shell that sparkled as the water splashed over them. In the distance birds were diving in the water and coming up with small clams that eventually they would drop on the sand and crack open. In one huge gulp, the birds would devour these tasty delicacies.

"Did you know that you can eat these clams raw? The birds do," Tony informed me. Tony then pointed out where he could put a mooring for his boat. Then Tony said the oddest thing: "I am just going to get a small boat to putt around in. I know, Hon, your days are numbered with the big boat." He knew he hit on a nerve. Ever since that awful experience in the fog, I really had very little desire to go out on the high seas. Tony could tell by my expression that this was a topic he could work on to get his way. "Let's face it, hon, you're still jittery after the fog experience." I didn't say anything—he was right. I was still on edge over that experience. Then he pulled out the ace. He laughed as he said, "Merry Christmas, babes, this is your new summer home! You had so much fun doing over the dining room. Imagine how much of a project this will be." Then he stated, "Start looking at plans for a small cottage." Before I could say a word, he grabbed me and kissed me. We kissed with two cold noses rubbing together. Somehow all I could feel was I was losing this battle. I thought about our friends. Tony must have sensed some apprehension. "Our friends will visit us, hon. Build it and they will come!" I became very quiet. Tony kept rambling on and on and on, and I kept telling myself that he would change his mind. I knew in my heart our course had been charted and this was the direction, like it or not, I was going in.

WHEN WE ARRIVED HOME I WAS exhausted. Part of me was tired from the ride, and the other part was mentally beat up. I went over to my mom's and asked her if she could give me some advice. She was older now, and I could see the fragility in her face. I began to feel that I shouldn't burden her with the Cape situation, but like all mothers she sensed that something was bothering me. She said, "What's wrong?" I told her what Tony had done. My mom was very surprised that he took the liberty to put a deposit on a property the two of us had not agreed on. Then she said the oddest thing: "You know, there are many types of men. There are the womanizers. There are the gamblers. There are the workaholics. There are the family men. What do you consider Tony?"

I laughed. "Ma, not the perfect man if that is what you want to hear."

"I will repeat my question, daughter. What do you consider Tony?"

"I guess he is a family man." My mom informed me that knowing

Tony all these years, she had never known him to put us in harm's way. The fact that he wanted to improve our life was a good thing.

Then she said, "Be honest with me—did you like the land?"

I said, "Mom, it was beautiful. The little beach with sand and wildlife was intoxicating. I just don't know if I am cut out for living in that area. I love my friends. What if the children don't want to come? What about you, Mom, will you come?"

My mom put her arms around me and said, "Your life is with your husband. Your children will come and go. They will leave the nest, and if you do not plant good seeds so will your husband. This is a good thing he is doing. Embrace it and have fun with it, daughter." I gave my mom a hug and informed her that I would try.

That night I heard Tony telling the children what we did on the Cape. What *we* did; he should tell them what *he* did. The children were positive. Naturally, when Mom and Dad are out of town and far away, the kids do play!

Chapter 26

Tony's Final Days as Commodore

DECEMBER WAS TONY'S LAST MONTH IN office. We wanted to go out with a bang. I had already ordered the canopy, which would be delivered for the Christmas dance. We would have large red ribbons on the poles with a banner that said, "Thanks for the memories. Our best, from the Commodore's wife and her crew." Tony would give his final speech, which he would revolve around the two fights, the profit, and the distribution of funds towards the new assessment. This would be one of his and his officers' contributions to the club that he hoped would be remembered for years to come. He would wish the club smooth sailing and thank them for the three years of opportunity that was given to him. Just like real politics, this was the final farewell speech.

The cold wintry days passed by. Tony was dividing his time between driving to the Cape and meetings at the club. Tony was beginning to show signs of fatigue. I could see that he was looking forward to less responsibility.

The farewell dance and party finally came. All Tony's rehearsing in front of the mirror paid off, and it all went according to Tony's and my plans. Ironically, there were no hitches. Past officers roasted Tony in a cute and comical fashion with lots of respect and integrity. I was extremely proud and yet quite sad to know we had cruised on our last big expedition. The waters around us would just be a puddle compared to the seas that had challenged Tony. The gift from me and my crew was very much appreciated. It actually graced the front of the club on Tony's last official night as Commodore. When Tony and I drove away, we glanced back at the club and the canopy and realized that a part of our life was over. I could honestly say I saw a tear in my husband's eye. Anyone who has achieved a high office for a long period of time knows the feeling of stepping down. Anyone who has taken the ride as I had with that person also knows the feeling that it's over. Tears, in this case, from both of us were justified.

Book 4

....

The Past Commodore

Chapter 1

The Cape House

DID TONY MENTION, "BUILD IT AND they will come?" By February of the new year, Tony had a foundation on the lot on the Cape. I had picked a three-bedroom cottage; it was actually two bedrooms downstairs with a huge loft above. This cottage was equipped to sleep ten uncomfortably and six to eight okay. There were two full baths and a half bath. I insisted on an outside shower, and Tony agreed. Tony felt it would be ready to occupy by spring. Of course, this meant if we didn't mind roughing it. Now that the dining room was done and christened during the holidays, it would not be that hard for me to take on this project. I was seeing my mom more, and with the children all so busy this gave her and me a project we could do together. Then I had the interest of my good friends Pat and Mary. First, Tony and I decided that we would concentrate on the basics. I was astonished that now Tony was asking my opinion on every detail. Some of the questions he was asking me were ridiculous. He would ask, "What kind of shingles do you want, hon? Do you want wood or asphalt?"

I would reply, "Tony, what looks good?"

He then would say, "If it's a Cape house we should use wood."

"Fine," I would reply. I thought Tony felt guilty about buying the property without asking me, and this was his way of saying, "Thank you for agreeing."

Then we had our first disagreement. There was no way Tony was going to win this argument. He said, "Oh, by the way, I am just going to install a builder's kitchen."

"What's a builder's kitchen, Tony?" I asked.

"A builder's kitchen is a small ell shape," Tony stated. "I will install basic oak cabinets, laminate countertops, an inexpensive dishwasher, a stove—"

"Stop right there," I demanded. I put my foot down with the stove and the cabinets. My days with my head in the oven cleaning a dirty stove were over. "Tony, you have gotten your way, and now it is my turn. This is what I want and need. I want a self-cleaning stove. I want strong maple cabinets that actually hold dishes. I don't want an ell shape kitchen unless I can have a small island in the middle. I love to cook, and the kitchen is my room." I couldn't believe how authoritarian I was. I must have picked it up from Pat. Pat would have been proud of me. Tony looked flabbergasted.

He then said, "Hon, I have never heard you so defiant."

I said, "Get used to it. I love you, but this is what I want. You convinced me to give it a try on the Cape. In order for me to give it a try, I need to have certain accommodations. The kitchen is important to me." Tony came over and gave me a kiss. This time I enjoyed it. I felt a small victory.

He smiled at me and said, "You will have your kitchen." We then discussed that a nice one-piece tile floor in the kitchen would be appropriate. My mom had an extra refrigerator that she was willing to donate. I laughed—we had told all our friends that all donations were accepted. In fact, Tony mentioned that my love of going to yard sales might come in handy. We needed dishes, pots, pans, etc. He said, "Call your pals and see what you can come up with." I thought this would be fun, though it might have to wait till warmer weather. But we could tackle it—I would ask Mary and Pat. I had something to look forward to with my friends.

Chapter 2

Tony's Tough Decision

I THOUGHT ABOUT OUR BOAT. I wondered what we would do with it. The boat was very large for the new summer residence on the Cape. It was a subject I thought about but wasn't ready to discuss with Tony. I felt when the time came Tony would be the one to bring the subject up because it was a subject I was staying away from. One morning when we were having a cup of coffee, Tony brought up the subject of *37 Park Ave.* I guessed it was the weather that put the idea to talk about the boat in his head. It was late March, one of those unexpectedly hot days. I knew that when those days took place after a cold New England winter boating fever started coming into play. Then Tony surprised me. He mentioned nonchalantly that he had offered our boat to the new Rear Commodore. At first I was confused and thought that during the week I must have missed a conversation. Did my husband previously discuss this matter with me? My mind was going faster than I could keep up with. I knew I was about to explode. I turned to Tony and not yelled but screamed, "Goddamn you, I am getting tired of you making decisions without consulting me first. Just because your club treats woman like second-class citizens doesn't mean you have to. That boat is mine too. I have a right to be involved or at least asked about its future." Tony fell silent. I then continued, "I know that I have been leery to go out on the boat, and I agree that it is time to talk about what to do with the boat, but for one of us to make a solo decision is not right."

Tony said, "Look, hon, I don't want to argue with you. I just felt that I have been in charge of the boat and that I continue to be in charge of the boat. No malice intended."

"Tony," I said, "When you purchased the boat it was our decision. Since you have been Thru the Chairs, you have seemed to have forgotten that we are equal. Woman may not be members of your club, but in this marriage I am defiantly a member and an equal partner. We both own the boat, and therefore we both discuss the boat's future. I do not want to be left out of any more major decisions involving our lives. Understood?"

Tony approached me. He gave me that boyish grin; the one he gave when he knew he was caught and was trying to squirm his way out. "Listen, hon, so far nothing has been agreed on other than the Rear Commodore is interested in our boat. Do you have any objection to selling it to him if we can agree on a price?"

"No, not at all," I stated.

He then proceeded to inform me that there was a smaller boat for sale at the club. It seemed one of the older members was thinking of giving up his slip and moving to Arizona to be with his family. In this case, Tony could keep the smaller slip and take the smaller boat down to the Cape when he wanted to. I looked at him. "Tony," I said firmly, "I would like to see the smaller boat that you are considering. I also would like to agree on the price that you will sell *37 Park Ave* for."

Tony said matter-of-fact, "Fine." I knew then that he realized that I wasn't questioning his ability to make decisions, just his lack of consideration toward involving me. I now hoped I had set the record straight. Time would tell. I did like the fact that we would still have the opportunity to be on the floats with my friends. If I chose not to go to the Cape by boat, I could always drive with the girls and the guys could take the little boat. The fact that he could handle the smaller boat and use it as transportation back and forth was very appealing to him and me. One other fact regarding the smaller boat was it would be easier to man. The children were not always around to help him man the large boat. Tony would never tell me he was getting tired of the responsibility of *37 Park Ave*, but I had seen the fatigue in his face lately. The house on the Cape was demanding a lot of Tony's time, and this would alleviate some of that pressure.

Chapter 3

They Came

MEMORIAL DAY CAME, AND ALONG WITH it, Jim, Mary, Pat, and Bob. It was nice to have Bob join us. Pat said to me, "You know Bob, he likes small gatherings. Bob never liked all the hoopla at the club. He is so unlike me. I thrive on it." It was nice having the six of us all together again. Tony and I were so excited.

We had made the deal with the Rear Commodore, who ended up with *37 Park Ave*. Tony and I ended up buying the little boat from the older member of the club. The new, little twenty-eight-foot boat, *Tony's Baby*, was in the bay. Of course I just assumed that both our names were a part of it; Tony and of course, me, his baby. When I mentioned this to him, he smiled and said, "But of course you're my baby."

Our children were all scattered in different directions, so we had the cottage to ourselves. Pat laughed and said, "I know you said we would be roughing it, but where are the beds?" The beds for upstairs had not come in time, so we just had the mattresses laid out neatly on the floor.

"Pat," I laughed, "just think—I don't have to worry about anyone falling out of bed."

Pat grabbed Bob. "Come on, Bob, we are going to take the loft because we are so adventurous."

Bob, who barely said two words, chimed in, "Bring a net—the Cape has bats."

"Bats!" Pat screamed. "Is that true, Tony?"

"Don't worry, Pat," Tony laughed, "they only come out at night and you will be asleep."

Pat looked at Tony and said, "I hope you are both joking about the bats." I did not have the heart to tell her Bob was right—bats did exist on the Cape. Jim and Mary were glad they were on safe ground in the bedroom next to us. The only drawback was the pole in the closet was missing, so they would live out of a suitcase or use my closet.

Jim blurted out, "Tony, I am going to put my clothes in your closet. This will give me a chance to pick and choose. You never know, I might go home with a totally different wardrobe."

"Suit yourself," Tony said.

I laughed. "Now I know where that saying must have come from." Our room was fine except the screens were backordered for the windows, and without them the bugs and black flies were horrendous. Tony considered this no big deal. It was a nuisance to me. Luckily I found an old pair of sheer curtains and used them. I tacked them to the border of the window, and hoped a breeze would come through. The bottom line was we were all together.

The next day, yup, you guessed it—yard sales. We all got up and had an early breakfast. The men had decided to go quahogging in the bay. This task had to be accomplished at low tide. The tide would be low by 7 AM. Tony had purchased huge rakes I called guest greeters. If I ever wanted to scare a burglar, I would just answer the door holding one of these rakes. They looked like giant dinosaur claws. They were on the bottom of a five-foot pole, and they were used by running them on the ocean floor and feeling the quahogs moving. Tony had a ring that he kept in his pocket. If the quahog could fit through the ring, he had to give it back to the ocean. There were strict laws regarding quahogging in the bay. Harvesters had to be a resident and had to have a license. These quahogs could be caught only once a week and each family had a limit of one bushel. A quahog was a medium-size clam and the best to eat. Tony was dying to make stuffed quahogs as an appetizer and clams and linguini in an olive basil sauce for dinner.

PAT FELT RIGHT AT HOME SKIMMING the paper for yard sales. We did have one problem—we needed a map because we were traveling in uncharted territory. I was still very unfamiliar with the Cape area. Pat found a map and also a yard sale fairly close to our house. We were excited about our new adventure. Upon arrival at our first yard sale, Mary spotted a seashell lamp. She said, "I am buying this for you so I can read at night." I laughed at Mary's reasoning because we were all aware of Jim's snoring at night. Jim not only kept Mary up during the night; if I didn't know better I would have thought our home abutted a lighthouse with a foghorn bellowing to guide ships to safety. Mary said, "The light on your guest bedroom ceiling is so bright. This will look cute on your little night table. It is just enough light to read by." Mary decided that this purchase would solve two things—a gift for Tony and me, and her ability to read during Jim's snores. I liked the lamp. It was cute, plus I could add more seashells to the glass base if I wanted to. It looked like a large apothecary jar. It had easy access from its bottom. I loved collecting sea shells, and now I had a place to display them. I accepted my first house-warming gift from Mary.

Mary was fiddling around with a lemon squeezer for ten cents. She said if the men returned with quahogs they might want to eat some raw. If that was the case, they were going to need fresh lemon juice. What a buy, what a mind Mary had. She was always thinking ahead. She laughed and said, "Ten cents." We all broke out in a chorus, "Ten cents a dance—that's all they'll pay me." This was a short rendition of a song that was popular in our mothers' era. We picked up a few more items and then decided to go to lunch. The lady at the yard sale recommended a cute place in the center of a nearby town. So with map in hand, we ventured out. When we arrived we noticed one of those stores where we could get our picture taken while dressed in cowboy or cowgirl costumes.

Pat looked at each of us and with a twinkle in her devilish eyes said, "Ladies, let's have some fun and go back in time. Let us see what it was like to dress and act in the wild, wild west."

"You know," I agreed, "this picture would make for a great memory of the three of us. I can hang it up in the new cottage." Upon entering the studio, a lady came up and before we could speak took over completely. I said to myself, *Oh my gosh, Dot reincarnated.* It seemed we were already typecast in her mind. We never had a chance to voice our opinion. This woman was very matter-of-fact. I thought to myself, *Pat is about to meet her match.* Our greeter had a cowgirl hat on and resembled Annie Oakley. She had on leather boots in various shades of red with pointed toes. They were so authentic that I was surprised she didn't have the spurs to go with them. Her skirt was also leather with large strips of fringe that greeted the tops of the boots.

She even talked with a twang. "Howdy, ladies, these are the clothes I feel are appropriate for this shoot."

Pat looked at me and said, "She is not letting us choose what we want to be." The woman must have heard Pat because she spun around with coat hangers and costumes in hand and said, "Ladies, I am a professional photographer. I do this all day, and if you want a great shoot, please allow me to dress you accordingly." Mary smiled and gave me a shrug. Pat, on the other hand was a little reluctant.

Mary grabbed her arm and smiled as she said, "Pat, let's have fun. It is only a picture." Pat and I were ladies of the night, and Mary was the Madame. The backdrop was a tavern in the bowels of the Midwest. The attire was very sparse.

I looked at my friends and said, "Should we be insulted? Do we look like ladies of the night?" Then the same devilish look Pat had previously was back on her face again. Ironically, Mary and I adopted the same look. I guess we really were going to have some fun. This was a different role to be typecast in. Annie Oakley, as we referred to the photographer silently and under our breath, had an assistant. He was a middle-aged man. However, I was surprised to see that he was out of costume. I expected maybe a Roy Rogers for an assistant. This man was extremely tall and built solid. I guessed if I had to cast him he would be one of those Dapper Dans seen gambling in a saloon, the man with that evil smile who always managed to pull out four aces. One thing that bothered us ladies was that he was very free with his hands when he placed the finishing touches on our costumes. Pat was in fuchsia. Her gown fell off her shoulders, revealing her bosom. She had a giant plume on her head. Dapper Dan placed a broach around her neck. He seemed to be taking a long time. I noticed his eyes were traveling further down toward Pat's ample bosom. I wasn't too happy with his actions, but Pat wanted this picture perfect. I was in royal blue. I also had ostrich feathers shooting out of my head. However, unlike Pat, Dapper Dan started stuffing with cotton areas on my body that God had forgotten. Honestly I was getting a little annoyed. I wanted to say something to him, but we were having so much fun with the different costumes that I let it pass. I became upset when he placed a ten-dollar bill between my breasts, and even Annie Oakley questioned his actions.

She said, "Don't you think you are going a little too far with your hands?" But he insisted that to make it look authentic I needed some money sticking out of my bosom. I looked at Mary, who was donned in black. She looked like a black widow spider. Mary had the appearance of a Madame that not only ran the ladies in the saloon with a strict upper hand but could dispense of any man that displeased her. Mary looked like a tyrant. Dapper Dan must have sensed her strong portrayal because he never touched her or her costume.

Mary saw my expression and said, "Listen, may we take this shoot before we all pass out in these heavy costumes? I never realized how bulky the dresses were way back then in the wild west. I am starting to sweat, and I am sure my friends are too." My concern was mainly if they had ten-dollar bills way back then. Anyway, the shoot went well, and as we were departing with our pictures in hand we noticed that the man we referred to as Dapper Dan was gone.

I asked our photographer, "Excuse me, where did your assistant go?" She turned around and removed her cowgirl hat. I could see that she also was sweating. Her hair was stuck to her forehead. The brim of the cowgirl hat must have been tight, for her hair was plastered in a slick, oily fashion. She seemed to be running out of patience now that the shoot was over.

She looked at the three of us and said angrily, "What assistant?"

I said, "The man who was adding all the props to me and my friend. The man who used his hands so freely when placing the different accessories on Pat and me." The photographer looked at us strangely.

She sincerely answered us, "I thought he was with you girls. After all, do you think I would let an assistant of mine use their hands so freely?" I looked at Mary and Pat, and they looked back at me. For a split second we just went blank, and then simultaneously we lost it. We howled with gales of laughter till our stomachs ached. We were actually bent over and convulsing. The photographer was not pleased by our demonstration. She was angry and firmly said, "I really think my job with you is done. I would appreciate it if you would kindly leave the premises." This only made us laugh more.

Pat said, "How naïve can we be?"

I roared, "We just assumed he worked for the photographer! He was just some stranger who walked in off the street. Some crazy man who figured he could take advantage of three foolish ladies. But then to be asked to vacate the store … I cannot believe this is happening to us."

Mary stayed calm. She grabbed both our arms as we exited and said, "We really need lunch now. We really need to calm down. We seem to be making a spectacle of ourselves."

"Sure," Pat giggled, "You never had that man all over you. Do you realize how stupid we both feel?"

Mary said, "Listen, no one knows us in this neck of the woods. And that is a good thing,"

I commented, "I guess, Mary, that is one way of looking at it"

"Pat," Mary said, "get out your map and let's find that bistro." Pat and I realized Mary was now losing patience with us. The worst part was Pat and I couldn't control our giggles. The only way was not to look at each other. We got in the car and tried very hard to accomplish this. We did not want to upset Mary. We finally arrived at the restaurant, and we ordered three strawberry daiquiris. We then toasted to each other and placed the pictures that we took on the table. No one would ever know but the three of us the procedure we went through to take these pictures. We toasted to secrecy, friend- ships, and naïveté. Pat and I still had the giggles, but Mary seemed to have mellowed since our arrival at the restaurant. That picture is to this day in our cottage, and when I'm down and out I look at it and I cry, laugh, and miss my pals.

Chapter 4

Time Goes By

THE FIRST YEAR IN OUR CAPE house was filled with friends and children, but as the years went by Tony went less and less to the club and more and more to the Cape house. The politics of the club changed with each passing Commodore, and some of Tony's old-fashioned ways were replaced with computers, cell phones, and fax machines. Tony had a hard time catching up to the new ways in which the club was being operated. Don't get me wrong, the club was doing fine—it was just that he wasn't needed as much anymore. Everyone was very respectful towards him, but each new officer had their own way and own crew to accomplish what had to be done in their own fashion. So eventually Tony became, "Tony Who?" as in most political situations. Do you remember the fifteenth president of the United States? I guess that is my point. Our gang was also getting older. Our pals were having grandchildren and our time was divided more and more with family, but we still managed to get together a few times a year with Mary, Jim, Pat, and Bob and had at least one weekend with them at the Cape house.

THE SIXTIES WERE NOT FOR SISSIES, and we were all now entering this age bracket. We were all feeling what this age brought. Boating was becoming a chore. It was a responsibility that older men sometimes traded for golf. Yes, Tony took up golf, and worse than that he made me take it up too. In the beginning it was the most humiliating sport I ever tried. I would swing and swing and not hit a thing. For days my body would ache. How the instructor dealt with me I'll never know, but because the instructor didn't quit neither did

I. Tony, on the other hand, was a natural, but most of all Tony was very patient with me. He wanted us to have something we could do together. Tony realized that the boat was just too much work, and the children who we relied on for help had fallen into their own lives and had their own responsibilities. When they were around they helped, but they were rarely around these days. With the undertaking of golf I saw my girlfriends less and less. They did not share my enthusiasm for the game. Did I say enthusiasm? Well, I was beginning to hit the ball—actually, my drive was pretty good—and I was actually having some fun. Nothing could explain how beautiful a golf course could be at 7:30 in the morning. It was so peaceful, the grounds were so manicured, and the coffee just tasted better. When it was over I felt like I had accomplished something. I also felt like I had exercised. Tony made us walk at least nine holes. The nice advantage that had was we feel better about ourselves, we felt we were doing something healthy. However, I didn't always feel great about how I played. Ironically, I couldn't wait to play the game again.

Chapter 5

Pat

I RECEIVED A CALL FROM PAT. We were planning a Labor Day weekend at the Cape house. I figured she was calling to RSVP. However, when I heard her voice it was disappointing. She said very quietly, "I am just calling to let you know Bob and I won't be coming Labor Day."

"Pat," I said, "why?"

"I am just not up to it." I was rather surprised. I continued our conversation.

"Pat, we haven't gotten together since July, and I know how much we all looked forward to reuniting Labor Day weekend. Is there something you are not telling me?"

"No," Pat said, "I want you and Mary to have fun. I am just a little tired."

"Tired from what, Pat? We are a trio, we need you to come." I could tell that Pat was getting annoyed by my constant plea for her to come to the Cape house.

Finally she pacified me temporarily by saying, "I promise I will think it over, and if I change my mind I will let you know. I have to hang up now—I am expecting another call." She ended by saying, "All my best to you, Tony, and the children." I got off the phone and called Mary.

"Mary, you wouldn't believe the conversation I just had with Pat." Mary listened very intently.

She responded by saying, "I can't believe Pat would react that way. I am very surprised, and I am going to have Jim call Bob tonight."

"That's a great idea, Mary. Maybe you can get to the bottom of this. It is not like Pat to bow out unless she has a very good reason. Let me know if you hear anything." I then hung up the phone and hoped for the best.

A FEW DAYS LATER MARY CALLED me back. Bob reluctantly told Jim why they were not coming. He did feel Pat needed her friends. He also felt he needed all of us because this was very difficult to handle alone. The news was bad. Mary could barely speak. She just blurted out, "Pat has breast cancer, the worst, and most aggressive kind. Even if they remove both breasts, the doctors' diagnosis was that it probably had gone into the lymph glands. Of course they will know more when she is operated on." Then there was the longest silence. Neither one of us spoke. I knew I heard Mary crying. I couldn't get the words out of my mouth. I had a choked-up feeling, and I felt my cheeks getting wet with tears. Finally I broke the silence.

"What should we do, Mary?"

Mary said, "Be there. Come back from the cape."

I stayed home more and visited Pat more. Mary also was there. The sickness came, and it came hard and quick. I watched my friend melt away piece by piece in front of me. I watched what was once a smile on Pat's face turn into a fine line that barely moved. I saw eyes that once sparkled be drained of all fluid. It was like someone took a magic marker and made two giant black circles. When I held Pat she was like a wounded bird. Mary and I tried our best to make her laugh, and Pat tried to accommodate us. I knew and Mary knew that Pat, our little wounded bird, would never fly again. Pat died within the year. She was sixty-two.

Chapter 6

The Wake

THE CASKET WAS CLOSED. PAT WANTED to be remembered the way she was before the illness took over. Lots of people attended, but it was the Commodores, past and present, in full uniform that made it so emotional. After the ceremony at the funeral hall, her husband decided he would have people back at the yacht club; there the new Rear Commodore had put a small buffet together out of respect. It had been about a year since Tony and I had been to the club. All the boats were in the water, and some were so large it was quite impressive. Pat's final wishes were to be cremated and have her ashes sprinkled in the waters of the club. This ceremony would be done on another day, when her family had enough time to adjust to this type of ceremony. Her family was Catholic, and at the time cremation was not an option. This, however, was Pat's wish. At the club today, we tried to share some of the different episodes we had enjoyed with Pat. Some of us brought pictures of Pat doing different charities at the club. I had one of her holding one of the reindeers we had created. We placed different pictures in a huge picture frame that her family could take with them. We spent time reminiscing over times gone by.

Chapter 7

Paul Adler

AFTER AWHILE IN PAT'S WAKE, I needed some fresh air, and where to get it better than the ocean. I sat outside the club in a quiet corner, reliving some of my own special memories of Pat. Paul Adler approached me. He just sat down next to me like we were old pals. He said, "I'm sorry about Pat. I know what it is to lose someone you love."

I said, "I know, Paul; you went through a lot with your wife."

He said, "I don't mean my wife. Yes, I went through a lot, but I never really loved her the way a man can love a woman." Paul looked straight into my eyes. "I mean the way I loved Jill."

"Jill," I said and looked right into his eyes. Then, overcome by my own grief I yelled, "How could you love Jill and make her do what you did?" He looked at me very perplexed, like I had three heads.

"What are you talking about?" he asked to me.

"I'll tell you what I am talking about," I replied. "I am talking about the extracurricular sexual activities you expected her to perform for certain favors, *Paul!*"

He shook his head and said, "Who told you that lie?"

I clammed up and said, "It really doesn't matter at this point. Paul, may I grieve my friend's death in peace?"

"*No*," Paul said, "you are going to hear me out. I loved Jill from the first moment I saw her. George sent her up; George was the one who had her engaging in those so-called sexual games you are referring to." Paul paused and then went on, "I started talking to Jill, and then one thing led to another. Yes, I slept with her. I would rather say I made love to her, and she knew it. She knew I was in love with her. She also knew I had a wife. I told her that I had to stand by my wife. I told her my wife was ill. I told her it was just a matter of time before my wife died. I said in time we would be together. I told her to stay away from George and any other men who were out to exploit her. If my wife wasn't so sick maybe we would have had a chance, but when Jill found out she was pregnant with my child the pressure was too much. I offered to send her somewhere were she would feel comfortable. She had always wanted to go back to her roots. I told her I would pay her and help support the baby. I wanted that baby so bad. I wanted a second chance. My wife never was a loving woman to me; the poor woman was always sick. I know she tried, and that was why I had to stand by her. However, I loved Jill and the thought of a child and a second chance was so great. But Jill was afraid. She thought I might go back on my word, and most of all she was afraid of George. She knew his reaction to all this would be disastrous. The bottom line was that the timing couldn't be worse." Paul was trembling as he spoke to me. His hands were shaking so much. His eyes were watery, and he actually had tears coming down his cheeks. He must have been holding all this pain in for a long time. It was pouring out of him. The problem was that I couldn't comfort Paul; I was missing one of my best friends. Maybe in a different time I could feel sorry for him, but this was neither the time nor the place.

He continued explaining how he could have been more support-ive to Jill, how his first obligation was to his wife. He rambled on and on. Paul had reached for that second chance; I guessed it was so close and yet so far. Paul asked me about my visit to Jill the time she was ill and said she had some woman problems. Paul then went on to say, "What Jill didn't tell you was she aborted the baby. My chance to have a child went out the window. Jill never discussed it with me—I was at the hospital with my wife. Jill just went ahead and had the abortion, figuring it was the best for all involved. Well, was it?" Paul questioned me with such pain in his face. His face was so contorted that I became frightened. I just sat there dumbfounded as Paul continued. "Here I sit today. My wife is dead, my girlfriend is dead, and my child is dead. So I think I understand what it is to lose someone." With that Paul Adler got up, turned around, and just walked away. Paul was right—

his timing for things was all wrong. Today was not the day to reach out to me. Even if I wanted to comfort him, I was drained from the loss of my friend. I had no comfort to give him. I didn't know about his relationship with his wife, and I couldn't understand why Jill had painted him the way she did. Maybe the baby was George's. I did know one thing—lost opportunities were horrible because they could never be had again, and in that I felt bad because Paul Adler truly was a beaten man.

Tony must have realized I was missing. When he finally located me in the corner, I was huddled like a ball. He came over immediately. "Honey, I was looking for you. What are you doing here alone? Someone said they saw you with Paul Adler. Did Paul upset you?"

I looked up at Tony all teary eyed and said, "Paul tried to comfort me, or maybe Paul tried to comfort himself." I had no intention of explaining all of Paul's conversation to Tony. Tony looked at me and decided that I had been through enough for one day. Anyway, it was getting late and we were scheduled to go back to the Cape. The drive back would be long, and we were both exhausted. I got up, went back into the club, and said my goodbyes.

During the ride back I was extremely quiet. Tony talked incessantly about all the new gossip. I guessed he was trying to divert my attention toward something that could cheer me up, but there was no cheering. Finally he started saying, "Hon, look, I know you loved Pat—" and I immediately stopped him.

"Tony, I need to be quiet right now. I am so sick inside. I don't know if this feeling will ever subside."

"What is it, honey?" he asked.

I looked up at him with tears running down my face and said, "Tony, it's *the lion's paw*. I now know what Mary went through." When we got back to the Cape house, I picked up the picture of the three of us dressed up as ladies of the night. We were so happy that day. We had laughed and laughed and laughed. I hugged the picture close to my heart, and I cried. I felt *the lion's paw* churn in my stomach, but then when I looked back at the picture it was like Pat reached out and reminded me of our secret on how the picture was orchestrated. Then and only then did I smile. Tony entered the room. He smiled as he held up two glasses of wine. As Tony placed the wine